The Rain

A Story of Noah and the Ark

By

Chris Skates
And
Dan Tankersley

PRESS

Tommy & Sherrie,

May God Bless.

II Peter 2:5

Chris Skate

Contents

"Just as it was in the days of Noah, so also will it be in the days of the Son of Man. People were eating, drinking, marrying and being given in marriage up to the day Noah entered the Ark. Then the flood came and destroyed them all." (Luke 17:26–27 English Standard Version)

Prologue

W e huddled together around the table, terrified of what was to come. Though we had been warned, the reality of what was happening was almost more than we could bear. We violently pressed our hands to our ears to block the sounds from those outside, but we could not keep from hearing their screams. The sound of fingernails clawing desperately at the sides of the ark went through us like a knife blade.

Nothing could be worse than this, I thought.

But it did get worse. I began to hear familiar voices. The cries of strangers were harrowing enough, but now I could hear the shouts of my mother's sister and her son. When my wife, Tamara, heard her mother's voice, she could stand no more.

"Japheth, we must help them!" she exclaimed.

Suddenly, Tamara leapt and ran toward the door. I rushed after her. I had to stop her from lowering the door. I was certain that if the door were opened, so many people would rush in that the ark would capsize. When we entered the ark, even though no rain had fallen, my father had been adamant that the door be closed immediately. Now, hearing the panic-stricken people outside, I understood why.

I could barely see Tamara as she ran down the dark passage. But I heard her hysterical cries. I grabbed her just as she clamored for the latch that I had made. God had not bothered to give any instruction as to how we were supposed to hold the door closed. Dad would not listen to my elder brother Ham's fears about how the door would be torn open in rough water. He would not consider allowing us to install the huge latches that we had built because he had received no "instruction from God" to do so. So on the day we entered the ark, Ham distracted Dad with one question after another while I bolted the latches. We placed fodder in front of the door to hide our handiwork.

Before either of us could utter a word, we suddenly heard a low growl, like that of a great bear, coming from the other side of the hull. The sound came with such intensity that it stood out from the cries outside and our own cries inside. The growl was followed by a pounding on the outside of the hull as if it was being hit with a sledgehammer.

A loud creak rose above all the sounds of agony and anger from outside. The hull groaned and popped. The ark tilted sharply. I held tightly to Tamara and cushioned her from falling into the wall. The ark was beginning to move. Would it float, or had our efforts merely succeeded in delaying our deaths?

It was as we stood there, trying to keep our balance, that we noticed the door. A few hours before, Ham and I hurriedly tried to seal the seam around the door with pitch because water was seeping in. Now there was no seam. In fact, the hull now looked as solid on this side of the ark as it did on the other. I tossed the fodder aside to reveal that our latches hung open, holding nothing. I was stunned.

In the months before the rain came, exotic animals we had never seen before began to congregate in the woods and hills near our home. Their gathering at a time so close to the ark's completion made me want to believe that God was with us. Still, I had so much doubt. But something about the now-useless latches touched me more deeply. It was as though

God was speaking directly to me, letting me know that the work of my hands could never save us. The latches and all the pitch would not have kept the water from rushing in the door. But God somehow had sealed it completely.

All that Dad had said was true. Dad never gave up, despite the years of ridicule and taunting he had endured. Even when he knew *we* doubted his sanity, he pressed on. This perseverance came because God *had* actually spoken to my father. It was almost too much to comprehend. My knees began to shake, and I felt faint.

Tamara noticed the door too. Her cries quieted to whimpers. Then she began again.

"We have to let them in," she said, now wild-eyed. She beat on the sealed door with all the energy she could muster. But her efforts were for naught. She could not open the door, no matter how hard she tried. None of us could. Even in the midst of being inspired by God's handiwork, I worried briefly how we would ever get out.

But that concern passed as I noticed that the cries of the people outside were subsiding. Tamara's cries stopped as she seemed to resign herself pitifully to the people's inevitable plight. I grasped Tamara in my arms, and our backs slid along the hull as we clung to one another. We couldn't cover our ears tightly enough. We could not escape the reality that people were dying just inches from where we sat. Everyone we had ever known outside our immediate family would surely be drowned soon. But for the word that God had spoken to Dad, we would have perished as well.

Shem told himself that he had to stand strong with his father, Noah, and their God. He wasn't sure that his baby brother, Japheth, and particularly his wife, Tamara, had the strength to endure what they were hearing outside. Shem knew that Japheth wanted to believe what Dad had taught them about God. At the same time, Shem realized that Japheth was sometimes too greatly influenced by their middle brother, Ham.

Our brother…humph, Shem thought.

Sometimes he wished that were not true. Since they had been small boys, Ham had always wanted things his way. In Ham's mind, all the rest of the family existed for his convenience. He had refused to help with the ark in the first two years that Noah, Shem, and Japheth worked on it. Finally, Dad forced him.

Shem had thought about stopping Tamara from running from the room. But she was Japheth's responsibility. He had his own wife, Prisca, and his mother, Sapphira, to be concerned with. He looked around at their faces and stopped on his father's. His long, gray hair and beard did not have the flowing quality Shem was used to. Instead, they were damp and stringy. His head hung down as he stared into his lap, yet Shem could tell he wasn't praying. He seemed frozen in that position. Sapphira had her head on the table, her face hidden. Her forearms covered her ears with her fingers laced behind her head. Shem wondered if she were having any success in blocking out the sounds from outside. The silent shaking of her shoulders as she sobbed answered his question.

Shem held his dear Prisca's head in his lap and stroked her hair. Prisca was a passionate woman, and she made no attempt to hide her grief. She sobbed openly and loudly. No one spoke against her. It was as if she expressed what they all felt. As he tried to comfort her, Shem could not help but wonder about his own behavior. He had heard the cries, but he had yet to shed a tear. He felt he was being strong, but maybe he was numb.

He couldn't come to grips with the fact that people outside were drowning. He kept thinking that, in a couple of days, they would open the door and see those who they knew standing there. Their loved ones would have been through quite an ordeal, but now God would have their attention.

Now they would admit that the warnings from Noah had been true.

Shem had these hopes. But deep in his heart he knew that it would not happen that way. Dad said that God had made it clear He had had enough. God had instructed them on building the ark. And soon, perhaps within hours if all that Dad had perceived from God came true, all those outside the ark would perish. Shem's mind just couldn't comprehend it. So he sat and stared blankly.

Noah was in shock. It had been nearly one hundred twenty years ago since God had told him this flood would come. Now that it was here, Noah couldn't bear it. The week before, when he and his family entered the ark and closed the door, Noah had been reeling from the loss of his beloved grandfather, Methuselah, who had died just two weeks before the rains came. If not for his grandfather, Noah might never have completed the ark. It was Methuselah who had encouraged Noah from the start and had been there in support during all the times when Noah doubted himself.

Noah understood quite well what was taking place outside and why God had determined it had to be that way. Despite that, the actuality was debilitating.

Why, oh why, did they not listen? Noah thought. He shed no tears. He had cried so much and so often in these recent days that his body could produce no more tears. He continued to stare into his lap. Noah wished the screams outside were not real. He wished to awaken from this nightmare. But he could only endure it. As the rain pounded the roof and the people outside suffered, minutes were like hours. Noah knotted his fists into his cloak and tried to hold on.

The sounds of agony from outside had gradually faded as Adina, Ham's wife, tried in vain to sleep. She sobbed loudly as she lay on her crude pallet inside a storage room within the ark. Her husband, Noah's middle son, lay beside her on his back, staring at the ceiling. Ham had forced her to move their belongings into the storeroom after only three days of being quartered with the rest of the family. Adina assumed he had not wanted to be near them. She hadn't been given an explanation. Ham wasn't in the habit of explaining his actions to her.

She didn't like it here. The pallet that Ham had fashioned for them was crude, made of the same straw that was to be used to line some of the animals' cages. After one night of sleeping in the dark storeroom, Adina longed for the comfort of the bed they had abandoned in the living quarters and for the welcoming glow of the fireplace there.

As she lay there crying, her back turned toward Ham, her husband rose up on one elbow.

"Shut up!" he bellowed. Adina jumped, then pulled her hands to her mouth in an attempt to stifle her sobs. Ham leaned toward her, his mouth so close to her ear that she could feel his breath on her cheek.

"Isn't it enough that I had to hear that," Ham yelled, waving his arm toward the hull. "Do I have to lie here trying to get some sleep and listen to your blubbering too?"

Adina cringed and tried to force herself to stop crying. Ham grunted in exasperation, pulled the blanket from Adina's back, and left the room. At that moment, Adina felt more alone than at any time she could ever recall. Left to shiver uncovered on the cold pallet, Adina longed for her parents.

She never really meant to leave them. Adina's faith in God was strong. Until a few days ago, however, her faith in the pending flood had not been so strong. She had walked up the ramp following closely behind Ham, yet she had done so primarily out of loyalty to him and respect for her in-laws. She really didn't believe at that time that she would never see her parents again. At that thought she abruptly sat up, stood, and walked to the far corner of the room, weaving through shelves of supplies and barrels of wheat. Her arms folded across her stomach, Adina leaned against a barrel and thought about praying.

She did not pray. She knew on a conscious level that God loved her. She didn't doubt that. She knew that, for reasons she didn't fully understand, He had spared her. Still, she didn't want to talk to Him. She wanted to talk to her parents. She wanted to wrap her arms around her mother and smell the familiar odor of lavender that seemed to always be present in her hair. Tears began to run down Adina's cheeks more rapidly now. Not knowing what to do with herself, she returned to the pallet.

Adina lay on her side, pulled her knees in close to her chest, wrapped her arms around her shins, and rocked slightly. She knew God loved her. She knew her husband loved her, despite his eruptions. She knew these things, but as she lay alone on the cold floor, she could not *feel* it. This was a moment when the love of an aloof husband was simply not enough. Even the love of God, whom she had never actually seen or touched, didn't ease her suffering. Adina could not remember ever wanting her mother and stepfather so much. As she lay there rocking, the flames from the candles flickered and then went out. Alone in the darkness of the storage room, Adina stopped fighting for composure and let the sobs take over her body.

She couldn't see the One sitting in the corner of the room. He wanted to reach out to her. He wanted to scoop her up in His arms and hold her as her stepfather had when she was a little girl. That opportunity would come, but it could not be today.

He sat and kept watch over Adina and the others. He had walked about the ark and laid His hand upon the animals so that they slept peacefully. He had stood for a time beside the table as Noah stared blankly. He looked at Tamara and

Japheth's faces as they first noticed the door after He had sealed it.

As He watched His people, as He saw the tears flow, He suffered in a way no one else on the ark could fathom. He suffered for those outside. He felt every tear that fell inside. Oh, that they could know how His heart broke for them. But they couldn't understand. He knew that. So He sat quietly with Adina and wept.

CHAPTER 1

The Absence of Innocence

*"And Cain went out from the presence of the Lord...
and he builded a city..."*
— portions of Genesis 4:16-17

After nearly five years of construction and preparation, it was almost time for us to board the ark and raise the ramp. My father's instructions from God were that we would begin living on the ark in just a few more weeks, even if it had not begun to rain. The entire family was working steadily, but not frantically, to finish loading supplies.

I was loading our largest wagon, for what seemed like the fiftieth time, with straw that would be used for animal bedding. This load would be the last one needed. My dog, Rowdy, lay under the wagon in the shade. I threw a fork full of the hay playfully across his back. He opened one eye and wagged his tail lazily.

"Japheth, look on the ramp," Shem called out to me. Everyone else, though intent on their own chores, stopped to look as well.

Suddenly, with no prompting from any of us, two young lambs, a male and a female, walked up the ramp and into the ark. Tamara and I rushed in behind them to observe their behavior. Once inside, the animals turned to the right and walked up the inner ramp to the mid deck. They continued calmly into a stall that was well suited for their size and began munching on the hay that had been loaded into each trough.

We had been using the evenings of the previous month to plan how we would get all the animals that had recently taken up residence in the vicinity loaded into the ark. With the sound of the lambs' hooves walking to the exact area we had intended for them, we realized our planning might have been unnecessary.

All of the supplies were nearly loaded onto the ark and that was fortunate, for the lambs had started a trend. Throughout the rest of the day, a few more pairs of animals of multiple types followed the lambs' example. The parade of animals was sporadic, which worked to our advantage as it gave us access to the ramp to load supplies.

After I completed my work, I approached Shem and Ham. Both my brothers were covered in dust. Their faces were smudged with dirt from their work, their hands blackened with a combination of pitch and grime. As instructed, we had thoroughly coated the ark in pitch. Now it seemed no one could get within ten yards of the vessel without getting some of the gooey substance on their hands, clothes, or elsewhere. I probably looked as grimy as they did.

I looked up to my brothers—literally. They were both big men. I was over six feet tall, and Shem stood a good four inches taller than me. Ham was the largest member of our family, standing nearly seven feet tall. Both men were strong and muscular. I was the wiry one.

Shem looked up first at my approach. His face was dark brown from spending most of his ninety-seven years in the sun. His pale gray eyes crinkled at the corners as he smiled in my direction. Shem was almost always in a good mood, and in that way he was the most like Dad. Dad had a very happy nature too, until he began to feel the pressure of the last few years.

Shem kept his sandy hair cut short, which fit his practical and unassuming nature. He and I were both clean-shaven. A casual observer would have guessed right away that Shem and I were brothers, since we shared facial characteristics and hair color.

On the other hand, Ham's hair and full beard were raven black. Like Shem, Ham was dark from the sun, though his tan came more from time spent at leisure rather than work. Ham let his hair grow thick. It spilled out from his collar and over his shoulders. Women had always found him very handsome. When we were bachelors, I often grew frustrated with the attention he garnered. His flippant attitude toward the women seemed to only increase their attraction to him.

"I've finished filling the storage bin with straw," I reported to Shem.

"Good," Shem replied. "We have all the grain, fruits, dried meat, and greens loaded. Gentlemen, I think we are ready to accommodate the animals. At least I pray that we are. We have followed Dad's instructions to the letter, so we should be prepared."

"I love the way we are basing all of our actions on whatever Dad comes up with," Ham retorted sarcastically. "Especially considering the fact that the most animals we have ever had on our farm at one time is a few dozen. If all the animals that have shown up around here end up in the ark, we will have thousands to care for."

"We're not basing anything on what Dad 'comes up with,' Ham," Shem replied. "Dad is telling us what God is telling him."

"Yes, how could I forget!" Ham rolled his eyes and walked back to the cart he had been loading. Shem shook his head, displeased with Ham, and turned back to me. As our eyes met, a smile crossed Shem's face.

"Little brother, I think we are actually going to pull this off," he said.

"What are we pulling off, Shem?" I inquired. "We may manage to get all these animals on board. We may even have enough food to sustain them for some time. But how long will we sit inside that stuffy ark before we give up on Dad's vision?"

"You still have doubts that the flood will come?" Shem asked.

"I don't know what to believe anymore, Shem. For so long I have felt as if we have been playing along, like we have come this far in order to humor Dad. Now that the time to actually follow through, to actually leave our houses and move into the ark is at hand, well, yes, I suppose I am having doubts. Aren't you?"

"I haven't had time for doubts, Japheth. I have been so focused on logistics and trying to make Dad's ark a reality, I haven't allowed myself to really think about it. As I stand here at this minute, I do believe. I believe the flood *will* come."

Shem and I were quiet for a moment. Then I turned toward the city. The spires atop the tallest buildings were visible on this crystal-clear day.

"If the flood does come, what do you think they will do?" I asked, nodding toward the city.

Shem wiped his hands together in a futile attempt to clean them off, then walked over and stood beside me.

"Haven't you been paying attention to what Dad tells us, Japheth? You know what will happen to them."

"Do you really think God will let all those people die?"

"It's overwhelming to consider, I admit," Shem replied. "I know I can't fathom it."

"I wonder how deep the water will get," I asked Shem. "I mean, maybe some of the people can live in the taller buildings until the water recedes."

Shem shook his head grimly. "No, I'm afraid that won't happen. God has told Dad that the water will cover the highest mountain. If that happens, even those tallest spires will be covered."

"What do you suppose the people in the city are thinking right now? Do you think they're scared, Shem?"

"You know how they have rejected Dad's warnings. They're not scared. They're complacent. They're going about their routines as they always have. The only way that our work may have affected them is that it has given them a common cause to mock and detest."

We stood for a few more minutes, staring silently.

"I know you two are busy staring into space," Ham called out. "But when you get a minute or two free, I could use some help over here."

Shem and I looked at one another and smiled.

"I guess we better get back to work," Shem conceded.

As Shem turned and took a step towards Ham, I said, "Shem, do you think there are innocent people there in the city? Perhaps we missed someone. Perhaps there is someone that hasn't heard our warnings who might be receptive to what God is saying through Dad. There are so many people living there. Could God have forgotten someone?"

Shem had stopped walking and was standing with his back to me. He looked at the ground for a moment and then looked up to the sky. The sun shone through the fluffy clouds overhead so that rays of light emanated from them and splashed across the sky. The sky had the pink hue of morning, and a soft southerly breeze brought the smell of distant spring flowers to our worksite. It was a breathtaking day.

"God hasn't forgotten anyone, little brother," Shem said, still looking towards the sky. "We have to believe that. We have to trust that."

We said no more. Shem picked up a large grain shovel leaning against a post and joined Ham. I took a final look at the gorgeous sky and then looked back over my shoulder toward the city.

"God help us," I whispered. "Let us be doing the right thing. And dear God, be with anyone who might not have heard our warnings."

Jerah knelt behind the manicured hedges that grew in front of the museum. Behind him, huge columns of pink marble, polished to a mirror finish, rose to support the imposing building that housed the finest art that had been created by men. Jerah had peeked inside from time to time. The art didn't appeal to him. He didn't understand what it was. All he had been able to see from his vantage point was a statue that portrayed several nude adults intertwined in an embrace. It made Jerah feel uncomfortable when he looked at it.

There were some paintings on the far wall. They didn't look like anything recognizable. In one of the paintings, he thought that perhaps he could make out a face, screaming as if in torment.

He wasn't interested in looking into the museum today. His mission was much more important. He was in search of any type of cloak that would help to keep his little sister, Shelah, warm. She was shivering all the time now, and her cough was getting worse.

They had made a home in one of the honeycomb of tunnels under the city. They had been living there for four weeks. A complex system of aquifers ran high overhead and brought running water into every home and building. The tunnels provided a path for the dirty water to flow back to the river. Jerah had fashioned a shelter in one of the recesses where the force of flowing water had created a small cave. No water flowed into the cave, but moisture constantly ran down the walls and it was damp. Jerah had considered building a fire but was afraid the smell of smoke might alert those on the surface.

There was one thing Jerah could feel good about: He was keeping Shelah well fed. At seven years old, he was a seasoned veteran at pilfering food. There was food everywhere as the people ate constantly. He and Shelah could get fat picking through the refuse of the poorest household in town. Jerah didn't bother with poor houses, though. There were plenty of places where he could get the finest cuisine. He just had to be careful.

He usually did his "shopping" at night. Shelah was afraid to be alone in the cave, but he lit a candle for her. Under cover of darkness, Jerah had become very adept at moving about in the shadows and collecting food and other things they would need. The cloak would be a larger challenge. He normally stuck with things he could carry in a small leather satchel. A cloak as heavy as what he had in mind would never fit and carrying it would slow him down.

He hadn't taken time to bring much with them from their old house. Jerah always thought of it as just a house. It certainly had never been a home. The woman who had given birth to him and Shelah made it clear that they were an unwelcome burden to her. She never lifted a finger to protect them from the parade of men who moved in and out of the house and their lives. Some of the men treated Jerah like a slave and beat him no matter how much he tried to do as they said. His "mother" threw back her head and laughed when one of her lovers held Jerah's hand over a burning candle simply because he had failed to fetch the man's horse quickly enough.

When Shelah was born, something awoke in Jerah. He felt a yearning desire to protect his baby sister. Though he was small, he determined that he would not let her endure what he had been through. Whenever his mother came home with a visitor for the night, Jerah made sure he had what he and Shelah needed to stay away for a day or two. Sometimes it was almost fun. They slept in the woods if it was warm and played together for a few hours without fear. It was during that period that Jerah had developed his skills of sneaking into the city and acquiring food and provisions.

When there was no man living in the house, their mother largely ignored them. She would occasionally slap Jerah, but she had only hit Shelah once or twice. Yet when there was a man around, his mother became more cruel. So Jerah developed a hatred for the men. He couldn't even remember their faces. There had been too many to recall. Only one stood out.

When Jerah turned seven, he thought his life was about to change. His mother took up with a man who spoke kindly to Jerah. He didn't order him around. In fact, he even prepared meals for Jerah and Shelah. Sometimes he brought them sweets.

After he had been there a few weeks, he would give Jerah and Shelah big hugs when he came home. At first the hugs, though strange for the two of them, felt warm and comforting. Then something changed. The man's hugs would last so long that they didn't feel good to Jerah anymore. Soon the man began to touch Jerah in ways that made him uncomfortable and frightened. Jerah looked to his mother when this would occur, hoping for guidance and help. She only shook her head and, with a scoffing puff of her cheeks, left the room.

As time progressed, the man grew bolder. He told Jerah it would be good for the two of them to play together in the way that he and Jerah's mother played. When Jerah refused, the man became angry.

"I thought you were my friend, Jerah. Haven't I always been kind to you and Shelah? If you can't show me that you care about me, then I don't want anything to do with you," the man insisted.

That night Jerah cried quietly in his bed. He hadn't done that in a long while. He thought he had run out of tears. But now he was torn. Was he wrong to refuse the man? He had shown

Jerah more kindness than he had ever known. Though it made him terribly uncomfortable, Jerah determined that it would be all right. He would go to the man in the way he wanted.

Jerah walked into the main room of their house late that night and saw that the man was sitting in a chair. As he rounded the corner he noticed that the man's arm was around Shelah. Why wasn't Shelah asleep? It was so late. Something was wrong. Shelah looked confused and afraid.

Something in Jerah rose up within him. He reached around and grabbed a poker from the fireplace. As the man turned to face him, Jerah hit him hard on the side of the head. Then, without thinking, he grabbed Shelah and ran out the door. He heard his mother hollering at them as they ran, but he couldn't make out her words. He heard a lamp that his mother had thrown crash on the ground behind him.

For a day they tried to live in the forest. But the weather was getting colder and Jerah knew they could not survive there. They needed shelter.

It had been difficult for Jerah to make it into the city undetected with Shelah, even at night. Shelah marveled at the spires and tall buildings that seemed to reach nearly to the sky. She wanted to explore, but Jerah couldn't let them be seen. He didn't feel he could trust an adult. In all the times Jerah had ventured into the city, he had never seen another child. In fact, Shelah was the only other child Jerah had ever seen.

At the first opportunity, he led Shelah to an entrance to the underground tunnels. The tunnels were Jerah's primary means of navigating through the city. They found the little cave right away. Jerah tried to make it somewhat comfortable, fashioning two small mats for them to lie on. He even made a tiny table out of a scrap board and a crate he found. He placed their candles on the table. He kept at least one burning at all times so that Shelah would not be afraid.

That had been a month ago. The nights had grown steadily colder, and Shelah had become ill in the damp cave.

As the sun went down that night, he made her as comfortable as possible and told her to wait. He promised he would fetch a cloak for her to wear.

That had brought him here to the museum. He had hidden in these bushes many times and watched the finely dressed men and women walk up and down the stairs. They all would be bundled up warmly. Jerah moved perilously close to the corner of the steps leading into the museum.

Suddenly, Jerah thought he had the opportunity he was looking for. A man stopped on the top step, removed and folded his cloak, and hung it over the railing. He was arguing with some women. As the argument got more heated, the man's arms began to flail in animated conversation. Jerah hoped the man would absent-mindedly knock the cloak into the bushes where he would be waiting to catch it. As he waited, Jerah could hear their discussion.

"I heard what he said perfectly well and, yes, I too have been out there and have seen the exotic animals gathering around his project," the man pronounced.

"Well, it just seems to me that it's at least possible that there might be some type of god out there. Perhaps it's a god of animals or something. I mean, why would they suddenly come around?" one of the women inquired.

"The presence of the animals doesn't prove anything!" the man responded in exasperation. "Don't you pay attention? He has been loading food into that thing for months now. He probably has put some type of bait in there to attract the animals.

"Think about the logic of what he is saying. You think there is a god that has the power to cover the whole earth with water? Look around you. No god built this magnificent city. That is one thing the founders all agreed upon. We didn't need any gods or temples to gods, and they have been proven right. We live in luxury and comfort and it has all been by the ingenuity of man."

Jerah wondered for a second who or what was this thing called God. He had never heard that name before. There was no more time to listen, for as the man spoke of the city, he walked to the opposite end of the portico outside the museum. The women followed. Jerah knew he had to move quickly. He climbed up and reached as tall as he could. In a second, Jerah had yanked the coat down and jumped to the safety of the ground behind the bushes. He had to get underground.

"I suppose you're right," the woman said, her voice getting closer. "If there is a god living out there with Noah, I don't suppose we've any need of him here. Let's go in. I'm getting a chill."

The last thing Jerah heard before he ducked into the tunnels was the man shouting profanities about his missing cloak. He had escaped in the nick of time.

Raamah couldn't believe what he had just seen. He had given up looking for children long ago. There hadn't been a child in this city in ten years! But as he loitered across the street from the museum, waiting for some easy target that looked like money to walk by, he was certain he had seen a boy. And the little scum was a thief too. Maybe he ought to take the kid under his wing and teach him how the pros did it. No, he had better plans for this one. There were folks that would pay big money for one that young.

When he was sure no one was looking, Raamah stepped from the shadows. It wasn't that he was afraid of getting caught. No one had the guts to try to stop him. Raamah stood nine feet tall and was nearly five hundred pounds of muscle and sinew. The tiny stubble of hair covering his head did not hide the tattoo of a pentagram that covered his skull. If he wanted, he could do like some of the others of his kind and openly victimize whomever he pleased. No one would dare raise a hand to him. And his victims' struggles were useless.

Raamah did his work from the shadows because his very appearance struck fear in everyone he encountered. Sometimes that led to a chase, and Raamah didn't like to run. Pulling someone into the shadows and snapping their scrawny necks was much quicker and easier.

As he parted the bushes and stepped from behind them, Raamah looked skyward and rolled his eyes. The kid had headed into the tunnel. Smart kid. This was going to be a real pain in the neck. He couldn't fit through here, but he knew a place where even he could walk in nearly standing up. An hour later, he was in the tunnel. He had banged his thick head a dozen times on the low ceiling and was growing angrier by the second. Where was the little worm?

That's when he saw the candlelight. He crouched down and inched closer. He didn't want to have him bolt when he was this close. When he peered around the corner of the cave opening, Raamah couldn't believe his luck. There were two of them, and one was a girl. Jackpot!

Jerah had Shelah so bundled up he could hardly see her tiny face.

"Are you getting warm?" he asked. He smiled when Shelah nodded happily.

Jerah turned to the little candle stove he had made. "Now it's time to get something warm into your belly."

He placed the metal cup of soup onto the candle, but suddenly it was knocked violently from his hand. He looked ruefully at the wasted soup on the floor before he realized that someone was grabbing Shelah. He never saw Raamah's face, only his giant forearms. With no fear for himself, Jerah wrapped himself around the arm and latched on with his teeth. He bit down as hard as he could until he felt warm blood spilling into his mouth. Raamah screamed in pain. As he did so, he slung Shelah to one side to free his right hand.

Jerah heard her head hit the floor of the tunnel and realized she was not moving.

With his right hand free and his mind clouded with rage, Raamah grabbed Jerah's neck. It was a few seconds before it occurred to Raamah that the boy was now hanging limp in his hand. He held the boy's now-pale face up to his own.

"Why did you have to go and make me lose my temper, worm? Oh well, no need in letting the two of you go to waste."

With that, he grabbed Shelah in his other hand and trudged back down the tunnel.

Jerah didn't see Raamah leave with his and Shelah's old bodies. The little boy was much too mesmerized by the light radiating from those standing before him. Then he thought to ask them to help Shelah. As he started to do so, he felt a tiny, warm hand grasp his own. He glanced over to see Shelah looking up at the adult nearest her. His little sister was smiling broadly. Both of the children felt something from these two that, prior to now, they had only felt from each other. Though they had never seen these adults, they didn't seem at all like strangers. One took Jerah's other hand, and one took Shelah's. With the four of them holding hands, the adult next to Jerah knelt down.

"Jerah. Shelah." The adult looked from one face to another as he spoke.

"You can come with us. We are going to take you to your new home. You'll never have to scrounge for food or be cold or frightened again. And there is someone who is very excited about meeting you and holding you in His arms. Come now, we'll take you to Him."

The four of them left the tunnel and began to rise high above the city. Jerah and Shelah turned to look back, momentarily watching the lights from the city come together in the distance until they looked like a distant star. Neither of them could have known it then, but their leaving meant that there was not another child anywhere in or around the city. Jerah and his sister had been the last two children left on all the earth.

The feeling of safety and acceptance that the two children experienced from the angels leading them was wonderful. Still, it would later be dwarfed by what they would experience in the presence of the One who they were going to meet. It was an emotion that they had never felt in their mother's house or with the men who passed through it. It was something that they never would have found in the city. The children were finally going to experience the greatest gift of all every moment of every day, forever and ever. They would be loved.

CHAPTER 2

Sin Enters In

Noah and his family knew nothing of the drama taking place under the streets of the city. They were much too busy with final preparations for boarding the ark. Soon, perhaps as early as tomorrow, the family would abandon the homes they had always known and begin life anew inside the confines of the ark.

The ark was nearly full. For most of the day, animals had marched up the ramp and into their cages. Almost all supplies were loaded.

At nightfall, Noah and his family congregated outside his house, as they had many nights before. Just as on those other occasions, they had come to wind down after the difficult chores of the day. Unbeknownst to them, it would be each couple's last chance to spend a night in the privacy of their own homes for a long time.

The warmth of the fire drove away the stiffness from their joints. The dancing flames seemed to mesmerize them as they sat in a circle, each person staring into the coals. Prisca broke the silence.

"We are nearly ready to leave, aren't we, Dad?"

"Yes, daughter, the time is nearly upon us."

"Would you tell us now?" Prisca asked.

Noah didn't have to ask what story it was that Prisca wanted to hear. He had been promising to tell them all, and he sensed they were now ready to hear it. It had been years since he had told it to his sons. And he had never fully told it to his daughters.

"We will be going into the ark very soon and leaving this place behind," Prisca continued. "I am ready to know what led to all that we will be experiencing. How did the world get to this point? How did we get to a point that, as you have said, God's wrath will be unleashed?"

Noah's stood and began to walk around the fire. He closed his eyes and took a deep breath. Noah, as his fathers before him, took this passing on of knowledge quite seriously. Therefore, the telling of this story would be more vivid and more engrossing than any that his sons and their wives had ever heard.

Noah had grown up in a world where rich oratory was the sole means of recording history. Like his grandfather Methuselah, Noah had developed a nearly photographic memory. Likewise, he was incredibly gifted in the art of storytelling. The most wonderful characteristic of all was that Noah and Methuselah's stories were all true and were told as the events had actually happened.

"Prisca, the world that you grew up in was very different than the world that God created," Noah began. "I want to tell you the story told to my grandfather face to face by our ancestor Adam. It is the story of a garden."

As Noah spoke, all the family members felt as if they had been transported back in time. It seemed that they were actually present in Eden on that most fateful day.

He brushed silently past the fronds of a giant fern as he moved slowly along the path. He could not help but admire the beauty of this garden that God had created. Fruits and fragrant blossoms seemed to spring from everywhere in a spectacular display of color. As he moved along, he noticed a pair of lions. They were lying on their bellies upon the cool moss, eating ripe papaya that had fallen from its tree and burst upon the ground. At his approach, they stood up and moved cautiously away.

He continued his walk until he came upon one of the garden's many pools. The shade of large trees nearly hid this one from view. But the telltale gurgle of a small waterfall gave the location away. The air temperature dropped a few degrees as he stepped into the shade and neared the water's edge. He walked around the pool until he came to the end opposite the little waterfall. The water's surface was still and calm here. This was where he came to see the one creation he thought was more enchanting than the garden or anything it contained.

He lay on his stomach and stared. He could spend hours just lying there staring at what he saw in the water. How marvelous he was. Nothing God would ever create could possibly be as beautiful as he.

A tiny bird flitted into view, landing inches away. Its flight momentarily broke his concentration. Absent-mindedly yet with lightning quick speed, he caught the bird in his hand. He hated it for the distraction it had created. He began to squeeze the bird's tiny throat with just enough pressure to stop the flow of air. The bird tried desperately to flutter its wings but began to grow faint. Another second, and the heart would stop. But he mustn't for he had no authority over God's creation. Not yet. He opened his hand and the terrified bird flew frantically away.

He glanced once again at his reflection. Only now his thoughts turned, as they so often did, to God. It must have been difficult for God, knowing that he had driven away his most wonderful creation. That was the only explanation that could be given for this elaborate "paradise" and its inhabitants. God was obviously trying to fill the void that had been left after he had been cast down. It was pathetic really. The anguish God must be feeling at His loss must be excruciating. Good.

As he lay there contemplating this, he heard them approach. Compared to him or even some of the animals in the garden, the man and his woman were clumsy and slow. He despised them both, yet he was strangely intrigued by the woman. He could approach her. He could appeal to her desire for the man to be more than he was. As he watched them laugh and frolic near the forbidden tree, he could barely contain his contempt.

How stupid, he thought as he watched them. *How can God favor them over me? They're sickening in their frailty. I could expose them. God takes pride in these two. I can show Him what they truly are.*

In that same moment he saw the serpent in the tree of knowledge. He would approach the woman through the serpent so as not to overwhelm her with his presence. He moved over to sit upon a rock. As he closed his eyes and concentrated, he could suddenly see through the eyes of the serpent.

Adam walked behind as Eve teased him about keeping up. All day they had frolicked in the garden. They had ridden two of the elephants for a while but had released them and were now on foot again. For the past few minutes they had been sampling some of the fruit that God provided. Eve turned and walked backwards to face Adam as she popped berries into her mouth. She smiled provocatively. She was considering running away again because she knew Adam would give chase. She loved that game. But just when she was about to turn and run, movement caught her eye.

The movement came from the tree of knowledge of good and evil. Eve was drawn at first by the movement then by the beauty of the tree. Adam called out to her to stay away, but by then she had seen the serpent. Of all the animals in the garden, she had never seen one quite so beautiful. Adam called to her again to stop and then he jogged to catch up to her. By the time he did, Eve was talking with the serpent.

Adam listened as the serpent reassured her about the safety of eating from the tree. He stood idly by as Eve took the delicious-looking fruit in her hands. And he watched in stunned silence as she brought it slowly toward her lips. At first she just looked at it as though she could see through it to its center. Then quickly, without warning, she bit into it. She closed her eyes and tilted her head as she let the juice run from the corners of her mouth and across her cheeks.

She told Adam that it was the most delectable thing she had ever tasted. Adam hesitated before taking the fruit she offered. But then he thought that perhaps now Eve would have wisdom that he would not. Or worse, perhaps she would consider him less courageous than herself. He knew full well God's rule about the fruit from this tree. But why should Eve get to enjoy something that he could not? She had partaken and nothing bad had happened.

The sweet taste exploded in his mouth. It was a flavor and sensation of which he had never dreamed. However, almost immediately after he swallowed, his stomach began to cramp and churn. He looked up at Eve to see her folding her arms across her stomach as well. A sour, vile taste rose in their mouths. It was as they tried to spit this from their mouths that they heard the approach of God. He mustn't see them like this. They were naked. They must cover themselves.

Adam tore fig leaves from a tree as rapidly as he could. The fruit still soured his belly, and he surmised that was the reason his fingers suddenly seemed so clumsy. He had expertly made things with his hands his entire time in the garden. Now every move required thought. He couldn't seem to do anything right as he tore the leaves and had to start over repeatedly.

The man felt something he had never felt. He gritted his teeth in anger at Eve and himself for their foolish disobedience and at his frustration with the fig leaves. God would be before them soon. He must hurry.

Once the deed was done, he no longer needed the serpent. He withdrew and returned to his perch on the rock near the pool. He watched, nearly drunk with self-satisfaction, as they stumbled clumsily into the area behind some fig trees. He had done it! He had created the crack in this perfect world that would bring it all crashing down.

And the most magnificent part was how little he had to do. All that was needed was to provide this man and woman with the opportunity to let their nature take control. When the situation suited them, they would believe him instead of God! *Aha! I'll use this tactic from this point forward*, he thought as he laughed to himself. They certainly had more understanding of evil now. That was the only point he had spoken truthfully to the woman about.

His smug satisfaction was short-lived. God entered the area, and familiar fear clutched him. He hated that he could not stop the fear. He shouldn't have to feel that way. He wanted God to fear him.

He listened with guarded pleasure as God questioned first Adam, then Eve. God then began to pronounce a curse upon the serpent. But as God uttered the words, "I shall put enmity between her seed and your seed. He shall bruise your head, and you shall bruise his heel," He no longer looked upon the serpent. Instead, He turned slowly to look through the thick brush, across the little pond, and straight into his very own "beautiful" face. The face of the great deceiver.

Ham placed another log on the fire as Noah paused in his story. The patriarch had been walking around the fire inside the circle formed by his family. Now a little tired, he plopped down heavily onto a bench. He motioned toward the kettle that hung over the fire, signaling to Japheth that he wanted some hot tea for his throat.

But the stories that Noah had grown up on were vivid in his mind now. After only a swallow or two, he began again. He spoke of the difficulty that Adam and Eve suffered upon the entry of sin into their world. Then he began to tell of the transformation that took place in the garden itself. Once again, the family was transported by Noah's vivid storytelling to a green patch somewhere in the center of the garden.

The small hare moved one deliberate hop at a time in search of the lush clover he had always enjoyed. Over the last few weeks it had not been so readily found in the meadow. To his left, his littermate ventured over the hilltop to search on the far side. Both stopped often to scratch behind their ears, something they had only recently begun to do.

Things were different in the garden. Before there had not been these insects crawling on their skin or the others flying about their eyes and ears. While he searched for clover, the hare occasionally nibbled on blades of grass. It too was scarcer, tougher, and much less succulent. As the hare foraged, every movement brought puffs of dust from the earth.

A horrible shriek pierced the air. It had come from over the top of the hill. The hare hopped to the crest of the hill, instinctively curious. There was no fear. The little hare had never had any use for fear. But what he saw over the hilltop stunned and confused him. There was clover, but it was covered in red. He looked a little further to see what he thought was his littermate. It couldn't be. There was too much red. What was wrong?

The wolves were standing all around his littermate. Were they trying to pull him away from the red that was covering his fur? Often he had grazed amongst the wolves, but they usually paid him no attention. Now they were all growling and snarling. The red was on them too.

One wolf began carrying his littermate away by his neck, but another bit into his hind parts. A shriek, worse than the first one, erupted, shocking the hare. In that same instant, the red splattered onto his fur and the sickeningly warm sensation of it made him jump. The movement brought the attention of one of the other wolves. It also awakened the little hare out of a stunned paralysis.

He turned to run. He ran faster than he ever had for his den at the bottom of the hill. He could see the large boulder under which the entrance was dug. He leaped as hard as he could, his belly only inches from the ground. The boulder loomed larger, closer, then his vision filled with gray. Suddenly before him were gray fur and sharp teeth.

He wheeled left and ran some more. Even in his confusion, he knew he must get far, far away. He ran until he couldn't bring air into his tiny lungs fast enough. His heart would surely burst if he ran much farther. He had to find a burrow. He had to find somewhere to hide. But where should he go?

He would try to make the stream. Perhaps if he could hop all the way across he could hide in the large rocks on the other side. He could feel hot breath on his back. He heard yet another scream, only this one came from deep in his throat. He had never known this terror before.

He rounded a bend and almost stopped. Before him was a wall of brush covered with sharp spines that had not been near the stream the last time he had gone there. He saw a very small opening in the thistle. He would have to try and jump through. He pushed with all the might in his back legs and stretched his body as his front paws reached forward.

He landed in a spot in the center where there was no growth. He turned around just in time to see the wolves run into the thistle and yelp loudly. They were all around him now. He hunkered as close to the ground as he could and backed deep into the center of the thistles. The wolves lunged in his direction several more times, only to pull back abruptly, sometimes swiping their noses with their paws.

After a long while, they gave up. The last one in the pack looked back over his shoulder at the thistle before following the others back over the hill. The hare panted. He lay on the cool earth until nearly nightfall before his breathing slowed. Finally, he raised himself upright on wobbly hind legs. He touched his nose lightly to one of the sharp spines. He had never seen a thistle before in the garden. But he would never venture far from them again.

"Noah," Sapphira scolded. "Why must you speak to these children of such things? It's gruesome and frightening. They all care for the animals we are tending. They mustn't be made to think of this bloodshed."

"Now, Sapphira," Noah said. "They are not children. They need to know. They need to know and understand everything, not only about the goodness of God but also about the darkness that is around us."

Sapphira sat back, still looking uneasy but nonetheless succumbing to her husband's judgment. Noah continued talking. Though the fire was burning down to a pile of red coals and all their eyelids were heavy, no one could go to bed. Even though Shem, Ham, and Japheth had heard these stories many times, they were as enthralled tonight as they had been as boys.

"So all of creation was affected by sin?" Tamara asked.

"Yes, Tamara, sin did not only corrupt man. In its insidious manner, sin infiltrated all facets of God's wonderful and pure creation. You see, once sin was allowed an opening, the perfection of God's creation was violated," Noah responded.

As Noah got his second wind and was about to continue, Japheth blurted out, "Dad, tell them about Adam's sons. Tell them what happened between the brothers."

"I will, Japheth. I will."

"No, no," Sapphira exclaimed, sitting up on the edge of her chair again. "I cannot stand to hear of it. It is too much. It is too sad."

With that she stood abruptly and headed to bed. Noah looked after her, a sympathetic expression on his face. Then he looked back to his sons and their wives. All six were wide-eyed with expectation.

"Eve had given birth to two sons." And on Noah went. Noah spoke briefly of Cain and Abel's childhoods. He spoke of what type of boys they were and of what type of men they became. He spoke of what was in their hearts.

Once the last piece of brilliantly colored fruit was in place, Cain stepped back. It was perfect! Every fruit and vegetable was without blemish or flaw. He had been meticulous in arranging his offering so that the color of one fruit accentuated that of a neighboring vegetable. There was just enough greenery to add contrast. The entire display glistened with morning dew.

God will be thrilled with such a gift, he thought. *And it is well that He should be. I have labored long for weeks to nurture every part of this offering. I worked the soil around each plant to remove weeds. I hauled water up from the river when the weather was dry to keep the roots moist. I was vigilant to keep pests and insects away from all my crops.*

Now that I have taken what I need for food, it is finally time for me to enjoy God's reaction to this fine sample of the harvest. He gave me this gift I have to grow things. I know He will admire and revel in how I have used it.

Not too far away, Abel was arranging the slaughtered offering of his first lamb on the altar. He had taken neither wool nor fat from the offering, though he could have used both to make clothing or as a preservative. In fact, he had taken nothing from his herd prior to this.

The first and best his herd had produced should belong to God. Abel felt that was the least he could do in light of all the blessings God had bestowed upon him. His flock was healthy and thriving. God had provided good grazing for them. They would produce fine, rich milk and thick wool.

As he looked at his rough-hewn altar with the firstling arranged on top, Abel felt ashamed and embarrassed. "I gave my best and labored long in preparing this offering, dear God," Abel prayed. "Still as I look at what I have brought, it does not seem worthy to give to One so holy and good." When he finished placing the firstling, Abel bowed and backed away with his eyes to the ground.

Cain beamed as he approached the area with his platter of fruit and vegetables. He smiled in anticipation of the blessings God would surely bestow in light of such an offering. But soon Cain realized that God would not give a special blessing. Instead, He rejected Cain's offering altogether.

Cain stood there, shocked beyond words. He had done everything well. There was no reason for God not to accept this offering. As he fought through the disappointment, he could hear God's words to Abel.

"You have returned the best of the first blessings I have bestowed from your flock. You have come to me in humility and with reverence. Well done, my good and faithful servant."

At this, Cain's shock wore off and he began to grow angry. He threw his offering on the ground and stomped some of the pieces. With his fists clinched, he began to walk back to his dwelling. On the way, he clearly heard the voice of God asking him why he was so angry and promising him that if he were obedient, he too would be favored. God also had offered a warning that lack of obedience is sin. But Cain didn't feel much like being obedient at that moment. All he knew was that he had been treated unfairly, and he was furious.

Cain covered his ears and turned to walk in a different direction. He did not want to hear God's suggestions. He wanted the credit that was rightfully his. When he thought of this, he stopped walking. He looked at the ground and turned his head to glare over his left shoulder. He watched Abel walk into the field with his staff, the remainder of his herd following behind. It was Abel's fault. Abel had taken his blessing from him.

Abel had taken the praise that should have been his. He had worked longer and harder on his offering than Abel had. How much work had it been to slit the throat of a lamb? Cain had worked for weeks tending his crops. Abel had done nothing to deserve God's favor. As he watched Abel walking closer, Cain's breath came faster and deeper and his nostrils flared.

Cain walked to the edge of the field toward his brother. Still in shadow, Cain bent to pick up a stone slightly larger than his doubled fist. He stepped out into the sunlight with one hand slightly hidden behind his back. Cain smiled as he approached Abel, who smiled in return.

"My brother," Abel began gently. He placed a hand on Cain's shoulder. "I know you worked hard, and I also know in my heart that you will present many offerings in the future that will be pleasing to Him."

"You are right, brother. God has spoken to me and told me that I too can be accepted," Cain responded, a tight smile spreading across his face. With that, he wrapped Abel in a firm embrace that allowed him to bring the rock unnoticed from behind his back. As they hugged, Cain gritted his teeth. Abel stepped back to face Cain and noticed the wild look in his brother's eyes and the snarl on his lips. He never saw the rock but heard the loud crack inside his skull.

Abel didn't know what was happening but instinctively raised his hands and stumbled to his left to escape the pain. Cain followed and lashed out again with the rock, striking awkwardly, wildly. His second blow grazed the opposite side of Abel's head and created a long deep gash that spurted blood. Abel went down to one knee, causing Cain to trip and fall. Dirt filled his mouth. Abel, struggling to stand, tried to cry out, but his tongue would not function. He merely managed a guttural screech.

Cain was up quickly and on his brother's back as the wounded man tried to crawl forward. Abel pushed back against the weight on his back as if he could shove it away. When the next blow came down hard on the crown of Abel's head, his arms buckled. He lost control of his bladder and bowels. As he lay sprawled on his belly, his arms and legs continued to flail weakly in a pitiful attempt at escape. Cain, feeling empowered by this victory, rose up on one knee and, in blind fury, rained down blow after blow upon his helpless brother.

Cain stood over the quivering body and tossed the rock into a deep pool of blood. A drop splattered onto his cheek, and he wiped it with the back of his hand. As he examined the red streak on his knuckle, he remembered with contempt Abel's blood offering. He took a step backward, smiling at the irony.

Noah sat down heavily on one of the benches surrounding the fire. He was exhausted not only from the day's work but also from the passion he had put into the stories.

"I never have seen why Abel's sacrifice was so much better than Cain's," Ham said. "He had to work just as hard to raise his crops as Abel did to raise the lamb."

"It is not a matter of how hard Cain worked, Ham." Noah stopped abruptly, rubbed his throat, and took a swallow of what was now lukewarm tea. He bowed his head in prayer.

Shem looked around and saw that the others seemed to want an answer to Ham's question. With Noah talking to God, Shem stepped in. "The short answer is, Cain wanted to do things the way *he* thought they should be done," Shem said pensively. "He was boastful and proud of his sacrifice. Abel approached the altar in humility and with a thankful heart."

Everyone either nodded slowly to indicate their understanding or looked at the ground as if in thought. Everyone, that is, except Ham, who stood, dusted off his hands and stared into the coals.

"It still seems pretty unfair to me," he said. Then he turned and began to walk toward his house. No more was said as, one by one, each family member headed off to bed. Finally, only Noah was left. He tossed the dregs of his tea onto the few remaining embers and stood for a moment watching the steam rise.

Noah had started to call out to Ham. He wanted to stop him and explain more. *There will be time for that later, I suppose,* Noah thought. Then he thought yet again about what he had wrestled with all during that day. He couldn't decide whether he should tell everyone that they would never spend another night in these houses.

The family had been living on the ark for a week in order to test the facilities and discover adjustments that needed to be made. Noah had encouraged them all to spend tonight back in their homes. Their beds and furnishings were still there. Tomorrow, even that connection to their past lives would be gone.

Noah looked around. This little cluster of humble homes was all he had ever known. He had been born less than a quarter of a mile from here. On most days, Noah's family had felt somewhat insulated from the evil that swarmed around them. Noah had felt blessed to have always had his sons and their wives so close.

At that moment, Noah made his decision. *Let them have one more peaceful night's sleep in their own beds*, he concluded. *Better that I tell them tomorrow afternoon just before we pull the door closed. There will be less time that way for them to second-guess and worry.*

Then Noah spoke just loud enough for someone standing nearby to hear. "My Lord and my God, I have passed on your instructions. I know that tomorrow must be the day, but I don't know just when or how. How do I break it to them, Lord? There are so many more little things that could be done. How will I know when we have reached the point where we are just busying ourselves and not truly accomplishing things that are necessary?

"Lord, I ask you now. Should we board for the final time in the morning or in the evening? Should I make a speech? Should we gather on the ramp for prayer? It is such a big moment, Lord, so much preparation has been done. I feel I should lead the family on board in some special way."

Noah stood for a time looking toward the sky and listening. After hearing nothing for several minutes, he dropped his head, a glint of disappointment showing in his face. Finally, he halfheartedly kicked some sand onto the embers and turned for home.

CHAPTER 3

Prisca's Heart

Prisca awoke early the next morning. All the other family members would sleep a little later than normal after staying up listening to Noah's stories. Prisca, however, was thinking too much for sleep. She rolled over and looked at her beloved Shem. She wished he was awake and that he would wrap his arms around her. But he needed to rest and she didn't want to wake him.

As far as Prisca saw it, she had just spent one of her last nights in paradise. Shem was ninety-seven now. Prisca was ninety-four. They were entering into the prime of their lives. Prisca knew how bad life in the nearby city had become. She understood most of what Noah had told them about sin and the origination of mankind's disobedience to God. After the stories of the previous night, she had accepted that the flood was inevitable. But it wasn't her desire.

If Prisca could have everything she wanted in life, she would stay right here in this little house with the man she adored. Shem had always kept her safe. And, before him, Noah and Sapphira had given her safety and love in their home.

Prisca's first memory of anything at all was the orphanage in the city. Its owners weren't caretakers; rather they depended on the free labor provided by homeless children. On her last evening there, a very cross-looking woman viciously scolded Prisca for not scrubbing the floor thoroughly, even though the eight-year-old could barely hold the large scrub brush in her little hand. The woman had left in a huff. Prisca had known that when the woman returned, she would have a strap with which to beat her.

It was amazingly simple to leave. Prisca just opened the front door and walked out. No adults had been nearby to stop her. As she had roamed the city streets, it seemed as if she was nearly invisible. As she lay here now next to Shem, Prisca realized that had been a miracle in itself. By all rights, she should have never been able to make it out of the city alive.

But make it she did. And she had walked straight to Noah and Sapphira's door. She had never been there before. She didn't know anyone in the family. Something just looked inviting about the home. When she had knocked on the door, Sapphira had answered and smiled down at her.

In an instant, Prisca's life changed forever. She found a household filled with love. There was love for one another, and the love for God was palpable. Prisca sensed that love and was taught soon after coming to live there who God was and how He loved her too. She learned to pray and feel God's presence in her own life.

Prisca quickly felt as if she were Noah and Prisca's own daughter. She felt like a sister to Japheth and, to a little lesser extent, to Ham, who was aloof even then. She never felt like Shem's sister.

From the beginning, Shem treated her differently than the others. On her second night in the home she went to her newly made bed to find a small wooden doll on her pillow. She picked it up, delighted. Shem blushed as she caught him peering over the edge of the loft where she was staying. She knew immediately that he had made the doll for her.

On some nights there were flowers waiting for her on her pillow. On other nights she would find a few sweet berries or an apple placed there. Soon Sapphira and Noah began to notice the two holding hands as they played together outside. What started out as puppy love grew as the children grew. Their love for one another never waned. There was never a desire for any type of separation.

As Prisca listened to the steady breathing of her husband, she rolled over and placed her head on his shoulder and her arm across his chest. Shem, still sleeping, brought his arms up to embrace her.

Why do we have to leave here? Prisca wondered as she looked around the small room. Shem had painstakingly built this home long before construction on the ark had begun. It was a good house. It was solid, as only Shem could have built it. He had designed it so that rooms could be added to accommodate children. Tears began to roll down Prisca's cheeks as she pondered the fact that children would never sleep under this roof.

Suddenly she decided there was no need in lying here. Gently she moved Shem's arm from around her and got out of bed. She looked around the room and sighed with resignation. She then proceeded to the main room of the house. Prisca moved across the room and stood by a window that looked out toward Sapphira and Noah's house. She would miss her morning walks over to visit Sapphira. As she stood by the window, Prisca noticed the charred stones of the outdoor fireplace where they had all listened to Noah.

Noah had spoken last night about how God had once created a perfect garden for Adam and Eve to live in. So what would God create to replace her home here with Shem? Was it possible that, if she trusted Him, He would give her just as happy a home in the future? Shem had told her that no one was sure how long they would be on the vessel, but none of them expected to be onboard forever. That meant there would eventually be an opportunity to build a new home, perhaps in some faraway land.

Then a thought occurred to Prisca. She wasn't leaving her home. All that really made this place home would be on the ark with her. Shem would be by her side every step of the way. And she would still have her morning visits with Sapphira. She just wouldn't have to walk nearly as far to do so. Prisca smiled reluctantly at the thought of living *that* close to her extended family.

Then she looked up at the sky and she knew. Prisca knew in her heart that whether she was in her house or sitting around the fire with her family or aboard the ark or even in some far-off place, God would go with her too.

CHAPTER 4

Wheat into Flour

Sapphira was upset and more than a little frightened. *How could I have been so forgetful*, she thought as she fretfully ran her hands through her hair. She and the other women had searched all over the kitchen aboard the ark. And the kitchens in their own houses had long since been emptied of anything useful. Still they could not find a small yet critical tool.

The mortar and pestle used to grind wheat into flour were nowhere to be found. Wheat cakes and bread would be primary staples of the family diet aboard the ark. Having the ability to grind wheat was critical to their survival.

Now Sapphira, Prisca, and Adina rode along in the ox cart, dreading the moment when they would see the spires of the city coming into view. Noah and the men were busily loading the last of the animals onto the ark. Sapphira had said nothing to any of them before they left. She didn't want the men upset at such an already stressful time.

Instead, she slipped quietly away to solve a problem that she felt she had created. She was afraid to go into the city alone, even in the morning. So she talked her daughters-in-law into going with her. Everyone, that is, with the exception of Tamara. After what Tamara had been through, there was no way Sapphira would ask her to go back to the city. Sapphira had not even told her she was leaving. There was no need for her to worry about the three of them. Besides, her talent with animals would be needed on this day.

The oxen plodded along with ease, pulling the empty cart. Their work was no challenge as the weight of the three women and the cart paled in comparison to the huge logs and beams they had been dragging in recent years to the ark. This was a relatively young pair of oxen, and this would be their last chore and exercise prior to boarding the ark themselves.

It was Sapphira's hope that they would be in and out of the city long before the thugs and hoodlums emerged from the hiding places where they slept off the previous night's activity. By mid-afternoon they would begin waking up and taking to the streets to terrorize whomever they encountered.

As they approached the city's outskirts, they had to stop the cart often. The city seemed to be bursting at the seams with all the activity. Carts and wagons filled the streets, crisscrossing in front of one another. Vendors lined the sidewalks and spilled into the alleys hawking their goods.

Mostly there were people. Everywhere you looked and as far as one could see down each street were seas of people. Most people lived to an average age of seven hundred years. In previous generations, families of twenty or more children had been common. The earth God had created and the farming techniques He had revealed to man provided plenty of the fruits and vegetables the people needed for a steady expansion of the population.

There were just over two million people in the city that morning. There were nearly four billion across the whole earth. However, the three women in the cart were not aware of these numbers. They only knew they couldn't wait to have their business conducted and to be away from this crowd and back at home.

As Prisca looked at the sea of faces from her seat on the cart, she was reminded of other trips to the city and how she was always stricken by the same sadness. She so desperately missed children. She knew Adina did as well. Sapphira had at least been able to raise Prisca and her sons, but she too ached for the sound of a child's laughter.

Tragically, this was not a time or a world for children. Children weren't wanted by the world that Prisca lived in. The city was devoid of any religion or references to it. However, pagan cults did exist in outlying areas. Many of these cults demanded that families sacrifice the firstborn male and female child to them. The ritual of sacrifice was so brutal that most chose not to have children to avoid the emotional devastation. Inexplicably to the women of Noah's family, the people would not abandon their pagan gods despite this fear.

Others did not believe in any god but instead lived for their own pleasure. Casual sex was not only acceptable but expected. Pregnancy provided an unwanted hindrance to the almost constant fulfilling of lustful desire. Therefore, practices and treatments could be undergone to end pregnancy before it progressed very far. If a pregnancy did progress and a baby was born, the parents were well within their rights to dispose of the infant. They need not provide a reason. Everyone could understand someone not wanting to be burdened with childrearing.

Ten years prior to the trek the women now made into the city, there would have been some little faces in the crowds. But only a few of those allowed to be born by their parents had made it to adulthood. In this society, where pagan temple ritual called for little girls to be given to temple priests to be horrifically used and then discarded as the priests saw fit, violence against children was rampant.

Once such a brutal example had been set by religious leaders, there was no determination on the part of society to protect children from routine things like beatings or even murder. Laws to protect children were first loosely enforced and ultimately abandoned altogether. The younger women in Noah's family grew up in a world where children were given no value and no protection. All three vowed never to bring their own children into such a world.

The little cart rolled past the museum. Prisca and Adina whispered to each other.

"Well, Adina, we always were curious about what was behind those grand columns. I suppose now we will never know."

"No, I suppose not," Adina replied as she looked at the polished steps. Neither woman knew that, just a few nights before, two children that the world had forgotten had fought to survive just beneath the street where their cart now traveled.

The women fought the crowds and eventually arrived at their destination. Though the weather was warm, they had the hoods of their capes pulled tightly around their faces. It was important that they get in and out of the city without being recognized. Many within the crowds at one time or another had made treks out to the ark construction site. They used these little day trips as opportunities to mock and deride Noah and his family. It was highly likely that some within the throng might recognize Sapphira or one of the other women.

Sapphira had guided the cart to one of the most affluent shopping districts in the city. Here she would pay more for the items she needed, but it was her hope that the people in this neighborhood would be less likely to recognize them or speak out if they did.

"Wait by the cart," Sapphira instructed her daughters as she parked in front of a shop. "I will do this as quickly as possible, and we shall be on our way."

She entered the shop to see a haggard-looking woman moving large earthen carafes of dried beans, tea, and coffee from one shelf to another. Sapphira began to look around the store, hoping to quickly find what she needed on her own so that she would not have to speak to anyone.

"What do you want?" the woman asked, impatiently turning to look back over her shoulder at Sapphira.

"I want to purchase a mortar and pestle." Sapphira kept her reply as succinct as possible.

The woman, who was nearly as old as Sapphira, blew her bangs out of her eyes and stared at her. Then she looked back toward the shelves, wearing an expression that looked as if she were sharing a private joke at Sapphira's expense with some imaginary coworker.

"I haven't sold one of those in years. I'm not sure I even have one. Besides, it would be in the back and I'm not going to look for it. I have too much else to do. You can buy something that you see on these shelves or you can go elsewhere. I could care less."

"Please, ma'am. I need to buy one today. And I really must not take the risk—well, I just can't go anywhere else."

"What's the matter, lady? If you don't grind some wheat today, is the world going to come to an end or something? I already told you I am busy. Go find your stuff somewhere else. You're starting to get on my nerves."

"Please. I am willing to pay more than these items are worth. I can make it worth your while. I am even willing to go in the back and look for it myself."

Sapphira held out a small leather pouch that contained enough coins to easily pay for half the cookware in the store. She had brought all the money she had saved through the last several years. She knew the coins would be worthless in the world that Noah assured her was to come. She found herself hoping, as she held out the pouch, that the word Noah claimed to have from God really had come from God.

The woman eyed the pouch. She had been a merchant a long time. She did not need to look inside the pouch to have a pretty good idea of what it contained. Her highly attuned ear allowed her to accurately estimate the value from the mere clink of the coins inside.

"I suppose I could accommodate you," she raised her eyes back up to meet Sapphira's. "But I don't need you rummaging around in my storeroom. You wait here."

As the woman walked through the curtain to the storeroom, Prisca and Adina sat on the back of the cart. Their heads were down as they hoped to avoid eye contact with those who passed by. Sapphira's strategy to encounter more agreeable people in this part of the city would not prove successful.

A group of three finely dressed men walked by on the sidewalk and stared intently at the women in the cart. Adina and Prisca saw them from the corner of their eyes and felt themselves being gawked at. Both women were thinking the same thing: *Please keep walking, please keep walking.*

"Well, what have we here?" one of the men remarked. He had lagged behind the other two and had stopped just even with the back of the cart. "What are you two ladies up to?" He addressed Adina directly now.

Both Prisca and Adina were attractive women. Adina, in particular, had striking looks which she modestly tried to dress down. She had purposely developed a habit of wearing clothes that were a little too large for her.

"Lads," he called back to his cronies. "Don't be in such a hurry. Looks like we have a couple of farm girls come to town." He then leaned down to attempt to look closely at Adina's face. She turned her head away.

"Now don't be like that," one of the other two men said to Adina. "We're just trying to be friendly. We don't get a lot of your kind in this part of town."

The first man reached out and began to run his hand down the rough homemade fabric of Adina's cape. It was obvious to everyone from their clothing that the women were not from this part of the city. The man grasped the front of the cape and tried to pull it open.

"Let's see what you have underneath here," the man said. "I have a feeling that you're hiding something that really should be shared with the rest of us," he said as he stared at her. Adina pulled her clothes tightly to her.

By now the other men had come around the other side of the cart and were standing alongside Prisca.

"This one's a little on the skinny side for my taste," one of them said. "But she certainly does have a pretty face." He lifted his hand and tried to stroke Prisca's cheek, but she abruptly turned away. Both women still stared at the ground.

A crowd was beginning to gather, yet no one had any intention of coming to the aid of the two women. Adina and Prisca were growing increasingly frightened.

The first man, feeling empowered by the laughter that was building within the gathering crowd, spoke once again.

"Come on, you," he grasped the lapels of Adina's cape. "Stand up and let us have a real look at you. We might want to invite you to play."

Adina was scared, but in that instant her mind went to Tamara. While she didn't know what had happened to her sister-in-law a few weeks ago within this very city, she did know how adversely it had affected her. Adina felt her face flush, and anger begin to boil up from her core. With all her strength, she brought both hands down onto the man's wrists, breaking his grip. For the first time she looked directly into the man's eyes, a look of defiance in her own. She saw a moment of shock in the man's face, which he tried to cover by smiling crookedly. He rubbed his wrist as he took a step back.

"Wow! This one packs a pretty good wallop."

Adina's hands were hurting as well but she dared not let it show. It was at that moment that Sapphira emerged from the store. The woman had followed Sapphira to the door and held the bag of coins in one hand.

"You must really want to grind some flour, lady," she said as she looked around at the gathering crowd.

"Get away from my door, all of you!" She yelled to no one in particular.

The crowd, completely ignoring the shop owner, turned its attention back to the activity near the ox cart.

Sapphira pushed her way through the crowd and sat the bowl down beneath the seat of the cart. The large pestle was still in her hand. Sapphira did not have to ask any questions to get a sense of what was going on. She stooped in an exaggerated fashion and walked up to the first man. In the best kindly-old-lady voice she could muster, she said, "If it please you, sir, my daughters and I seek no trouble with you. This one is sorry if she has offended in any way. If you would be so kind, we would be on our way, sir."

"Oh, there is no offense taken whatsoever, old woman," the man replied. "But you won't be going anywhere just yet. Why, we were just getting to know one another."

Sapphira was already sorry she had brought Adina and Prisca along. Now she realized that one old woman traveling alone likely would have been ignored. She had made more than one error in judgment today. However, she wouldn't have that error result in harm to these precious young women.

Sapphira was old. But she had spent her life in hard labor, first on Noah's farm and then often working side by side with him on the ark. She was both fit and savvy. And she now understood that the time for talk had passed.

She didn't hesitate. She gripped the pestle tightly in both hands and stepped forward as she drove it with all her weight into the man's solar plexus. Not expecting such a move from one who appeared so frail, the man was caught completely off guard and crumpled into a heap on the street. It took his mates a moment to realize what had happened. When they did, one made a move toward Sapphira. As he did, Adina stuck out a foot, tripping the man. As he fell, Sapphira swung the pestle with both hands in a backward arc, landing it squarely on the man's nose. As she did so, her hood came off and fell to her shoulders.

The crowd at first cheered and laughed at the plight of the three men. The remaining man, embarrassed and having seen enough of the abilities of these farm women, ran off down the street. The crowd would have just as readily cheered if the assault on Adina had continued. They were only interested in a show. Any show would do.

Two of the people in the crowd were a man and woman who recently had spent an evening at the nearby museum. The man still had not replaced his stolen cloak. He spoke to his female companion.

"Say! You have been curious about Noah's ark," he said loudly enough for all to hear. "Why don't you ask that old lady? After all, she is Noah's wife!"

The situation was deteriorating rapidly. Sapphira boarded the seat and got the oxen moving as rapidly as possible. The oxen were relatively slow on an open road under good conditions. Now, with the traffic and the suddenly pressing crowds, their progress was even slower. Those who had gathered at the storefront began to follow them. Word spread rapidly as to who the women in the cart were. Though some in the gathering mob had never heard of Noah, those who had quickly convinced them that anyone associated with his family was deserving of whatever verbal abuse they wanted to hurl at them.

"What are you doing here with the damned?" one woman inquired.

"You should be back in your wooden crate looking down on us vile sinners," another added sarcastically.

Sapphira wanted to stop the cart. She wanted to plead with the people and assure them yet again that Noah and their family did not look down on them. She wanted to remind them that Noah had tried desperately for years to include upon the ark any who would repent and come aboard. But there had been no takers during those repeated attempts, and Sapphira knew there would be none now. The only thing to do at this point was to continue moving toward the country-side and hope that the crowd did not turn violent.

Suddenly the man from the museum spoke again. "These women want to live amongst the animals. Why don't we make them feel at home?" With that, he reached into the street and scooped up a handful of mud mixed with horse manure. He threw it toward the cart, hitting Sapphira hard on the side of her head. The swelling crowd roared its approval.

The hood of her cloak provided little protection from the sting. Sapphira first felt the sting and then the disgusting warm wetness on her cheek and in her ear. She kept one hand on the rod with which she guided the oxen. With the other she reached back to pull her hood more tightly around her face.

The man had started something, for now many in the crowd began to search for animal droppings to throw. Soon Adina and Prisca were crouched down as low as possible in the back of the cart, trying desperately to protect themselves. The oxen were being pelted as well. They were startled but continued to plod along at a slightly more brisk pace. As Sapphira was hit repeatedly with the foul-smelling projec-tiles, she felt her eyes well up with tears. She was deter-mined not to give the people the satisfaction of seeing her cry, still she felt so very humiliated. Not only that, but she was deeply angered that her daughters-in-law had to endure this type of treatment.

Finally, after what seemed an eternity, Sapphira could see the edge of the city as they topped a hill. She was counting on the people's laziness to keep them from pursuing them any further than that. Some already were losing interest and drifting away. Frighteningly, the core group that remained seemed to grow angrier. Some were beginning to throw rocks. As the three women finally passed an abandoned building at the outer edge of the city, Sapphira heard Prisca cry out as a rock landed with a thud against her rib cage.

"Don't think that we are through with you!" a distant man's voice declared. "We shall be out to visit you and your ark shortly."

If Sapphira and the other women would have had the opportunity to look inside the old building they were passing, they would have seen a rather odd-looking little man. Tiptoeing, he was just tall enough to leer at them over the sill of an upstairs window. The man had coarse, gray hair that almost completely covered his arms and legs. His legs were short and stumpy. His midsection was nearly as big around as the man was tall.

He watched the three women roll along the road and out of sight. Then he looked back towards the city and saw the crowd beginning to disperse. He waddled back over to the middle of the room and eased into a sitting position. He looked over at Sapphira's mortar and pestle, which he had stolen from her kitchen two days before. After peeking in Sapphira's window as he had just peeked out this one, the little man had waited for an opportune time to sneak inside the house and take the tool. Now the man reached out and picked up the mortar and turned it over in his hands. Then, placing a chubby hand on his head, he ran it across the patch of long hair that grew only around the perimeter of his skull.

What would he do with this now? he wondered. Leave it here, he surmised. As he stared off into space he smiled a little, revealing three pointed teeth. His master, the Prince of the Air, would surely be pleased. By choosing the mortar and pestle to steal, he had forced Sapphira to come into town and incite the crowds there. Now a mob would be formed in the city that would go out and destroy the ark.

At least he hoped a mob would form. That was the plan, after all. He pulled himself up to the window and looked toward the city again. All the people had melted back into the hubbub of the city and abandoned the chase. *Hmmm,* he thought, *it appears that our work must continue.* The people would need to be reminded how angry they were at Noah and his family. He and a few of the others could see to that. A whisper here and a rumor there, and they could have an out-of-control mob together in no time.

As he had heard the Prince say many times, Noah and the others must not be allowed to shut the door of the ark. God would not allow the Prince or any of his workers to enter the ark when the door was sealed and the window was closed. The Prince's plan was nearly complete. With the children wiped out, it would only be a matter of time before all of mankind would die off from the earth. Then what seed of the woman would be left? Crush the Prince's head, would He? God would never succeed in continuing the Son's line with only the protection of such an ugly wooden box. Why, the thing didn't even look like a boat!

The man stood stiffly. To an observer he would have looked on the verge of collapsing from a heart attack. That is, until he leapt from the upstairs window and landed with a perfect somersault on the street below. He sprang to his feet and a dust cloud arose from where he had landed. He began to walk towards the city to look for just the right person to incite. He laughed at the thought of God's folly. "Crush the Prince's head indeed," the little man croaked. Then with his next step he disappeared into thin air, leaving only his hoof prints in the dust of the street.

CHAPTER 5

Inciting the Crowd

Noah walked out to meet the cart as the women approached. He had walked up the road a full mile and was just coming even with the back of the line of animals that were walking in an amazingly orderly fashion up the ramp and into the ark. Sapphira could readily see at a distance that Noah's piercing blue eyes were aflame. His tunic was covered in dust from his work. His stark white beard and long hair, though dingy with dust, flowed in the light breeze.

"Sapphira, where have you been?" Noah asked sternly. "And what have you been doing? You are all filthy!"

"We had to go into town, I –"

"*Into town?* On this day of all days?"

"Noah, you know I would have never taken such a risk if I hadn't had to." Sapphira never stopped the cart as she spoke. She continued on toward the ark, subconsciously seeking its refuge. All of the ladies looked pitiful. Their clothes were filthy and their hair was caked with manure. Adina and Prisca didn't realize that they had not even looked up to make eye contact with their father-in-law, but Noah did. Based on his own experience, he had an idea of what the women had been through.

"Is anyone following you?" he asked.

"We have not seen anyone on the road behind us," Prisca finally spoke, still looking at the floor of the little cart. "But some in the crowd threatened to come here."

Noah was angry and worried. But it was apparent how badly Sapphira and the girls felt. There was nothing to be gained now by chastising them further. Instead, Noah stared back down the road toward the city as the women continued toward the ark. He knew they had at least two more hours before the last animals would be loaded, although the work would go faster now that the women were here to help. Still, the last of the loading had taken significantly longer than Noah or Shem had estimated it would.

"Lord," Noah began to pray, "let us at least be inside before anyone comes."

The parade of animals finally ended, hours later than Noah anticipated. At frequent intervals, Noah nervously glanced over his shoulder toward the city. Each time, he saw a vacant road. No one was approaching the ark.

The women worked as hard as the men in completing last-minute preparations to make the family's living quarters tenable and helping with the animals. Sapphira, Prisca, and Adina had gone about their tasks grimly, their clothes still covered by the putrid stains of their attack. Except for a partial cleaning in a wash basin, there had been neither time nor adequate water supplies for them to enjoy the luxury of taking a bath or washing their clothes and hair.

As the women continued working inside, Shem suddenly found himself standing outside near the bottom of the ramp. For the first time in years, he realized he had nothing to do. For so long, he had kept a running list in his mind of what task he needed to accomplish next. With no fanfare, Shem now realized there was nothing left on the list.

He looked around and then up the ramp as if he might see something that would jog his memory and get him started on something new. As he looked up the ramp onto the lower deck, he saw Tamara leading two zebras around the corner toward their stalls. They were the last ones.

Shem looked all around. The open field around the ark was empty for the first time in weeks. There were no animals standing about. Except for Noah, every other family member was on board busily going about their own tasks. Shem couldn't believe it. He knew this moment would come, but it had snuck up on him. Could it be possible that years of work were finally complete? Shem walked up to the top of the ramp for a better view of the surrounding area. Surely there must be a stray animal somewhere that they had forgotten. He saw nothing.

Shem cupped his hands around his mouth to shout at Noah, who was heading toward the ark from some distance away. "Dad, I actually think—," Shem quickly stopped talking. There was a dust cloud on the road. Someone or something was coming. Shem squinted in that direction. He saw torches. Again, he cupped his hands and shouted forcefully this time, "Dad, get over here fast! There is a crowd coming up the road."

Noah's eyes grew large for a moment and then the older man began to run. Shem met him at the bottom of the ramp and grasped his arm, nearly carrying him up the ramp. When they got to the top, Noah turned toward Shem. With a tight grip on both Shem's forearms, Noah looked him in the eye and said breathlessly, "Call for your brothers. We have to get this door closed now."

Sapphira and Adina, unaware of the drama unfolding, walked up to the men. "We've decided to get some extra plates from Adina's cupboard," Sapphira commented.

"No," Noah said, still catching his breath. "No one is going back out. Shem is getting his brothers, and we are closing this door."

"Right now?" Sapphira asked, incredulous. "We aren't quite ready," she went on. "We need to—" Noah held up a hand and shook his head.

"Sapphira," he said sternly, "it is time. I asked God last night to tell me the precise time that we should board. He has just answered my question. I know this seems abrupt, but I am certain of it. The time is now."

A few seconds later, the boys manned the ropes that would close the ramp. Noah bowed his head in thanks as the door closed with a solid thud. His family was safe inside for now, although everyone except Shem looked more than a little unsure.

As if on cue, menacing black clouds began to roll in. Noah and his family climbed a ladder to peek through the narrow window at the top of the ark. Undeterred by the change in the skyline, the crowd continued their approach. The group was much larger than the one the women had encountered.

Through the window, which ringed the upper deck, it was possible to look out from the ark's gabled peak to the sloping roof over the main part of the vessel. Because of the angle, there was no way to see the ground directly around the ark from the vantage point of the windows. In fact, someone would have to be standing at least a hundred yards away from the side of the ark to be seen from the window. So as the crowd rushed closer to the ark, Noah lost sight of them. But they could be heard clearly.

It was readily apparent that those speaking were drunk. Their speech was badly slurred.

"Hey, Noah!" called out a strange man who was apparently the group's leader. "Come on out here and tell us if these are the clouds you have been waiting for. Guess you were right after all. Looks like it might rain," he continued sarcastically.

At the sound of the man's voice, Japheth's dog, Rowdy, growled quietly, a deep rumble coming from his chest. Japheth knelt beside his companion and wrapped his arms around the big dog's neck in a soothing embrace.

Many in the crowd began picking up construction debris, rocks, and anything else they could gather. Noah knew what was coming. He only hoped the ark was strong enough to protect them.

His biggest concern was that the people would focus their efforts on forcing open the door. If they thought of that, there was nothing to stop them from coming aboard. They would have been welcome under different circumstances, but it was clear that these people had nothing but ill intentions.

There seemed to be no plan for any type of attack as some stumbled about and laughed hysterically at what seemed like nothing in particular. Many of them seemed perplexed as to how to approach such a large vessel. Suddenly, the first man who spoke stepped back to speak again. As he did so, Noah saw that he carried a heavy axe.

"If you're not coming out, maybe we should let ourselves in!" the instigator shouted. With that he unleashed a guttural roar that continued as he ran toward the ark and threw the axe. The others, following his lead, began to throw whatever makeshift projectile they had in their hands. The axe hit the hull sideways and glanced off the thick boards. The rocks and sticks pinged off the ark's exterior. With the exception of a few seconds of loud clattering and banging that startled the animals and set Rowdy to barking, there was no damage done from the first volley.

Realizing the futility of their attack, the throng of people began to mill about and formulate a plan. The torches were handed off from one individual to another until they were clustered in the center of the group. Noah, understanding their intentions, felt fear grip him.

"Dear Lord," he whispered to himself, "if they are able to get the pitch on the hull to ignite—"

Noah didn't finish his prayer. As he spoke, he saw from his vantage point in the window little spouts of dust kick up from the ground in various spots around the ark. Before he had a chance to realize what he was seeing, he heard a roar. Those who he could see in the crowd crouched down and threw their arms over their heads. The distant roar was moving toward the people and the ark from the west, and the spouts of dust became more and more prevalent. Noah stuck his hand out the window, then quickly jerked it back in when balls of ice stung him.

For a few seconds the ice hit the roof of the ark with such force that all on board subconsciously did as the crowd outside and crouched. Then, just as quickly as the hail started, it stopped. In its place, great drops of rain began to fall. Like the hail, the rain fell slowly for a few seconds then came down in a torrent. The intensity of the rain made the crowd begin to disperse.

Noah, standing once again, saw that some of the torches were flickering out. The man who had done most of the talking threw his torch halfheartedly toward the ark. Then he and a few others broke away from the group and headed in the opposite direction towards Noah's house.

"Everyone, start closing these shutters," Noah said calmly.

The rain continued without let up. Shem, who had taken over Noah's post at the window, had seen no one from the crowd for several hours and assumed that most sought shelter inside his house and the houses of his family. In any case, they were not attacking the ark. And that was good news.

Shem couldn't take his eyes off the rain. He and his family had rarely seen rain in their lives. In the world that had existed since the Garden of Eden, most of the earth's moisture was delivered in the form of a thick cool fog that shrouded everything during the night and through the early morning. Only once or twice per year had rain ever fallen, and never before had it come like this. Its arrival provided a sense of validation for the years of work Shem and his family had done on the ark.

Still, Shem could not envision the puddles of water that were forming outside ever getting deep enough to make the ark float. He found himself simultaneously hoping that such a flood would occur and praying that it would not.

So many times, he had wanted some assurance that his trust in his father was justified. He had wanted some way to know that Noah was not insane. At the same time he could not fathom everything and everyone in the world being destroyed. If that is what it took to prove that Noah actually had heard the voice of God, Shem didn't want proof.

Winds kicked up and rain began to blow sideways onto the narrow walkway that extended the length of the ark's window. Shem reached out to grasp the last open shutter and pull it towards him. Before he did so, he reached up above the window and pulled a rope that would raise a diverter gate. The gate had been installed in the gutter at the roof's edge. Normally, rainwater from the roof was intended to run down the gutter the length of the ark and dump off the back. With the opening of this gate, water was diverted to a secondary piping system, where it traveled inside the ark and spilled from a header into a series of barrels.

As God had instructed Noah, the family had spent no time and energy in hauling large amounts of water to the ark. Despite the fact that no rain had fallen during the final months of preparation, God had promised Noah that he would provide clean water for the family and the animals. Once again, things were happening the way that God had promised Noah that they would.

The water fell from God's heavens and landed on the roof of the ark. It was a rain of provision and a rain of cleansing. As the other barrels filled, one had been removed. In its place was a tub where Adina rested.

Sapphira knelt by Adina's head and guided the spout of water from one of the openings in the header onto her hair. At the same time, Tamara helped Prisca to wash the stains from

69

the women's clothes. As the rainwater and soap was worked into the fabric, the stains became fainter until eventually they could not be seen at all. The therapeutic hair washing process would be repeated for each woman. Sapphira had insisted on going last.

Eventually, the water would cleanse from their hair and clothes the last vestiges of humiliation that the women had suffered in town—just as it washed over the earth, settling the thick dust of drought that had covered it. Ultimately, the rainwater would be God's means of cleansing the world from the evil that had consumed it.

CHAPTER 6

The Waters Rise

R aamah had spent the last few hours soaked to his skin on
the roof of a house. It wasn't his house. The house had
belonged to a couple who had run back into town with a large
group. Raamah had overheard some in the crowd talking
about having been out to Noah's ark, whatever that was. From
their conversation, it was clear that some in the group who
had thought this Noah a crazy man were suddenly beginning
to wonder if perhaps he were perfectly sane. Raamah had not
given their babbling much thought. His primary concern had
been getting in out of the driving rainstorm.

The only reason he chose the middle-age couple as his
hosts was that their house was the first one the crowd came
to. The couple turned and left the crowd and walked a short
distance up a street to enter their house. Raamah could see
from his vantage point in an alley across the street that it was
a good-looking house. It looked solid and dry and was likely
well stocked with food. Raamah decided it would do quite
nicely and that he should invite himself to be the couple's
houseguest.

Raamah looked in the window, deciding how he wanted
to do this. He could see the stricken faces of the two of them
and could make out most of their conversation.

"But we have never seen rain like this in our lives," the woman was saying. "Is it possible that Noah and Adina were right?"

"It has rained hard for a few hours. It has to have done this before somewhere. It will take a little more than this," the husband declared, raising his hands overhead to indicate the rain, "to make me admit that that fanatic, that kook Noah was right."

Raamah made a mental note to find out more about who this Noah was and where he could be found. The husband continued.

"I'll tell you one thing; as soon as this lets up I am going right back out there and demand that our daughter be released. This has gone far enough."

"Perhaps she is safest there for now," the wife replied. "I haven't spent my life protecting her to place her in jeopardy now."

As Damaris spoke about the safety of her daughter, she suddenly looked very familiar to Raamah. Then it hit him. He had seen this lady before. His old man took him to this lady's village when he was a youngster. Or at least Raamah thought she looked familiar. It was hard to keep all the saps whose lives he had destroyed through the years straight. Their faces all ran together. Raamah decided not to give these two any more of his time. He was getting wet.

With one blow from his forearm, the front door to the house splintered and the giant bent down to step through. His head touched the ceiling slightly as he said, "Thanks for inviting me. I'll be staying here awhile."

Then he said to Damaris, "What I need from you is a plate of hot food." The woman had dealt with giants before for her face had blanched a pale white and abject fear was in her eyes. "Get up and fix me something to eat now!" Raamah bellowed as he reached to jerk the woman up by the arm.

It was about that time that his plans were ruined. As was sometimes the case, the woman's husband suddenly decided to be a fighter. Before Raamah could lay hands on the woman, Othniel whacked him as hard as he could across the shoulder and back of his head with a broomstick. To the powerful giant it felt like a polite slap on the back. Raamah's incredible reflexes went to work. He thrust his dagger into the side of the man's neck.

Damaris screamed like a cornered animal, rose from her seat, and dove for Raamah, clawing at his eyes with her fingernails. Her sharp nails were enough to make Raamah wince and his eyes water. He struck her as hard as he could in the side of her head with his fist. The woman went limp and fell to the floor in a heap.

That had been a week ago. Raamah felt bad about having thrown out the rubbish, as he had called it, when he threw the couple's bodies out into the street. He felt bad not for the couple but for himself. Without the woman around to cook, he had been forced to eat cold food from the kitchen. At least he had been able to entertain himself by trying to predict when the ever-deepening waters in the street would rise high enough to wash the bodies away. That had occurred the day before yesterday.

It had rained extraordinarily hard for an entire week, and the water was almost all the way up to the edge of the flat roof. Raamah looked up at the black sky and cursed it for making him so wet and miserable. There was no need staying here.

Raamah remembered what he had heard about the man named Noah who had built an ark. Raamah didn't know much about it, only that there was food inside and it might be dry.

As he stood on the roof he saw a door floating down what had once been the busy street. Without giving it much thought, Raamah jumped toward the door and into the churning brown water. The door turned over once, then twice, as he tried to secure himself on it. He flailed wildly in a near-panic when his head went under the water. Suddenly, his feet touched something solid, and he used the leverage to get the upper half of his body onto one end of the door. Turning it into a makeshift raft, he kicked his powerful legs and pointed himself in the direction that the couple had been walking from.

Hours later, Raamah was able to see the ark in the distance. It was surrounded by others who, like him, had managed to ride on anything that would float to this point. As he drifted closer, he could hear the people screaming to be let in. Many were standing on wobbly legs on their rafts as they reached up futilely toward the top of the ark. Others clawed pitifully at the hull as if they could scratch their way inside.

Once Raamah and his door were beside the ark, one of the other people fell from a log onto the door. Raamah, despite his size and physical strength, could not swim. He went into the water with his eyes wide and his limbs flailing. He stretched to his full height but his feet did not touch bottom. He felt himself sinking but then threw his arms over the now-abandoned log previously used by the man who fell onto the door. After an exhausting struggle, he was able to straddle the log and paddle with his hands to come alongside the ark.

He placed his huge hands on the hull for balance. Then he doubled his hand into a fist and pounded with all his might on the hull, breaking his right hand in the process. He was now desperate to get inside before the water rose higher. He drew back his fists to pound again but his action was stopped by a loud creaking and popping from the hull. With a great screech, the ark floated free from the scaffold and stands upon which it had rested during its construction.

The ark lurched abruptly toward Raamah, knocking him from the log. Again, he tried to flail and fight to keep his head above the surface. His arms were heavy now from his struggle, his strength was failing him, and he was overtaken by the massive hull. He felt himself being pushed down deeper and deeper towards the bottom.

For the first time in his life, Raamah knew terror. He knew what Jerah, Shelah, Adina's parents, and dozens of his other victims had felt at the sight of him. In a last fit of anger, he pushed up hard from the bottom in an attempt to break through the surface for a breath. Instead, the crown of his head hit hard on the bottom of the ark. Stunned, he tried to stand again and again until finally he could hold his breath no longer. He opened his mouth to scream in defiance. Raamah, eyes bulging, felt the murky floodwater filling his lungs. It was the last sensation he would ever know in this life.

CHAPTER 7

The First Morning

I woke with a start as Rowdy was licking my face. At first I was disoriented and not sure whether the horrors of the previous night had been a dream or reality. Had I really chased my hysterical wife down the passage? Had the ark actually broken away from its scaffold? One look up at the perfectly sealed door brought me fully awake. Yes, it had all been real.

Presently, the sounds from outside had faded. I could still hear people calling out as if in the distance and could only assume that they were now clinging to distant treetops. As near as I could estimate inside the dark confines of the passageway, it was early morning. We had survived the first night of being afloat.

As I shook off the effects on my mind of restless sleep, I looked down at Tamara. The normally beautiful brown hair that flowed across her shoulders and down her back was now tangled and stuck with perspiration around her face. Her mouth gaped open and she almost seemed to have fainted more than to have fallen asleep. My wife normally had a lovely fair complexion. On this morning, her face looked pale and almost waxen. It had been a very difficult night for all of us, but Tamara had such a gentle spirit. I found myself worrying and hoping that she would recover emotionally.

I tried to ease her head off my shoulder and rise from my uncomfortable position alongside the passage wall. Despite my best efforts not to wake her, Tamara stirred and then opened her pretty brown eyes. They were clouded with confusion and red from hours of crying. As I stood stiffly to my feet I stumbled to one side and then the other. The ark was gently swaying. We were actually floating!

With the exception of some tiny craft that we had fished from on the lake, none of us had any prior experience with or use for boats. So it was that throughout construction, Shem, Ham, and I often discussed whether the ark would be too heavy to float. Except for Father, none of us was even sure if the floodwaters would come. If they did, my brothers and I all had visions of the hulking, fully loaded ark remaining on the ground as the waters rose. We worried that the water would eventually rise up and spill in through the window that ran along the very top of the ark, filling it with water and dooming us all.

The ark was large and heavy. It would take a great deal of water for it to float away from its stands. With that much water, I surmised that the one I had heard pounding on the hull the night before must have been holding onto whatever he could find that would float.

I reached down and helped Tamara to stand. We began to shuffle slowly down the passage and back toward the living quarters where we had left my mother, father, Shem, and Prisca. We stumbled often as we struggled to walk. I noticed that Rowdy was even unsteady as he followed me.

Tamara and I hadn't spoken to one another in several hours. Both of us were too much in shock to speak. For my part, I felt that if I began to talk about what we had just experienced that I might become emotional. Tamara didn't need that now. Perhaps the sounds of our footsteps alerted the animals to our presence for many began to vocalize as we passed.

"I am going to have a look at some of the animals," Tamara said, breaking the silence.

"Yes, that would be good. You go on ahead. I'll check on the others and join you in a while," I replied.

I encouraged Tamara to be with the animals she loved so much. I knew that she would find some small comfort in being near them.

The first member of the family that I found was my brother Ham. At the last moment, he had insisted that he and his wife Adina move away from the rest of the family. The two of them had made makeshift quarters in one of the rooms where food was stored. As I arrived at the storage room door, they were lying awake on the bed they had fashioned from straw.

Ham looked disheveled and angry. He was angry often. He was angry before Dad first mentioned the ark and was much worse after. I was not thrilled with having to work on the ark, but Shem and I had too much respect for Dad to disobey. Ham was different. For the first several months he defied our father's orders and went out riding horses across the countryside with his friends or into the city while the rest of us worked.

Ham was the strongest physically, and we needed him. One night when Ham came home, Father was waiting for him. I don't know what was said, but early the next morning Ham joined us in the work. He had been a reluctant participant ever since.

"Where have you been?" Ham asked accusingly. "You weren't in the living quarters where you were supposed to be. That's not like you, oh dutiful son."

His sarcasm didn't sting anymore. I had grown accustomed to it long ago.

"Tamara was very upset by, by what we were hearing. I was with her."

Merely speaking of it made my throat ache and tears well up in my eyes. I stared at the floorboards for a long moment while my mind filled with pictures of horror-stricken faces.

"Tamara is a weak-minded fool!" Ham snapped. "Why doesn't she spend her energy worrying about us floating around in this wretched box of your father's?"

I ignored the insult to my wife and blurted, "Ham, God is real! He sealed the door, and He really did speak to Dad."

"You bumped your head chasing around that stupid wife of yours! Of course, God is real, but God didn't seal the door. We did. We did it because Dad was probably off somewhere on board praying or building an altar or some such nonsense to give any thought to the door. What kind of madman would build a door for a floating box with a crack as wide as two of my fingers all the way around?"

"You're wrong. The pitch would have never kept the water out. Our latch is hanging loose." I replied. "The pin came out and the latch fell open, yet the door held. God sealed the door so that you cannot even see a seam. Go look for yourself.

"Not only that but you just said yourself that we are floating. We were not even sure that the ark would float. The plans God revealed to Dad were correct. We are going to be safe in here."

Ham stared back at me, puzzled now. He knew I was almost as good a carpenter as Shem and would know if something had changed on the door. He pushed past me gruffly and headed out to look at the door.

Adina said nothing during my exchange with Ham but instead looked glumly from one of us to the other. I noticed that she wore the same blank yet pained expression that I had seen on Tamara. I wondered if I looked the same. Neither of us spoke. She stayed there wrapped in her newly washed cloak as I stood searching her face, worried how she would react to all of this.

We were nearly married ourselves once. But she was closer to Ham's age and, when we had started spending time together, he had stepped in. I never felt that Adina had fallen in love with Ham so much as given up on resisting him. I still cared for her. I found her large brown eyes mesmerizing and, at times as we worked on the ark, her smile still made my breath catch in my throat. Nevertheless, my love was for Tamara alone.

We both noticed the rain as it pounded the roof with even more fury and looked up as if we could watch the drops fall. When it first began, the rain had protected us from attack. The rhythm of it upon the roof had provided an almost calming sound. Now the rain fell in heavy sheets, making a frightening roar against the roof and sides of our new home.

"Do you suppose my parents survived, Japheth?" she whispered.

I waited a long time before answering, and then stammered, "Perhaps, I mean, they might—"

"No," she replied, "I suppose they are gone now." Her eyes began to well up with tears.

"Noah warned them," she went on, more loudly now. "They wouldn't come with us. Why wouldn't they come with us?" She didn't expect an answer. I wanted to comfort her but had no words that were adequate for such a time. As her large eyes stared toward the roof and the sound of the unceasing rain, I moved quietly out the door.

I met Ham in the passage.

"This gopher wood must have swelled when it got wet. That's why the door is tighter," he said.

"Tighter? The seam is gone! The wood could not have swelled so true. There would at least be a ridge between the door and the hull. God sealed the door, Ham!"

"I am going to talk to Dad," Ham said as he pushed past me.

We all needed to talk to Dad. We should have already been in the living quarters. It was safer there.

Tamara approached the horses' stall slowly and quietly. It may have seemed odd to the others that she would go to see the stallion at such a time, but she had to seek him out. She was certain that her mother had died in the flood, along with countless others. Her husband, Japheth, was the only immediate family she had left. She knew she loved and was loved by the rest of Japheth's family, but she had known the stallion longer than any of them.

He had been the one that had begun Tamara's fascination with animals. He and his small herd were the last of the wild horses anywhere around. Tamara had first spotted him a few years before the flood; it was the year before she met Japheth. She was in the fields helping her father in his work, and the stallion brought his herd thundering over a distant hill.

It was a magnificent sight. The stallion's roan coat practically glistened in the sun. And his platinum mane and tail billowed freely as he ran. In her innocence, Tamara waved and cried out a greeting to the stallion. The second she spoke, he stopped running and looked at her. He tossed his head and fluttered his lips with a snort. Then, as if he were returning Tamara's greeting, the mighty horse reared on his hind legs and pawed the air with his front hooves.

Tamara had seen the horse many more times once work was begun on the ark. She worked diligently to approach him, to pet him. But he would never let her come any closer than ten feet. So Tamara was thrilled when, on the day the animals began entering the ark, she saw the stallion come over the horizon. This time he only had one mare with him. He watched from a distance for awhile. Then when there was a brief break in the line of animals entering the ark, he came charging toward the ramp with his mare in tow.

There was no doubt that he was used to being in charge, for he marched right into the stall planned for the horses. Noah was going to bring two of his own smaller horses aboard. But he realized immediately that these were the two God intended for the journey.

Now Tamara approached the stall rather than to deal with her sorrow or with what was happening outside. The stallion's eyes locked on hers immediately, and his ears went erect. He tossed his head in the way that was now familiar to Tamara and stepped in front of his mare as though he were protecting her. He snickered, a deep rumbling sound coming from his chest, perhaps to warn his caregiver or to comfort his mare.

"Easy boy," Tamara said as she slid one foot slowly in front of the other. "I only want to be friends."

With that, the stallion reared slightly and whinnied loudly. He tossed his head more vigorously and stomped the floor of his stall. Tamara took two steps back.

"I would never hurt her," she said as she looked toward the mare. As if following her thoughts, the stallion stepped across the stall and draped his muscled neck across that of the mare. The mare turned her head toward him and nuzzled his shoulder.

Tamara continued to back away. "Not ready to accept me as a friend just yet?" she asked. "I'll come back and try again later."

She walked away, tears of shame falling to her cheeks. *How could I allow my focus to leave those who suffered outside these walls? I can only assume that my own mother died last night. So what kind of a person was I to think of a horse at such a time as this?*

The truth was, Tamara had to think about something else. She was not sure she could bear it if she let her mind dwell on what her mother and the others outside had endured. And it had been the stallion and many of the other animals that had helped her to cope with what had been, until last night, one of the darkest periods of her life.

Noah spoke for the first time in hours. He spoke quietly so as not to awaken Prisca and Sapphira as they slept fitfully.

"Shem, the ark seems to have floated away from the scaffold. We should check all around for leaks."

"Shall I fetch Japheth and Ham to come along as well?" Shem inquired.

"No, it will soon be time to tend to the animals. The two of them will need to be rested for that."

Noah and Shem climbed the ladder from the kitchen that led to the very top of the ark. Shutters covered the window now. The shutters swung up and out to open. Shem was proud of the craftsmanship. Each shutter fit tightly in its opening. When closed, even in a driving rain, the shutters had not leaked. When opened, each shutter provided a type of awning for the casement. The family could float along in a relatively hard rain with the window open. As long as the winds were not too stiff and the rain came mostly straight down, very little rain water would enter the ark and the window would provide all the ventilation needed.

For now, the window was closed and latched. The air inside the ark was getting stuffy and filled with the smell of animals. Noah reached several times to open the window, but each time he had pulled his hand back abruptly. They sat silently and still now, afraid of what they might see if they looked outside.

Only weeks ago they had sat here together, wondering when the rains would come. That day they had enjoyed a beautiful sunset and a rare opportunity to rest. Although construction was complete, supplies were still being stored. More and more animals were gathering near the ark. The labor had been difficult during the past five years of construction. That evening, they had been enjoying the rare opportunity to take a break from all the hard work.

They had opened the shutter and when they looked out under the fading sunlight, they had a spectacular view. To the west they had seen the countryside, which was bathed in the rays of the setting sun. The giant lizards, or behemoths, as Noah's family called them, grazed not far from the ark. Noah and Shem had enjoyed the rare vantage point from a perch that was higher than even the behemoths' long necks could reach. The ark itself was made of gopher wood but they still needed wood from the local trees for scaffold and support structure. That wood had been hauled from the forest, which was visible in the distance. That way Noah and his sons were able to leave the nearby trees alone. Noah felt that if they rendered the immediate area devoid of trees, there might be a backlash from their neighbors.

To the east, but not as far away as the forest, were the outskirts of the city. The buildings and structures had looked almost inviting. In years past, Noah and his sons had gone into the city and listened to Noah's grandfather Methuselah and Noah's father, Lamech, present vivid oral histories of their generation. It was from these talks that Noah and his family learned the names that Adam had given the animals now aboard the ark. To go to the city and listen and learn had been great fun and a great privilege for Shem, Japheth, and even Ham.

But as they had sat high up in the ark that evening before the rains began, Noah and his eldest son realized that the sun would soon go down. Once it was dark, the city became dark as well. The issue was not physical darkness, lanterns lit every street. That which concerned Noah and Shem was the darkness of evil. Though Shem had some fond memories from his early childhood, the city and many who spent time there had been consumed with evil since he had been a young adult. The actions of some were unspeakable to Shem and his family. Noah had taught them that lying, cheating, stealing, and violence had been present to some extent even when he was a young man. But by Noah's five hundred and fourth year, just one year after Shem had been born, things got much worse.

When Noah was a younger man, those who preyed on helpless citizens lurked in the shadows. By the time Shem turned sixty, those acts began to be committed in the open. The hoodlums who committed them defied anyone to stop them or to bring them to justice. And there were other things. There were awful things that people did to one another. Shem shook his head. They were too sad, too painful to dwell upon.

"I think it would be alright if we looked out," Noah said, bringing Shem's thoughts back to the present.

"We need to see if we can get an idea of how far we have drifted, I suppose," Shem replied.

Their hands began to push out the shutter at the same time. The rain beat on it steadily as they pressed against the handles. They were only a few hundred feet from where the ark had rested before the rains, and only yards from where they had spent the last years in fervent labor.

Noah and Shem moaned in agony at what they saw. There was death and devastation as far as they could see. Hundreds of carcasses of drowned people and animals were bloated and bobbed in the filthy water. The spires of the distant city were still exposed above the surface of the water. Only now, people covered them and were clinging to the wood like ants. Others held to floating logs, pots, and pieces of furniture, anything that would float. They all seemed limp, saturated, and exhausted by the torrential rains. But they were alive.

In the distant, flooded forest, Shem could barely make out people, birds, and animals literally fighting one another for the right to cling to the few remaining treetops. The sight of the devastation was overpowering. Shem and Noah held on to the windowsill and one another for support.

"God, spare us from your wrath," Noah said in a hoarse whisper, the knuckle of his trembling right hand pressed hard against his lips.

"And dear God," Shem added, "have mercy on these who suffer."

"Shem," Noah choked through streaming tears. "it is now too late for mercy."

With that Shem turned away from the window and looked at the floorboards. He began to move toward the ladder that led back to the living quarters. He wanted to be with Prisca.

"We mustn't tell the others about this, Shem. They are not ready to know."

Shem hesitated briefly, knowing that his father was right, then headed slowly down the ladder. Noah wanted to slam the shutter closed. More than that, he wanted to turn back time. He needed another chance to warn them. If he could go back, knowing what he knew now, perhaps he could speak to them with greater passion, greater eloquence.

Everyone now aboard the ark had tried to warn others, but none would listen. They only laughed. If only they had tried harder or warned once more. It was as Noah sat there, looking out, shaking his head in disbelief and debilitating sorrow, that he heard the rumble.

The water that was all around began to move as if about to come to a boil. Some on the rooftops lifted their heads weakly to look. Suddenly, huge columns of water off in the distance began to stretch toward the sky. First, only one or two were visible. Then every few seconds another would appear. Spouts of water suddenly shot skyward in huge columns many feet higher than the ark itself. Then they would come crashing back down with a splash. These columns began to appear all around. And then the water began to rise. He noticed it first in the forest. Treetops that seconds ago were ten to fifteen feet above the surface began to be covered. There was a wall of water rising and moving across the forest. And it was headed straight for the ark.

CHAPTER 8

Impending Danger

A puff of dust rose from the rabbits' small trough as Adina poured in some grain. She held the empty scoop in one hand and reached up to absent-mindedly stroke the male rabbit's long ears with the other. It was already apparent that she would be able to complete her chores without thinking about them. The work was physically tiring, not mentally challenging.

She decided to take a brief break. Wiping her hands on her apron, she spent a few moments tying back her long, dark-brown hair. She had asked Sapphira to cut her hair short for the voyage, but Ham threw one of his boyish fits. Adina chose to see such an outburst as Ham's odd way of showing that he loved her. She had to search for little hints of his love where she could. Ham certainly wasn't going to tell her that he loved her or that he thought she was pretty or even that he liked her hair.

Adina's thoughts were still on her parents. She had managed to stop crying, but as she thought of her parents now, tears again welled up in her eyes. She began to think of what it must have been like for them in the end. She had avoided that line of thought. She wished she could put it out of her mind now.

She couldn't forget the sight of them. Adina had seen them on the day that the mob had arrived. They were standing well behind the crowd. She knew that they had not come as part of the angry crowd. They would never have joined in such activity. That day Adina had looked down on them from her vantage point at the window of the ark some forty feet high. Though they were distant, she could see the worry on their faces. Othniel and Damaris were worried for her. Even at that last moment before the hailstorm started, Adina sensed they had no belief that they should worry for their own safety.

The tickle of a tear running down her cheek brought Adina's mind back to her chores. She dabbed her eyes on her apron and turned her attention back to the animals. The rabbits didn't seem to be too interested in their grain today. Adina stuck out her bottom lip in sympathy.

"I think I have something here that you might like better," she announced to her charges as she stood and walked over to the storage shelves. Adina reached up to the highest shelf and retrieved a light crate. The crate contained greens and a few carrots. These were intended as treats for the voyage ahead, but Adina had already given the animals several things from the box.

"Yes, you like that much better, don't you?"

With the first hint of a smile on her face, Adina returned the crate to its spot high on the shelves. All the other women on the ark, as well as Noah and Japheth, would have needed a stepladder to reach the top shelf. But at six feet four inches, Adina did not. Adina had never met another woman as tall as she. Despite her height, Adina was pretty, perfectly proportioned, and not at all masculine. She and her ruggedly handsome seven-foot-tall husband made a strikingly attractive couple, with Adina coming just to his shoulder.

It had been Ham's height that initially attracted Adina to him. Adina had met and spent time with Japheth several times prior to being introduced to his older brother. Though she did feel some attraction to Japheth, she also felt self-conscious standing near him as he was nearly three inches shorter. When she was around Ham, she felt she could be herself, stand up straight, and not have to hide who she was.

Adina had spent her life trying to hide her heritage. Perhaps overcome was a better description. Adina was not just self-conscious about her height, she was embarrassed by it. She was embarrassed that her height came from the fact that her biological father was a giant.

As an infant, Adina was despised by the other women of the small village where she and her mother, Damaris, lived. The women hated her for being the illegitimate child of one of the giants who had razed their village and killed their husbands.

On the day of the attack, the men were in from the fields for the midday meal and were gathered with their families around tables outside their huts. But everyone stopped eating and watched in horror as the giants approached the village. They had all heard the stories of the giants and their capacity for violence. The men stood and desperately grasped whatever crude weapons they had. But they knew they would be no match for even this small group of the powerful invaders.

The giants first overturned the village idols as the villagers stood and stared impotently, wondering why their gods did not defend themselves. One villager, an impetuous young man betrothed to Adina's mother, moved to take action. He kissed Damaris and then ran forward to meet the attackers on his own. Though he was brave, his tactic had been foolish. He was killed before he could raise his sword.

In the end, tactics didn't matter; all the men were killed that day. Some of the women died from the brutal assaults visited upon them by the giants. Damaris too had been assaulted. It would be weeks later before she realized that she was pregnant.

Long before Damaris gave birth, the women in the village wanted to take the child. Despite the horrible way in which she was conceived, the young mother-to-be loved her baby and was determined to protect her. After Adina was born, her mother struggled desperately to keep her and her baby safe. What began as merely sneers and looks of disgust from the other women in the village eventually deteriorated into verbal assaults and even physical attacks. As time went on, it became apparent that Adina and Damaris would not be able to survive in the village. They would have to take their chances in the wilderness.

One night, Damaris slipped quietly away from the village huts, her baby bundled tightly to her chest. It was two weeks later, when both mother and child were dehydrated and nearly starving, that Adina's stepfather, Othniel, found them. He took them both in, fed them, and gave them a place to sleep. He never attempted to take advantage of their situation, but instead showed them respect and considerable kindness. Eventually, he and Adina's mother fell in love.

Adina learned early on *what* her biological father was. She had never known *who* he was. She didn't want to know. Instead, she had lived her entire life afraid of what might lurk deep within her heart and in her mind. Did she possess any semblance of the terrible character of the giants? Was she capable of harming someone or of inflicting physical and mental anguish on others? Adina determined from an early age that she would not allow any influences from the rogue who had attacked her mother to control her life.

As a young girl, Adina sought to be a good person. She made every effort to show love and kindness to her parents and to others. Likewise, she had a strong sense at a young age that there was more to life than that which she saw around her. She questioned her parents about this. Damaris taught her a little about the gods that she had once worshipped when she lived in the village, but there was no passion in her lessons. Nor did she seem to truly believe what she was teaching Adina.

Othniel was just the opposite. He was very passionate in his beliefs. He was passionate in his belief that no God or gods existed. He believed that anyone who placed his faith in some wooden statue or, worse yet, in a God he had never seen or heard was a fool.

"You had best learn to depend on yourself in this world, young lady," Adina had heard him say many times. "Strength comes from inside each of us. You're a smart girl, you're pretty and, most importantly, you are kind to others. Those attributes will take you anywhere you want to go. Don't waste your time and energy on some mythical being that you think is living in outer space somewhere. Save yourself lots of heartache. There is no one out there. We are on our own."

Adina loved her parents, but her heart told her that neither of them was right. As a teenager, Adina would sometimes lie on her back on the flat roof of their city home and stare at the vast sea of stars in the night sky. She knew there had to be more. Sometimes she would try to talk to "Him" but she didn't know who or what she was talking to. If there was a God, how would a young girl, raised in a home of unbelieving parents, approach Him? Adina didn't know it at the time, but the God who she was trying to talk with had placed her exactly where she needed to be to find the answers to those questions.

The sound of heavy footsteps interrupted Adina's recollections. She looked around quickly for a broom or something to fill her hands. She knew it was Ham, and she didn't want to be caught standing idly. Before she could occupy herself, Ham was standing before her, a familiar look of disapproval on his face.

"You haven't finished tending to your section yet?" Ham asked with an irritated edge in his voice. "Do you realize I have already hauled food for every animal on the port side of the lower deck? Do you have any idea how much the animals on my deck eat compared to these?" Ham smacked the side of the rabbit cage with his open hand. Adina jumped, then crossed her arms over her chest and looked at the floor. The rabbits ran around their cage in a panic, eventually ducking inside the covered shelter in the back.

"Please don't do that," Adina said evenly, still afraid to look up. "You mustn't frighten them."

"To heck with them," Ham shot back. "Stop standing around and get busy. I'm not coming up here to finish your work for you. And when you finish this, get to the kitchen and fix me something to eat."

Ham turned on his heels and walked back to the ladder. In a moment, he was gone. Adina was relieved. She was momentarily angry but soon her chin quivered. Why did she always seem to disappoint him? Then, when she was certain that Ham was well out of earshot, she retorted, "When was the last time I asked you to do anything for me?"

Our living quarters were near the center of the ark. According to Father and Shem, this would provide us with maximum stability if the ark pitched in the floodwaters. As with all critical things relating to the design of the ark, God had led Dad to locate them there. The passage where I had caught up with Tamara was built to the right of center. It was used to move from the living quarters to some of the food storage areas.

Most of the ark was open so that someone caring for an animal in a pen on one side could be seen from the other side. Likewise, there were many areas where one could see all three decks from one vantage point. But the living area was walled along with the passage to the rooms that contained the family's supplies. It was as if there was a small house built in the center of the ark. This too was at Father's direction. He felt that we would feel more comfortable if our living quarters were as separate as possible from the animals.

Ham and I had just finished putting some supplies away in the storeroom. We were walking down the passage toward our quarters. Even after showing Ham the sealed door, I had been unable to get him to admit God had done it. The passage had always been the darkest place on the ark. Now for the first time, someone had lit the lamps that lined the walls so that we could see our way.

The brighter light of a cook fire spilled from the kitchen, which was at the farthest end of the passage. Once inside, I saw Mother busying herself over a pot of porridge. This was her way. She would keep as busy as possible to escape the thoughts of what had happened outside. Prisca, Shem's wife, was moving as one with Mother as she pursued her duties. Mother used to joke that God had intended for Prisca to be her biological daughter. She said that when Prisca had come to live with us as a little girl, it was God's way of rewarding her for putting up with three cantankerous sons. The two of them always worked so well together that it almost seemed true. Now their faces were red from their labor and their eyes, like Tamara's, were still bloodshot and red-rimmed.

Shem sat at his place at the opposite end of the table, putting together a set of pulleys with some rope. He would use these for moving tools and supplies between decks. I had never seen him look so drawn and haggard. He was staring at the length of rope in his hand but didn't seem to really see it. No one, it appeared, was getting enough sleep.

Shem had developed great strength in his hands from carpentry. He had been known for miles around for his skill in building. He could build anything from furniture to barns to houses. When Dad had first mentioned the dimensions God gave him for the ark, it was Shem who best visualized them. He was very enthused at first. It was as if he was the only one who truly understood the instructions Dad was bringing from God. But over the years he too grew weary and wondered if we would ever complete such a massive project.

Shem shot us a look as we entered the room.

"It's time you two moved back in here," he said to Ham. "Your sleeping quarters are much safer than that supply room."

Shem had built beds for each couple that were cushioned on four sides and the bottom. Straps were included to hold everyone in place. To show us how secure we would be in them, he had strapped me in and turned one of the beds on its end while we were constructing the ark. I was able to stay in place with little effort. It had become a game that day, with everyone taking turns. There had been much laughter then. The rains had seemed so far away.

"You tie yourself up in your coffin, Shem." Ham snapped back. "I am fine where I am."

"What about Adina?" I asked.

As I asked this, Adina entered the room.

"It's about time you showed up to fix my supper," Ham said to her.

Before Adina could move toward the cupboard, Mother spoke to Ham. "There's porridge simmering in the pot. What's wrong with you? You can't ladle some into a bowl after it has been cooked for you? Shall I chew it for you as well?"

Ham glared in her direction, but even he knew better than to say a cross word to our mother.

Instead, Ham ignored my question as he approached the porridge. While Mother worked vigorously on bread dough, he shoved the ladle deep into the pot and greedily poured porridge into his mouth. He shrieked and spat as the bubbling food scalded him.

"Curse it!" he exclaimed as he threw the ladle across the room. Mother wheeled toward him.

"Mind your tongue, boy! You don't want your father to hear that kind of talk."

Ham started to speak again then turned for the water barrel we would use for drinking water. He plunged his grimy hands into our supply of drinking water and splashed water onto his face and into his mouth. In one quick movement, Shem traveled across the room and grabbed Ham's left forearm with his powerful right hand.

"Use a basin, you pig! The whole lot of us has to drink from this!"

Ham stood to his full height. At seven feet, he was six inches taller than Shem and more muscled. Yet Shem squeezed Ham's arm hard enough to make him wince. Ham drew back his right fist and the two locked eyes for what seemed like a long time. It had been years since my older brothers had fought. The last time things had grown so intense that we all feared one of them would be killed. Thankfully, my father had stepped in then—and he stepped in this time too.

"Ham!" Father's booming voice filled the room, freezing both my brothers in place.

He climbed down into the room from the ladder that led to the top deck.

"Ham!" he repeated as he approached my brothers.

He was not as tall as Shem or Ham, but he was an imposing figure. His long gray hair and beard accentuated his piercing blue eyes and hid the deep lines in his face. The wrinkles of age had turned his thin lips up at the corners so that he seemed to always have a slight smile.

When my father looked you in the eye, you could sense his wisdom and feel his strength. While Shem had been the construction expert on the ark, it was Dad who drove us to complete it. No matter what obstacle we encountered, no matter how many times finishing seemed hopeless, Dad had always been able to encourage and motivate us. My father commanded respect in our family. If only the community had held him in that same respect, perhaps more would have believed his warnings.

He was a kind man who, when we were children, laughed readily. However, Mother told us that the word he had received from God had brought out a single-mindedness that was fierce even for him. As he approached now there was an expression on his face more intense than any I had ever seen.

"Ham, Shem," Dad spoke again sharply. "There is no time for this!"

He placed a hand on both their shoulders.

"Something is happening. The waters are rising rapidly."

At that very second we began to hear a roar. It was faint and well in the distance at first but then became much louder, like the sound of a great wind building from the west. We looked from one face to another, searching for someone who would tell us what was happening. Then Shem grasped Prisca's hands.

"Get to your beds," Shem announced. Authority was in his voice. As he spoke, he moved rapidly to extinguish the cook fire.

"Get to your beds and strap yourselves in!"

CHAPTER 9

Fountains of the Deep

Tamara clutched Japheth's hand as the ark pitched hard towards its starboard side yet again. In his excitement, Japheth had pulled the straps so taut that she felt short of breath. She looked around at the others. Most were staring at the ceiling, wondering when this would end. Finally, her eyes met Mother's. Mother closed her eyes as if passing an embrace to Tamara and even managed a little smile of encouragement.

Several times they all feared the ark would capsize. While they thought the rain of the previous days would surely pound right through the roof, it came even harder now. It seemed to come in sheets. Outside the living quarters it was eerily quiet. Tamara thought of the animals and hoped they were alright. She wondered why they did not cry out.

"This box will end up turning over before this is all over!" Ham yelled over the roar from outside.

"God would not have brought us this far only to have us drown," Noah replied. "He will deliver us from this." And then he added almost hesitantly, "He has to."

The ark had pitched so far starboard this time that they were nearly lying on their sides. The straps burned their skin as their bodies moved back and forth beneath them. A moment later, they were on their backs yet again, and the ark seemed to be in its normal position. Then just as quickly they were nearly in a standing position, looking down at the end of their beds.

Shem struggled bravely to keep calm. Being the most meticulous of the family, he occupied his mind with detailed thoughts about the pens and corrals he had built. The animals had the advantage of their wild agility. But he worried that many would be injured from being thrown into the sides of their enclosures. And what would happen to the larger, heavier animals? Even though God had sent juveniles of animals like the dragons and the elephants to the ark, Shem wondered if the corral walls could withstand the weight of a large falling animal. His thoughts were brought back into the room as Prisca became ill. Shem tried to assist her as best he could, but he was struggling to keep his own equilibrium.

For his part, Japheth looked frequently over at the crate he had made for Rowdy. Shem had helped him in lining the crate with cushioned sides and fixing it firmly to the floor. Still, Japheth worried about his old friend and how he was faring.

Afternoon turned into evening, and hours turned into days. At times there were lulls when the ark was stable enough for the family to attempt to sit around the table or check on the animals. However, the breaks were brief.

After three days of torturous movement, there began to be periods of brief calm. Shem insisted that the family use these opportunities to check on the animals and take in water. But all of their stomachs were so queasy that the water was not welcomed.

On the fifth day, Sapphira used one of the lulls to make some herbal tea and wafers. She had to force everyone to take a little of each. But when they did, their stomachs actually began to calm. Sapphira had the gift of healing, and she had great understanding of the healing properties of herbs and roots. She had used some of them in the wafers and tea.

The animals on board were ill as well. Rowdy would not eat, but Sapphira managed to get him to lap at a little of the tea. Most of the other animals lay down in their enclosures, disoriented and frightened by the violent movements of the floor beneath them. The family worked diligently to get the larger animals up if only for a few minutes. Where it was possible, they led them up and down the aisles between stalls. They knew that it was not good for the larger animals to lie on their sides for too long a period. A large, heavy animal lying down for an extended time could develop breathing problems.

Each time there was a lull, the family took the opportunity to drink some of Mother's tea and to work with the animals. Finally, a night came when the waves were almost as violent as when they first hit. By that time, everyone had taken turns being ill and wanted desperately for the movement to stop. They thought nothing of the future and little of the past. They only wanted to be able to lie still for awhile.

Then, as if the fountains beneath the surface had finally exhausted their energy, the movements of the ark began to calm. As the motions became less dramatic, they also decreased in frequency. After all they had been through in what had now been nearly a week of rough waters, they slept so deeply that they awoke the next morning with their brains shrouded in fog.

They looked around blankly at one another. All tried to sit up before remembering the straps that held them. As they loosened themselves each person sat up slowly, eventually swinging their feet to the floor and sitting for a long while on the side of the bed. They were sweaty and each looked slightly pale. They looked as one who had fought fever throughout the night. Now they were rising, surprised and relieved that the fever had broken yet still feeling its effects.

Japheth and Tamara, the youngest couple, were the first to their feet. Tamara surprised Sapphira by immediately fetching a cloth and water from one of the barrels. She began to clean. Feeling guilty for allowing anyone other than herself to begin the unpleasant chore, Sapphira tried to get to her feet as well. She would have fallen were it not for the steadying hand of her ever-present Prisca, who was suddenly there beside her.

"Help me up, Japheth!" Noah croaked through a dry throat. "We must go and check on the animals."

After I had helped Father to his feet, I had to beg him to sit for a while and try to take a little water. We were all parched with thirst, but he and Mother were older and did not need to push themselves so hard. Tamara and the other younger women took care of the cleaning while Mother collected herself in the living quarters.

Our living quarters were at mid deck, which appropriately housed mid-sized animals. From the kitchen table area, one could open a hatch to climb down to the first deck where the largest animals and their bulky food were housed. Or one could climb up the ladder to a hatch that opened to the top deck where the smaller animals lived. Once on the top deck, it was a shorter climb to the narrow walkway that spanned the length of the window at the very top of the ark. There was no outside deck; only the sloped roof that could be seen from the window.

I told Rowdy to stay by the hearth in the kitchen while Shem and I went to the lower deck and spread out to check for injured animals there. Ham and my father were checking mid deck for the conditions of those animals. I was sure that my wife would rush through her cleaning duties to check on the animals at the upper deck. The animals coming to the ark seemed to provide much comfort to her. At the least the care that she lavished on them helped to occupy her mind.

As I walked by each stall, I immediately noticed that many of the animals were lying down again in the center of their areas. My checks of the animals were done from outside their enclosures. We had always had some wildlife near our home outside the city. However, I had never seen most of the animals that were on the ark until the day God drew them to the area. I had no idea how many of them behaved normally or if they could be vicious. None had shown any type of threatening behavior, yet I did not feel comfortable entering many of the stalls or pens. I was particularly cautious now that some of the animals might be sick or injured.

After two hours of careful observations, none of the animals seemed to have been injured, which was a blessing. The bottom deck of the ark was set up with slated floors. The animals' waste could fall through the slats, keeping their bedding areas relatively clean. The waste then fell to the huge pit whose walls formed the bottom of the ark. Just like with our penned milking cows back home, in a short time the waste material began to pack. As long as it remained relatively undisturbed, the odor was tolerable.

Shem had begun counting animals as they entered the ark. His count continued once we started living aboard the ark and throughout the early days of rain. The day before the floodwaters got high enough to float the ark, he had a fairly meticulous count. There were 15,754 animals onboard, although Shem was sure he had missed counting some of the insects that were likely hiding in the darkest recesses of the ark. There were so many varieties that I still personally had not seen them all.

We had each volunteered to be responsible for certain animal areas of the ark. Tamara and Adina did almost all the work with the smaller animals on the top deck. Mother and Prisca helped Father with the mid-sized animals on the second deck. Ham normally would work with Shem and me on the lower deck with the largest animals.

Our reasons for splitting the work in this manner were twofold. First, by having the same family member see the same animals over and over, he or she could get to know one another. This would help us to be better caretakers and help the animals to be more comfortable and at ease as well. Second, the heaviest physical work was required to haul the food and supplies for the largest animals. Therefore, it made sense for the three brothers to be assigned the lower deck. Likewise, Tamara and Adina, though quite busy, were able to handle the upper deck without being overwhelmed by the physical work.

The smaller animals required much less heavy lifting for their care. The top deck was also home to the insects, and it contained worm beds where the women raised earthworms and mealworms for the feeding of some birds and reptiles. Father had used God's guidance to design things on board so that as many animals as possible could maintain their normal diet. However, due to constraints on some of the foods that were available to be placed on board, some animals had to be trained to eat grains or plant material that they normally might not eat.

After we had verified that there were no injuries, we began feeding the animals. Even with the work broken up, the chore of feeding the animals required the entire morning and into early afternoon each day. Late afternoon was dedicated to the men cleaning or doing any maintenance as needed while the women prepared our meal. After our evening meal, we had duties that involved our own wellbeing or maintenance of our living area.

After completing my chores on the lower deck, I climbed the ladder to the kitchen to meet the others for what would be our simple noon meal of dried fruit, bread, and some cheese. Once there, I bent to scratch Rowdy behind his ears. He seemed to be perking up and looked more like his old self. Prisca, Adina, and Mother were slicing bread and placing wooden plates on the table. I immediately wondered where Tamara was. Mother caught my eye and nodded toward the sleeping quarters. She wore a look that showed concern as well as slight irritation at Tamara's absence.

As I entered the sleeping quarters, the room still smelled of Mother's homemade soap from the scrubbing it underwent early that morning. The floors were still damp. I saw Tamara sitting on the edge of our bed, gently hugging a kitten. Baby animals required less floor space and food. As much as possible, where domestic animals were concerned, we brought young that had already been weaned from their mothers.

Tamara loved petting and caring for these animals especially. She rubbed her cheek against the soft fur of the kitten's back as she stared blankly at the wall. She looked at peace, and I told myself not to disturb her. But I couldn't help myself. I wanted so much to hold her the way that she clung to the kitten. I wanted to feel her hair on my cheek. The time we had spent clinging to each other as the ark floated away that first night was the longest embrace we had shared in a long time. In this moment, Tamara seemed so peaceful and like the Tamara I married. I just had to reach out to her.

As my hand clasped her shoulder, Tamara jumped. I had startled her. But then she stiffened. I had some sympathy for what she must still be feeling. Yet I had grown frustrated with waiting for her to come back to me emotionally.

"I finished my chores. I just came in here for a few moments away from the others," Tamara said, her body still rigid beneath my hand.

"I understand," I replied. "I merely wanted to join you."

"Of course," Tamara began nervously, "sit down here with me. I'll introduce you to my friend."

I didn't want to meet her friend. I wanted her to forget the animal and throw her arms around my neck as she used to. After all, we had not seen one another all day. I wanted to take the kitten from her and toss it out of our way. I was becoming angry. But I knew anger would not help us. So I took a breath and reached out to pet the kitten gently between his ears. We sat there for a while, not looking at one another. As we both continued to stroke the little creature, Tamara placed her hand on mine for a long moment. Then suddenly she stood up and left the room.

CHAPTER 10

Realization

They had eaten lunch in groups of two and three as everyone reached a stopping place in their work at different times. Now as the family came together from different areas of the ark for their larger evening meal, each one dropped exhausted onto the benches. The family was used to hard work. For many years they had been working on their farm during the day and working in the evening on the ark. If anything, their workload was less now that the voyage was underway. The fatigue did not come from the workload but from all of the emotions they had experienced in the past month.

It had been nearly three weeks since the rough waters had settled. They sat around the table not speaking, many with their faces in their hands. Adina tried to lay her head on Ham's shoulder. At first, he jerked his shoulder away, commenting that he was tired too. Then, when he saw the hurt look in Adina's eye, he put his arm around her shoulders and tried in vain to pull her back to him.

Mother and Prisca, who had left tending the animals early in order to prepare the meal, began ladling a stew made from vegetables and spices into everyone's plate. The stew had been a favorite meal prior to the flood. The ingredients were abundant and easily stored, making it a perfect food for the journey. By the time the trip was over, however, all aboard would be happy if they never saw a dish of the stew again. Finally, Mother sat beside Noah as Prisca came over with two loaves of dark bread, still steaming from the cooking fire. As she took her place between Shem and Tamara, she noticed that everyone was suddenly looking at one another.

They had all noticed it at the same time. The rain was softer now. For the first time in weeks, the sound of it hitting the roof was much less intrusive. By comparison, the ark seemed consumed by an overwhelming silence. One at a time they realized, without speaking it, that it was very quiet. There was no sound of birds or wind in tree branches or even of water lapping the sides of the ark.

Shem and Noah made eye contact for a long moment. Both wanted to go back up to the window but neither dared. The images from the last time they had looked out were burned in their memory. Since then, the scene had played over and over in their minds. Even with their labor, they could not keep busy enough to block it out. Japheth broke the silence by stating what everyone had already thought.

"It's so terribly quiet."

Then Ham responded, "I want to have a look outside."

Noah reached out to stop him, thought better of it, and pulled his hand away from Ham's large forearm. He knew they would all have to face what must surely be out there. He too would have to face it.

Noah felt suddenly weak-kneed and was the last to rise from his seat. By the time he put a shaking hand on the ladder, he looked up to see Shem staring at him from the upper hatch.

"Come on, Father," Shem said softly. "I'll help you if you need it."

As they had before, Noah and Shem approached the window cautiously. Even the normally impetuous Ham did not reach to push the shutter open. The women stood at a distance, anxiously awaiting what they would see. They looked to Noah.

Before his sons were born, Noah had been led to build this ark. God hadn't led him to begin actual construction until a few years before the flood occurred. When a problem was encountered in the design of some component of the ark, though Shem often constructed the solution, it was Noah who went to God in fervent prayer to seek it. He sometimes fasted and prayed for days. But he always came back with an answer. Often times the family had failed to appreciate the genius in the answers he would return with. Now each family member had to credit their survival to the grace of God and the obedience of Noah. So it was that at this moment they looked to him.

Noah reached for the shutter and abruptly, as if to keep himself from turning back, shoved it open. He then quickly looked out the window. After looking out for only seconds, his knees buckled and he went down. He was suddenly unable to stand. Had it not been for Shem and Japheth at his sides he would have fallen to the floor with a thud. Instead, they caught him by the arms and gently lowered him to a sitting position.

"Dad, are you alright?" Shem inquired.

"Are you hurt?" asked Japheth.

Still in the midst of the concern for their father, neither could look away from the window for very long. Likewise, the women glanced with concern at Noah but looked back to the window as well. They were all fascinated, shocked, and terrified. For as far as they could see, no matter how hard they strained their eyes, there was only water. There was no sign of another creature, living or dead. There was only calm, still water. As the soft rain continued to fall, they realized for the first time the magnitude of God's word to Noah. They realized that what God had spoken was truth. With the exception of fish and sea creatures, they and the animals on this ark were the only life left on earth.

CHAPTER 11

Inside Our New World

They ate a late supper of cold stew in silence. They ate without tasting. They ate from necessity; there was no pleasure in it. Shem had actually carried Noah over his shoulder down the ladder as Japheth and Ham waited at the bottom for added security. They had all gathered around him as the women tended to him. Noah gradually sat up and finally returned to the table. He stared at nothing now as he methodically chewed his food.

They had survived, but to what end and for what purpose? What would their lives consist of from now on? So far they seemed quite safe and secure in the ark. They were dry and warm. The storm or waves or whatever had occurred a few weeks prior had frightened them, but they were uninjured. The animals still seemed unsure and were not eating well. But with the exception of minor injuries, they too seemed unhurt physically.

Shem was strong and had always been a man among men back home. But now he too was afraid. He looked around at the faces of the others. First, he watched Prisca. Her eyes stared at Dad but did not see him. Ham had moved his gaze from Japheth to Adina and to the table in front of him.

Noah, sitting at the end of the table next to Ham, took his hand. With his left hand, he reached out for Sapphira's. Then for the first time in hours, he spoke.

"Join hands, everyone. All of our hearts are breaking. And we are still exhausted with everything we have been through. I'm sorry for any burden I placed on you. I simply was overwhelmed. God told me this day would come, and for so long I have dedicated my life to insure that we all were obedient and prepared for it. Still, I am stunned by the magnitude of this reality.

"And yet at the same time I feel as if I have carried a great burden for a long time. When I saw the water surrounding us, I felt I had to lay the burden down. I suppose I have focused and driven myself so hard for so long to insure that you all survived—" Noah's voice faded.

"Now that we have reached this point, I don't know what to expect next. God has not told me anything past this point. But he has provided for us and prepared us for a long stay here in the ark. Let's pray together."

Ham seemed to soften at Noah's touch. Japheth was surprised to see him bow his head. As he did so, his long black hair covered his face. As they all held hands, Noah began to pray.

"Almighty God," he began. "Give us your strength as we have so little of our own left. We are weary, God, and we don't understand all that you have chosen to do. We are overwhelmed and ask for you to help us with those feelings. Most of all we pray for you to heal our hearts from the pain we all feel for those who are gone. Comfort us as well for we feel lonely and afraid."

Noah prayed for some time. Toward the end he prayed again for those souls that had been lost. As he did so, Shem heard the sounds of quiet sobbing. He glanced up to see Ham's shoulders shaking and tears falling from his face and into his lap. Noah finished praying and stood to place his arm around his middle son's shoulders. Ham shook his head and wiped his face brusquely with the back of his hand. He looked up as if issuing a challenge and everyone looked away. Noah, wisely seeing through Ham's bravado, chose to let his son go and not embarrass him further. He eased back onto his bench at the head of the table and they all sat quietly for a while.

Adina was angry. Last evening, she had been as stunned as the others to look out the window and see the water surrounding them. She had sat by the fire, alone, well into the night, unable to sleep. She had seemed incapable of any rational thought as she stared into the glowing coals.

Despite a mere three hours of sleep in the rocker by the fire, Adina was up at the first light of day. She had awakened surly, and her mood was no better now. She went about her chores slamming and banging noisily. Tamara looked up at her several times but remained silent until she could take it no longer.

"Adina, what's the matter?"

"Nothing," came Adina's abrupt reply.

"Adina, please tell me. If you are angry at me, tell me what I have done."

"I'm not angry with you, Tamara."

Tamara knew Adina wasn't mad at her. She was just trying to get her sister-in-law to talk. Unfortunately, Adina was in no mood to talk and had no idea what to say if she had been. She didn't know herself what it was that was bothering her.

With the early-morning chores completed, the family began to trickle into the kitchen for breakfast. Everyone was quiet this morning, but as Adina looked around at the faces no one else seemed to share her frustration. Ham came in last, took one look at his wife, and started to speak. She glared back at him, silencing him in the process. Instead, he sat on the bench next to her.

Adina did not place any of the bread or preserves that Sapphira had served on her plate. Instead, the plate remained empty as she watched the others begin to eat. No one looked up but kept their focus on their food or an opposite wall as they chewed. As Adina watched them, she inexplicably felt tears welling in her eyes. She felt her face growing hot and knew that her ears and throat must be turning crimson red.

"I hope you are all enjoying your meal," she shouted. The sudden outburst was as much a surprise to Adina as to the others. She wanted to stop herself, to gain control, but she couldn't seem to do that. With everyone now staring at her in shock, Adina grasped the plate before her and hurled it toward the fire. The wooden plate clanked loudly against the hearth and to the floor. Then she grabbed her cup and hurled it in the opposite direction, narrowly missing Japheth's head.

"Hey! What the—" Ham's words trailed off as he reached out to grasp Adina's wrist. She jerked away from her husband's reach. Sapphira got to her feet, a flash of her own anger in her eyes, until a raised hand from Noah stopped her. Sapphira read her husband's expression of caution and sat back down.

Adina began pacing around the room. "Should we just sit here and eat? Let's all enjoy the sweetness of the lovely preserves. What is wrong with all of you? Everyone is dead! My parents. Tamara's mother. Sapphira, I heard your sister and nephew that first night right outside this ark. His wedding was to have been today. Do you realize that? Does anyone *care* about that?"

Noah knew how out of character this was for Adina, and he wanted to let her vent some of her frustration. But when he saw the hurt she was now inflicting in his own wife's eyes, he knew he must step in.

"Adina, my daughter, of course we care. We are all hurting just as much as you."

"No, you're not," Adina fired back. "You and Mother have your children. Your sons have their parents. I, I have lost my parents. They never hurt anyone or anything. They were good people. They should be here with the rest of us."

Noah pursed his lips, unsure of how to respond. He said a quick, silent prayer before continuing. "Adina, your parents were indeed good people. I cared for both Damaris and Othniel very much." As he spoke these words Noah stood and moved toward his daughter-in-law. He grasped her hands in his and continued.

"That is why I went to them so often and tried to convince them to come with us. But Adina, no matter how hard I tried, and I know that you often tried as well, they would not even acknowledge that God existed. God didn't want your parents to die in the flood. He did not want anyone to die. God understands your anger, Adina, and He shares your hurt. That is why he made provisions for others on this ark. That is why we have more food than the eight of us can possibly eat. That is why we have room on board for many more.

"God instructed us to build this ark so that people like your parents could be saved. But they wouldn't listen to us and they would not accept God's provision. Adina, your parents' goodness could not save them. It wasn't merely deep waters that ended their lives."

Adina yanked her hands away from her father-in-law's and once again walked toward the fireplace.

"Then what do you think killed them, Noah, because it certainly seems like God killed them to me?" Adina's words became barely intelligible as she once again began to cry.

"Sin killed them, Adina. Sin killed your parents and all the others as well. Sin, and the way that it consumed all of the beauty that God had created. Sin destroyed the earth as we knew it."

"I don't understand what you are talking about, Noah. Can't God control the weather?"

"Yes," Noah answered. "But God is also holy. He cannot abide the presence of sin. It is not merely that he doesn't want to. He cannot allow sin to flourish. It is completely contrary to his nature."

The rest of the family had watched the conversation between Noah and his daughter-in-law with more than a little interest. Initially, they were all amazed to see the normally respectful and quiet Adina look Noah in the eye, ask him difficult questions, and even call him by his name. Normally, a young woman would have been expected to call her father-in-law Father or Dad. For his part, Noah seemed unconcerned about Adina's seeming lack of respect. Instead, he was completely consumed with helping her.

"My mother and father were not sinners, Noah," Adina was getting choked up as she spoke. "They had kind hearts. They always treated you well. They always treated me with nothing but love even though they didn't care for my beliefs — or yours."

Noah walked over to join Adina at the hearth. He placed his hands gently on her shoulders and guided her over to the rocker.

"Adina, this is why I told you those stories on the night before we boarded the ark. Adina, your parents were good people just as Adam and Eve were. Your parents were also sinners, just like Adam and Eve. And, for a time, sin separated even Adam and Eve from God. The difference between your good parents and good people like Adam and Eve and you and me is just this: We believed God.

"I have sinned in my life as have you. But we listened to God when he convicted us of that in our heart. We recognized and acknowledged that we needed God and we met Him on His terms. We believed God when He said there can be no forgiveness of sin without the shedding of blood, and we accepted that forgiveness through our sacrifices to Him."

"*That* was the rest of the answer to Ham's question that night before we left our homes. Abel recognized and acknowledged by his obedient sacrifice that he needed the forgiveness of God. By refusing to offer a sacrifice that included the shedding of blood, Cain would not acknowledge his need for forgiveness.

"Adina, I know it doesn't take your pain away, but your parents would not acknowledge God's existence. Therefore, they also rejected their need for forgiveness. Without God's forgiveness, none of us would be on this ark. And that includes me, my daughter."

Adina looked up for the first time in several moments. She did not speak. Yet Noah could see as she looked into his eyes that she sensed that what she was being told was true. With her brown eyes glistening, she continued to look into the old man's face for a moment longer, searching for more. Noah felt that he had said enough now and only returned her gaze. She looked around at the others. All of them looked humble and pensive.

Her eyes stopped on Ham's face. He looked up at her and to her surprise, he smiled. It was a smile that she had not seen in a long time. It expressed sympathy and understanding. Ham stood, crossed the room, and held his hand out. Adina took it and found herself pulled into her husband's arms. Adina, overwhelmed, buried her face into Ham's long hair. One by one, the family filed from the room and left them there.

CHAPTER 12

Shem Hears

S hem rubbed his rough hands across the surface of a bowed length of wood. The wood was to be shaped into one of the rockers on Sapphira's new chair. Shem had stashed some choice wood in this far corner of the ark as the supplies were being loaded. He wanted to build his mother the rocking chair she had always wanted but never had. He wanted the chair to be a pleasant surprise during a difficult time for Sapphira. But he also wanted the moments of relaxation that only carpentry could provide during the voyage.

Carpentry and woodworking had always been Shem's passion. He loved everything about it. He loved the smell of the wood, the feel of a smoothed piece of stock in his hands, and the satisfaction of creating something. Tonight, however, even his beloved hobby would not bring him peace. Shem could not turn his mind off.

He tossed the rocker onto his workbench and puffed out his cheeks as he let out a slow breath. He turned around, looking at the floor as if he had misplaced some tool, but he had not lost anything. He only knew that something had not yet been found. Shem looked up toward the high ceiling of the ark, buried the fingers of both hands in his sandy hair, and shut his eyes tightly.

"Oh, my God," he spoke aloud. "Help me now more than ever. Help me to be up to the task before me. And Lord, help me to be worthy of the responsibility you will surely place upon me."

Shem fell to his knees as he spoke these words and then placed his face in his hands as he continued.

"Lord, I remember. I remember when I was but a small boy, an only child at the time in a world gone mad. Mother and Dad had to fear for my life any time I was out of their sight. But God, even back then I found my solace in Your presence. I remember how I would sense You with me as I roamed the forests and fields. I began at a young age to pray and to talk to You.

"I continued to walk with You as I got older. After Prisca came into our lives, I prayed all the more that You would help me to be the kind of man such a beautiful woman would want to marry someday. You heard me, Lord, and You have allowed us to be together for all of these years. I prayed every day in our old home that You would give me strength and wisdom to honor You. You have always been with me, Lord. You are my life.

"So God, why? Why won't You speak to me the way You have spoken to Dad? I need that from You, Lord. I am not ready or able to take Prisca into whatever awaits us without strong guidance from You. I have always been able to sense you leading me. But I have never been allowed to hear You the way Dad has. That is why I doubted.

"I doubted when Father told me You spoke to him and that he wanted me to help build this ark. I doubted because I thought that I knew You so well myself that You would surely give me confirmation of the coming flood and the need for this ark. Surely You would speak to each of us prior to such a monumental event. But You didn't, and everything that Dad said came to pass. I have had no inclination of Your will or desires since this voyage started except through Dad. Have I displeased You, Lord? Did my doubts drive You away?

"I marveled at Your power when the rains came and again when the ark began to float. But then I shook with fear of You as I heard the people outside suffer. I have always sensed You and felt You to be a God of love. This too gives me worries and doubts. Did I ever really know You as I thought I did? Were you really there with me on all those walks? I never feared You then. These are things that are on my mind, Lord, and I confess them to You now. To deny them would be futile.

"And then, Lord, I doubt myself. How can I be capable of starting over in a new world when I have such thoughts and fears as these? I am the eldest son, and Dad will not be here for me that much longer. It will fall to me to lead us in the world we are heading to. I don't feel I am ready for that, God. I bark out orders to everyone but Mother and Dad on this ark. Father has chosen me to manage each detail of its running, yet I wonder every day if my decisions are the right ones. I show a confident face to the others here in this vessel. But this is a very different situation than we will face when the time comes for us to step outside.

"Lord, I can't do it. I am not capable. I need You to work through me. But I haven't heard from You. I feel I am connected to You by my presence here on this ark. Yet I don't feel the strength I will need from You.

"All that Dad has shared with us as being from You has held true. So I know, dear God, that You hold us in Your hand. But Lord, I am afraid of my own frailty. I am afraid of my own inadequacy. I need to feel Your presence now more strongly than I ever have. Lord, I need to hear a word from You. Won't You speak to me, God? I am humble before You, Lord. I am listening."

Shem waited a long while there in the quiet of the ark. He remained on his knees until the rough floor began to hurt his knees. Finally, he opened his eyes and rolled over onto his hip. He sat up, his right elbow hooked over his right knee.

"I didn't hear You, oh Lord. I don't understand why You won't let me hear from you."

Tears of frustration and disappointment welled in Shem's eyes. He began to feel anger building up from deep inside. Shem hung his head and looked at the floor. He swallowed hard and tightened his lips to block words he would regret from escaping.

"I must believe it, Lord. I don't understand what You are doing now. I have never in my life heard your audible voice. But I know You were with me on those walks in my boyhood. I know in my heart You gave me Prisca and placed us here. I don't understand the way You chose to do this, Lord. I don't feel confidence in my ability to lead us through whatever comes. Still, I will obey in what You would have me to do today. You have brought me to this point. Surely You will not leave me now."

Shem stood up a little stiffly after having spent so much time on the floor. He looked back to his rocking chair project, but his heart wasn't in it just now. He would go on up to bed and get some sleep. He was still hurt and disappointed. Just as he was about to take a step toward the ladder leading upstairs, Shem caught movement out of the corner of his eye.

He dodged as something seemed to rush towards him. It was only after it moved further away that Shem could focus his view enough to realize it was a dove. The dove had flown just past his ear the first time. It now circled the large open area in front of the lower deck enclosures and glided back toward Shem. Intrigued now, Shem stood as stiff as a statue to see how close the dove would come. To his amazement, the dove glided to a landing on Shem's right shoulder.

Shem was amazed that he could just barely feel the little feet gripping him. The beautiful snow-white bird seemed almost weightless.

"Well, you are friendly, aren't you? Now how did you get out of your cage?"

Shem was used to interacting with the large animals, so he was unsure of what to do with the tiny bird. He held out a forefinger. The dove stepped easily onto it. It was a beautiful bird actually, and it seemed to positively glow. The dove seemed to be looking directly into Shem's eyes. He was not turning and cocking his head the way birds normally did. Shem smiled to himself and shrugged. Then he moved carefully up the rear ladder of the ark. He would climb all the way up to the small animal deck from here, thus avoiding the crowded kitchen and family area.

As Shem approached the cage where the doves were housed, he held the dove out to sit on top of the cage. The dove, as if reading Shem's mind, stepped obediently onto the cage.

"You just sit right there, and I will get this latch open," Shem said. As his large fingers fumbled with the latch, he couldn't help but notice there was nothing wrong with the cage and that all the other doves appeared to be in place. Shem counted them quickly, one, two, four, seven, twelve, fourteen. Wait a minute. Only fourteen doves were brought onto the ark. Shem had catalogued them himself. He must have miscounted. He counted again. There were fourteen doves in the cage.

Shem looked up abruptly. The dove was no longer sitting on the top of the cage. He looked around the upper deck. The dove was not there either. He looked over the rail and down to the lower deck. Still nothing. After much searching, Shem finally gave up and gave thanks to God. The fifteenth dove had vanished.

CHAPTER 13

Brothers' Oath

I banked the coals in the fireplace to make it easier to start a fire in the morning. Before heading off to bed, I looked up at the flue. As Father had assured us it would, the smoke indeed was escaping through the side of the ark. He had directed us to build a type of square tunnel for the smoke to travel through. It led to a hollowed log that penetrated through the side of the ark and turned downward in such a way as to let smoke escape without rain coming in.

I sat down on the rug in front of the hearth, the whispers from my father as he knelt in prayer in the sleeping quarters penetrating the quiet. I stared into the coals and contemplated how much calmer the movement of the ark had seemed in the last day. Rain still fell without let up. Yet the torrential rains of the first weeks had not returned. Despite the calmer water, there was still a constant sensation of the ark moving in the currents. I wondered how far we had drifted and where we were.

The women headed to bed. Adina looked back over her shoulder at the rest of us as she followed Ham out of the room. She looked to be deep in thought. I sensed that rather than welcome the opportunity to be alone with Ham, the time she spent in that little room was lonely for her.

Shem walked past me and bent to cuff me lightly on the shoulder. He motioned with his head to let me know he wanted me to follow. We walked out the passage past the main sealed door of the ark and ducked through the door that led to the mid deck. Some of the animals stirred but did not startle as we each lit a candle from the one already burning on a stand near the wall.

We continued to walk without speaking until we stood in front of the cage that held a pair of the large cats. Adam had named them tigers. Shem and I were fascinated by their size, power, and the way that they moved. They stirred and looked up as we approached. The big cat stared unblinkingly at us as we spoke. There was nothing threatening in his behavior, yet there was an air about him that was awe inspiring.

"Look in his eyes, Japheth. There is absolutely no fear in them."

"Yes, but he doesn't know what we face."

"Still," Shem replied, "he is completely outside his normal surroundings. Everything he faces is new and unknown to him. Yet he never shows fear. Instead, the feeling I get from him is that he waits patiently for an opportunity."

I chuckled as I said, "You mean an opportunity to eat one of us?"

"Hmm, a distinct possibility, I suppose," Shem responded, a smile spreading across his face. "But something tells me God will keep that from happening. I think he awaits his opportunity to leave this ark, escape, and roam the forests once again. But more important is his demeanor *while* he waits. There is no fear or panic."

"Shem, you spoke of the tiger once again roaming the forest. There is no forest. Everything is gone! Do we even know if things will ever come back to the way they were?"

"Japheth, I know it is frightening to look out and see only water. No, we don't know when or if we will see forests or even land again. But God has brought us to this point and provided for us. We must believe He will carry us through.

"I'm afraid too, Japheth. I am very afraid. But I cannot show that to the others. Neither can you. You saw what happened to Father when he saw all the water surrounding us. He is tired now. We have all leaned on him since the first beams were cut for the ark. Now it is time for us to be there for him to lean upon."

"Shem, I am here to stand beside you and lend a hand no matter how hard the labor or what storms we face. But beyond that I have no idea what to do or how we should proceed. I don't hear God speaking to me. And I never asked for any leadership role in all this."

"You didn't have to ask, Japheth," Shem responded. "God has thrust it upon us both. Surely He would not have done so unless He felt we could handle the responsibility."

"So what are we to do, Shem? Call the others together and tell them what to expect? We have no idea ourselves. Will the fountains open up again, or will the waters remain calm? How will we ever see forests again with it raining continuously as it has? We don't know what the next hours will hold, much less the next weeks."

"Think about the amount of food God had us to store on this vessel, Japheth. We are not going to be here for weeks. We are going to be aboard this ark for months."

I had never considered that as a possibility. But Shem was right. It made sense. At the rate we were using supplies, we would indeed have plenty for many months. And most of the animals had eaten less each day since the storm. At the same time they were all sleeping more and were quieter. Did they sense the need to prepare themselves for a very long stay?

"Shem, we have everything we need here, but I am not certain I can stand being trapped inside this dusty box, as Ham calls it, for months without seeing the sun or walking the hills."

"I don't want to think about that either, Japheth. But we owe it to the others to steel ourselves and prepare for that possibility. We don't know how the others are going to respond. Dad is suddenly weaker. We have to be prepared to step up and give him as much support as he needs. Not just physically, but as leaders. We may even have to take over for him at some point."

"Father was called to this, not us. We do not have the word from God that he has. We cannot suddenly presume to be what Dad has been."

"To be certain," Shem replied, "we can never be Dad. But do you think we are on this ark by accident? These animals didn't walk up that ramp by chance, and neither did we. God placed us here too, Japheth. There must be a reason why."

"Ham is older than me. Let him—"

Shem interrupted. "Ham can't even deal with the fact that he won't get to go into the city and carouse with his friends. He is more concerned about not having his favorite food and drink. He certainly is not going to step in for our father."

"So what do you propose we do?" I inquired.

"We do what we have seen Dad do. We pray."

"I already pray to God, Shem. I prayed aloud during the storms when I thought this ark would capsize."

"We have to go beyond that, Japheth. We have to pray regularly throughout the day. We have to get to know God the way we know Dad because we are going to have to look to Him soon. We are going to have to look to Him the way we have always looked to Dad. In the meantime, we have to encourage the women, and we may have to counter Ham's negative attitude."

"Yes, but who knows how long it will take for us to truly hear God's voice? What do we do in the meantime? What do we do today?"

"Don't be surprised if you hear God sooner than you think. Until then, we can immerse ourselves in caring for the animals. And we make sure the others stay occupied as well. As the days grind on, it will be tempting to throw up our hands and give up. Our chores will become repetitive. We may dread getting up and getting started each day. We can't allow ourselves or the others to be consumed by that attitude, no matter how monotonous it may seem. We were called by God to perform this work. We must keep at it and keep busy. Besides, it must be important to God for every one of these animals to survive. We can't let even one be neglected."

"We can't work constantly, Shem. It won't help us to overwork either."

"There will be a time each day for the rest we need but not for idleness. If we give ourselves much time to contemplate the vastness of what lies before us and try to handle it with only our own understanding, it is very possible that one of us may lose our sanity."

"Shem, what did you mean we might hear God sooner than we think? Have you heard him?"

"Yes, Japheth. Yes, I have."

"Shem! You heard God's voice. Why didn't you tell me?"

"I didn't hear an audible voice. But I did hear from God. I heard him very clearly. And I was reassured that He didn't put us on this ark to leave us."

I didn't know exactly how Shem had heard God, but I knew that my brother had sensed God's presence very strongly. Some of what he had said was unpleasant to hear, but there had already been times when I had held my head in my hands and felt I had to press against it to keep it from bursting. The expanse of water all around us, the complete lack of any landmark or knowledge of what tomorrow might bring was more than I could bear on my own. I knew from Dad's behavior that neither he nor anyone else aboard the ark knew where we were to go from here.

Before the rains had begun, we were following God's guidance through Dad. Yet each night we had returned to the familiarity of our own homes. There was always the possibility in the back of our minds that the flood would never come and that our lives would return to normal. That possibility was gone now. It was buried under unknown depths. The only safety and security we could cling to from now on was our trust in God. He had gotten us this far.

CHAPTER 14

Ham's Greatest Love

Muscles rippled in Ham's back as he shoveled corn into a wooden chute. The corn traveled down to a hopper, where it came in contact with round cutting wheels and grinding stones. There, it was combined with the dried beef he had previously loaded to form a thick paste. The addition of corn or wheat allowed them to stretch their meat supplies for the animals.

The large dragons were the largest eaters of meat. Their smaller cousins preferred vegetables but would eat grain if that is what they were given. Over time Ham, as instructed by Noah, would add less and less meat, gradually shifting all the animals to a diet of grains or plant matter. Ham didn't think this would work, but his father assured him that it would. Ham tossed the meat paste into the dragons' trough and then stood back to watch. He had seen adults of this type run down frail deer with their long strides and clamp down on them with their giant mouths. Their rows of sharp teeth did the rest. This juvenile stood only a foot or so taller than Ham's seven feet. The dragon always stood on his hind legs; the front ones were very short compared to the rest of his body and stood straight, like tiny arms that seemed terribly out of place with the rest of his bulk.

As Ham finished his feeding duties, he pushed the cart back to the feed mill and wiped sweat from his forehead. He gathered his tunic and walked over to sit in front of the horses' stall. He had wanted to bring his own horse, but Noah had decided that the stud was too old to be a reliable sire in the future. He sat for awhile and watched the horse eat, then leaned back and closed his eyes. His work had long since become automatic and mindless, and his thoughts had been wandering throughout the day as he worked. For now, he thought about what he had heard his brothers saying about him the night before.

Japheth and Shem had not known that Ham had been listening as they talked last night. "I hope they don't think I care about their opinion of me," Ham spoke aloud. "I am as capable of leading as either of them. They have spent so many years cooped up working on this box that they don't even know what the real world is like." Ham stopped himself short. He recalled yet again that the world he knew was gone. Ham's nostalgia for that world had brought him to tears during Noah's prayer. Ham grew teary-eyed now as the reality of the situation came crashing in on him once again.

What Ham did not realize on any conscious level was that his tears were not for those lost but for himself. Ham was distraught over what *he* had lost. The time so far on the ark had been all work or long periods of boredom. Sitting around in the evenings whittling or listening to the others gab endlessly about the next day's activities did not compare with the evenings he used to enjoy. And Adina, never the most fun-loving woman in Ham's opinion, had turned out to be almost as much of a religious fanatic as his father.

Ham initially had been attracted to Adina by her statuesque beauty. In addition, by the time he had met Adina it was clear that Japheth was already starting to have feelings for her. Ham had enjoyed the challenge of taking a woman away from his brother. He was confident he could do it too.

Women had always liked Ham. He sensed that they liked his looks and, more than that, were attracted by the element of danger in his personality.

Adina had been no different. Once when Adina came to visit his parents and Japheth, Ham had made a special effort to smile at her and turn on the charm. Then once when Japheth went into the city to see her, Ham had tagged along. In no time, Ham had Adina's full attention.

Unfortunately, Ham's plan had worked a little too well. Before he knew what happened, Adina was pledging her love for him. He had never had a woman really love him before. He got caught up in it and asked her to marry him after a few weeks of courtship. He did love Adina. In fact, he didn't think he had ever loved anyone as much as he loved her. It was just so hard for him to tell her in a way that she believed it. He got sick of her asking him all the time to tell her. Telling her made Ham uncomfortable, but he did want to tell her—sometimes. For some reason, he just never did.

Ham believed in the God his father taught him about and that Adina so often talked about. But he had never seen a need to constantly dwell on the matter. In his life prior to the flood, Ham had always felt that God would not have minded one of his children enjoying all that His creation had to offer. Shem and Noah didn't agree, for it seemed to Ham that he was always receiving one lecture after another about his exploits. The speeches and disapproving looks only seemed to make Ham more determined to live as he wanted.

He frequently got into fights while in the city and on one or two occasions had succumbed to the temptations of another woman while Adina waited alone at home. No one knew about those instances, and it would be best to keep it that way. He had actually felt badly enough about those dalliances to attempt a mumbled but sincere prayer and offer God a sacrifice of one of the kids from his own small herd. Noah had taught him that practice. He insisted that Ham offer a sacrifice following times that he had struggled to "live righteously," as Noah always put it.

Though Ham somewhat understood the need for the sacrifice, he thought it was much ado about nothing. He had witnessed much worse behavior by others and nothing bad happened to them. Ham was sorry to admit it, but most of his family just didn't get it. His mother and father had long since forgotten what it was like to be young, and his two brothers just were not normal. They were as sanctimonious as their father, and Ham often felt uncomfortable around them.

Ham didn't want to think about it anymore today. What he really wanted was for things to loosen up on this ark. He wanted to forget all his troubles and recall some of the good old times. He had a good idea of how he could help himself do just that.

He made his way to the far corner of the ark. He glanced over his shoulder toward the door leading to the passageway and the family's quarters. He opened a trap door in the floor and climbed into the manure pit. He had done such a good job of hiding his little cubbyhole that it actually took him a moment to find it. There was the pouch. And inside were the flasks. He climbed back up with one flask and closed the trap door quietly. His father would surely go berserk if he knew about Ham's little stowaways.

A few long draws on the bottle and he would forget all his troubles. Just like back home.

CHAPTER 15

Tamara Remembers

Tamara had come to the third deck and was performing the second cleaning of the day on the small mammal's cages. The cages were built on stilts so that the animals themselves were almost at eye level. Beneath each cage was a sharply angled board that allowed waste to fall through the slats of the animal's enclosure and then be easily scraped into a trough. The trough was built even with the front edge of the row of cages. The trough itself could be scraped out with a tool designed for the job and then flushed with a minimal amount of water that flowed from barrels in the center. The trough dumped at either end of the ark into an opening that led to the waste pit on the bottom deck. With this design, Tamara and Adina could keep the area clean with plenty of time left for other caretaking chores.

The cages didn't need a second cleaning. She didn't like to sit quietly for very long for it was then that she began to remember. So she stayed busy. She talked to the animals constantly.

She felt sorry for them caged up this way, even though the animals seemed resigned to it. "I can hardly wait for the day when I can open all the doors and set you free," Tamara pronounced to her charges as she stopped in front of the cage of small monkeys. At the sound of her voice, the little female monkey was at the cage door in two quick bounds.

With a quick look around to insure that she was alone on deck, Tamara opened the latch and reached in. The female practically leaped into her arms. Their little visits together had become a daily occurrence. The less sociable male stayed inside his shelter at the rear of the cage. Tamara latched the door closed and began to hum as she continued her rounds. The monkey that she simply called Little One found a comfortable perch on Tamara's left shoulder.

Sapphira didn't like Tamara having the animals out of their cages. Noah was more understanding. He was most appreciative of Tamara's gift with the animals. And she did consider it a gift from God.

Tamara didn't know that her gift had a purpose until the work was nearing completion on the ark. In the year and a half before the family boarded the ark, she had a wonderful confirmation that all that Noah had been telling them was true. That confirmation was the large number of diverse animals that came to live near their home. Animals that had never before been seen in that area were suddenly coming from places unknown to them.

It was fascinating for everyone to witness. But more than anyone Tamara wanted to become familiar with all the animals she could. At first, the animals would flee at her approach. But just like Little One, she eventually won many of them over. She worked with them and trained them to eat out of her hand. That made their transition to life on the ark much easier. Noah quickly realized the benefits of her actions and gave her all the free time she needed to roam the woods and fields to search for newcomers.

Sometimes Tamara sensed some resentment on the part of the other women who were working very hard to prepare all the food and supplies the humans would need in the ark. While she never heard them speak a cross word about it, she really didn't have time to worry about what they thought. Just when she was getting to work with one type of animal, another would show up that she had never seen before.

As the time of departure drew nearer, Tamara felt God's presence in her work. Some of the animals that had seemed impossible to approach, like the tigers and zebras, suddenly began to let her walk up almost close enough to touch. The animals that initially only wanted to eat live prey began to accept the alternative foods that Tamara offered them.

"Help me check on the others, Little One," she said softly. As she went from cage to cage, she held the little monkey so she could see the other animals and be introduced to them as if a monkey could understand what she was saying. Being with the animals gave her a peace that she couldn't seem to find anywhere else. Yet, as she finished the introductions and stopped to sit on a stool, she felt the familiar knot in her stomach. *I mustn't let myself remember*, she thought.

The whole deck was dimly lit, even in the daytime with the window opened. Now, in the evening, only a few lanterns kept the animal deck from total blackness. As Tamara sat and stared at the flame of a lantern nearby, she tried to keep her mind occupied by talking to and playing with Little One. Nonetheless, she began to feel nauseous. She didn't want to think about this today. She had almost made it through since last evening without thinking about it, and she wasn't going to bring it all back to mind now. She stared at the flickering flame and, even as she shook her head no, the memories came back again.

"Tamara," her mother yelled impatiently as she shook the empty wineskin for the last drops. "Take these coins and go into town to trade for more wine."

As she spoke, her mother held out a small leather bag containing enough coins to buy a large flask of the more expensive wine. The amount also would have been enough to buy enough food to last the month.

"But Mother," she had protested, "it will be dark soon. Japheth doesn't like me to go to the city even in daylight." She hadn't said so, but she also didn't like the wine that her mother drank more and more of lately. The wine that her father used to make was sweet and good and she had never felt any effect from it. But since her father's death at the hands of a roving band of thieves that barged into their home one day three years ago, Mother had bought wine from a man in the city.

This wine had a very different and bitter taste that Tamara couldn't stand. And when her mother drank it, she became irritable and angry. She took this anger out on Tamara. Recently, during one of her wine-drinking bouts, she had slapped Tamara across the face. There was no explanation offered. Her mother just flew into a rage over something that was said or inferred. Tamara didn't want to visit anymore, but her heart broke at the thought of her mother sitting alone in the room she had been forced to rent.

Tamara's mother had lost everything that her husband had built soon after he was murdered. Tamara couldn't help but notice that her mother seemed more disturbed by her financial losses than by the loss of her husband. Japheth and his family had repeatedly offered help and reached out to her, but she rejected them out of hand. Her husband had thought very highly of his son-in-law and his family but then, in his wife's opinion, he had always been easily fooled. It was obvious to her from day one that Noah was a sanctimonious fool, always talking about God and the need for righteousness. And she felt certain that Japheth would grow up just like his father.

Lately, Tamara herself had been coming around warning of some giant flood and expecting her to move in with her husband's family of fools into a floating barn full of stinking animals. She had lost her husband and her home, and now her daughter had turned into some religious zealot. She hated them all, including Tamara.

"I swear, you are no help to me whatsoever, Tamara," her mother began. "Why do you bother to come here? All you do is preach to me as if you are better than I am. And now I ask you to run a simple, brief errand and you have to cry like a child about your fear of the city. Lots of people trade in the city every day and nothing happens to them. You know I can't sleep without a little wine at night. It helps me to not dream about your father. But that is of no concern to you. You have a husband. So go home to him. It is best that I, a widow, go myself. I'll make my way into town and fetch my own things."

The words stung.

"All right, I'll go. Just let me wait until Japheth comes to take me home. He will take me."

"Oh wonderful! When Japheth gets here he can lecture me again about strong drink as if I need to hear anything from him or his crazy father. Forget it! I don't want anything from you. Why don't you start for home now? Japheth can meet you along the road."

"Mother, don't be like that. I'll go. I'll get your wine."

Tamara walked nervously down the steps of the house where her mother rented the room and turned toward the noise of the city. She had taken this walk before and, though the winemaker made her uncomfortable, nothing had happened the other times. She convinced herself she was being silly and clutched the small bag of coins more tightly as she sped her pace.

As she approached the block where the winemaker sold his products, the streets became crowded. People danced and laughed raucously. Most drank from large cups but many hovered near pots, inhaling smoke that drove them into a frenzy.

On one corner, two scantily clad women cavorted with a group of men. A box in which the men could place their money rested at the women's feet. Through an open doorway across the street, hysterical laughter mixed with screams as spectators watched some animals fight to the death. This was the latest Tamara had ever been here and the busiest she had seen it. She walked rapidly, wanting to get this errand over with. She finally stepped into the winemaker's shop.

He was a repulsive man to look at, with rotting teeth and a massive, crusted cavity where his left eye had once been. He reeked of a combination of his own product, sweat, and urine. His stringy hair, beard, and hands were filthy. Every time Tamara had seen him he wore a leering grin. He stared at her in a way that made her skin crawl.

In a far corner, a man lay with an empty jug still clutched in his right hand. He appeared to be breathing but not conscious.

Japheth will be furious if he finds out I came here again, she thought as the winemaker spoke to someone in a back room.

"Boys, you might be interested in what we have out here." A moment later, three equally dirty men about Tamara's age emerged from the back. Their eyes were bloodshot, and they staggered a little as they moved toward her.

"Well, well," the tall one with red hair said as he sidled up to her. "Someone brought us some money." With that he wrenched the bag from Tamara's hand and threw it to the winemaker, who looked at it with disgust and let it drop on the counter. "What else did you bring us?" he continued as he reached for her arm.

Tamara said nothing but wisely stepped back toward the door. As she did so she fell into another one of the young men who had come up behind her. She turned to push away from him, and he grabbed her face painfully in his grimy hands. Unlike the winemaker, his teeth were not rotted but were instead coated in green. His breath made her retch as he clamped his mouth onto hers.

"Tamara, are you alright?" At the question, Tamara wheeled around to see Adina standing behind her. She then realized how her hands shook. Little One had managed to open a food bin and was making a huge mess. Tamara didn't recall that the little monkey had ever left the perch on her shoulder. Adina reached out, but Tamara drew her arms up to her chest and turned her face away.

"It's all right, Tamara," Adina said, holding her hands palms forward as she took a step back. "No one here is going to hurt you. We all love you."

Tamara looked at her. Adina noticed that her eyes were wide with fear. She didn't approach her terrified sister-in-law. Adina continued to hold her hands out to Tamara and waited. Tamara pressed her fists to her mouth and tried to stifle her sobs. Then suddenly she stood from her stool, knocking it to the floor with a thud. She ran across the floor and fell against Adina, who wrapped the younger woman tightly in her embrace. They cried together as some of the animals seemed to look on. Little One made its way over and sat on Tamara's feet. The area was quiet except for the sound of muffled sobs and the occasional creaking of the hull as the ark gently swayed.

Ham walked the decks searching for Adina. He was relaxed for the first time since they had closed the door on the ark. He smiled to himself, realizing he was maybe even a little tipsy. In any case, he wanted to find Adina. He wanted her. He heard the sounds of crying before he saw Adina. He tiptoed closer and saw his wife holding his sister-in-law as Tamara cried. He didn't have to ask any questions. Ham knew what Tamara was crying about.

He forgot his amorous urges as he stepped back into the shadows. Neither woman had seen him. Ham felt badly for Tamara. He wondered once again if he should share with her all that he knew. *No*, he thought, *it's better just to let it go*. There was no need to dwell on it now. Nothing would be gained by it. Ham had done some things in his life that perhaps he should not be proud of. But there had never been a night like that one. It was better that he just forget about it. It had all been a horrible mistake, and he couldn't change it now. He never wanted things to unfold the way they did that night—at the winemaker's.

CHAPTER 16

Wise Counsel

More than a week had passed since the night of Tamara's painful recollection. Now Noah dealt with memories of his own. He sat on a stool he had placed on the narrow ledge in front of the window. There was a stiff breeze coming in, but it was not strong enough to drive rain into the ark. By now everyone in Noah's family had realized that they needed their time by this window. Even though there was nothing to see but steady rain hitting the water and a gray sky, they still needed time to breathe fresh air. For Noah, it was also a time to think and pray. As he sat there this day, Noah thought yet again about the faces that he had left behind.

He thought about sermons he had preached to jeering crowds. Was he too forceful? Or had he preached with too much gentility and love? Perhaps he should have attempted to frighten the people even more regarding the coming destruction. Or perhaps his message had been rejected because the listeners resented his warnings as an attempt to exploit fear in order to turn them back to God.

Noah had followed God's direction to the letter regarding provisions and supplies for the ark. And he knew that they had significant storage room left over. They could have turned some of it into more sleeping quarters and accommodated many more on the ark. Had that been God's plan? Had his weakness and failings prevented others from joining them?

Every time Noah and his message were rejected, it hurt. Each time he watched the crowd slowly break up and walk away with their heads shaking and mocking smiles on their faces he felt like he had failed them and God. Rather than receiving applause and acceptance, on more than one occasion he would be pelted with stones or clods of dirt before he even completed his message. So many times he had not wanted to go back out. He sometimes delayed getting up in the morning because he dreaded what he would face. But he had persevered.

Each day throughout the years prior to construction, he would dedicate the morning and evening to preaching. Most days he had taken his message into the city where most of the people were. But there were times where he would pull a cart to nearby farms and small communities. He would use the cart for a stage and preach with the same passion he used in the city. But the rural people were no different in the reception they gave him.

Perhaps his worst experience had come during his first sermon. He had received God's revelation about the flood only two weeks prior. It would be one hundred fifteen years before he would begin the actual construction of the ark. It was during those first weeks after God spoke that Noah had tried to warn his closest neighbors. He had never had a good relationship with them. They resented Noah for his faith. So his neighbors felt no remorse as they dragged Noah from his cart and beat him so severely that he lay until well after nightfall in a trench beside the road, trying to gather the strength to stand and make his way home.

"Dear God, I know that you spoke to me," Noah prayed through gritted teeth as he fought waves of pain in his stomach and ribs. "You told me about a great flood that you will bring. Why did people react so violently to me when all

I am trying to do is to share your words? Please, God, speak to them the way that I heard you speak to me." Noah lay there awhile longer and realized that God would not do that. For reasons he did not understand, God chose to use Noah to warn the people.

"God, I am not suited for this," Noah prayed again. "Perhaps I should not be so certain it was your voice that I heard. Could I have been only dreaming?" As pain wracked Noah's body, he continued to pray but his words were jumbled as he fought to prevent passing out. Then, as Noah lay holding his side as his face pressed against the cool rough sand of the trench, he felt a hand on his shoulder. Without looking, he knew who it was.

"Grandfather, how did you find me way out here?" Noah said with a grimace.

"I didn't come looking for you, my son. God told me to leave my fireside and start walking. He led me this way. You are hurt. What has happened to you?" Methuselah said as he helped Noah slowly to his feet.

"I gathered the people to warn them," Noah explained. "They would not receive my warning. They fell upon me and beat me."

"What warning are you speaking of?" Methuselah asked.

"Grandfather, two weeks ago as I was tending to my crops I heard the voice of God."

Noah went on to tell Methuselah some of what God had said about the world being consumed by sin and His cleansing of the earth by a flood.

"Why did you not come to me immediately? I could have been here to support you, Noah!"

"I worry about you, Grandfather. I see how you struggle now to rise from a chair or to walk. At your age, you don't need to be exposed to what I went through today. Now you have been dragged into it anyway. I don't want you worrying over me."

"Stop talking about me as if I am already sitting on the edge of my grave," Methuselah retorted. "I can take care of myself and I should be there when the one I love so much needs me."

Noah smiled at this despite the pain. The old man's blood was up, and Noah could see that he was ready to use his cane on anyone who would raise a hand to his grandson. The smile faded quickly as Noah's thoughts returned to his doubts.

"Grandfather, do you believe what I told you about a coming flood? Do you think God spoke to me?"

With those words, Noah looked up until his eyes met Methuselah's. In the watery blue eyes of his grandfather, Noah saw complete trust.

"Speak no more of it here upon the road," Methuselah said. "Come, I'll help you to my house. It is closer than your own. Your muscles will loosen by the heat of the fire, and we shall talk."

As Noah sipped tea and sat at Methuselah's hearth he recalled many other such occasions under happier circumstances. Since boyhood Noah had roamed the hillsides with Methuselah, enjoying the lessons he learned about God's creation and enjoying being in the woods with his beloved grandfather. After their days together Noah would return to this same hearth and listen as his grandfather and his father, Lamech, told their stories.

On this night, however, it was Noah who told the story. He told Methuselah in great detail how God had spoken to him and instructed him to build an ark.

"You should have come to me sooner, boy!" Methuselah said again, growing a little agitated. Noah smiled again at being called a boy. He was four hundred eighty years old at the time.

"I know, Grandfather. I suppose I felt this was my responsibility alone."

"No, it is not. God would have me to support you in this. I know that He would. There is no need to doubt this word from God, Noah. What you have experienced is from God and it will happen."

"How can you be so sure, Grandfather?" Noah asked.

"All my life I have wondered about my name," Methuselah replied. "Now, for the first time, I know what the meaning refers to."

"I don't understand, Grandfather."

"Have I never told you in all the times we have talked what the literal meaning of my name is, boy?"

"No, Grandfather, you haven't."

The old man pushed himself forward on the arms of his rocker. The light from the fire gave his lined face a slightly eerie glow. Noah could see fire in his grandfather's eyes as well as he leaned close and spoke in a whisper.

"Methuselah means *When he dies it will come.* I don't know how much longer I will be with you, Noah. But however long God gives me will be the same length of time you have to complete your ark."

"Grandfather, I have enough heaviness on my heart. I don't want to think of your passing. I need you beside me on the ark."

"You must be at peace with it, my son," Methuselah warned. "We all must die. And when I pass, know that the great flood you speak of will begin very quickly."

Noah had his grandfather for another one hundred twenty years after that night. Those years had been filled with sermons of warning for the people, many times with Methuselah standing alongside Noah. Years later, when hard work began on the ark, Methuselah was unable to do much physically. But he helped wherever he could.

Finally, with the ark completed and the provisions loaded, Methuselah had slipped quietly away in his sleep.

Though Noah had promised his grandfather many times that he would be by his side when that time came, he had not been. He had seen his grandfather earlier that day, looking frailer than he had ever seen him. Still the old man had been bright and alert so that Noah had no worries about him as he left to load supplies.

Later that night, he had gone by Methuselah's home to check on him again. At first he had thought that his grandfather was sleeping deeply. But as he approached his bed more closely he knew that was not the case. Noah had recoiled when he touched Methuselah's hand and found it cold.

That night and the next day Noah mourned. But he had never had the opportunity to mourn in a way that was fitting for such a great man. For when he found that Methuselah was gone, he recalled the old man's words. He had to push aside his sorrow and encourage his family even harder to complete the preparations of the ark. Just as Methuselah had predicted, the rains had begun two weeks after his death.

Tears welled in Noah's eyes and brought him back into the present with a start. He jumped slightly as if awakened from a dream and wondered how long he had been sitting there. He could not afford to sit and dwell on these things any longer. There was work to be done. He stood and began to walk slowly and stiffly to the ladder. He was six hundred years old now and though he could still work alongside his sons, it took him longer to recover the next day. He placed a wrinkled hand on the ladder but stopped before he put his foot on the first rung. Something was different. It had stopped raining.

CHAPTER 17

Spiritual Heritage

A dina squeezed cool water from the cloth and let it run over her neck and shoulders. Despite the family's efforts to keep the animal cages as clean as possible, the ark was a dusty, grimy place to work. It felt good to get clean at the end of a long workday. Sponging off in the basin had become a nightly ritual for Adina. It helped relax her, and she slept better because of it. There was plenty of water in the barrels for an occasional bath in the large wooden washtub they had brought along. But drawing a full bath was so much extra work that Adina simply didn't have the energy tonight.

As she finished her bath and changed from her work dress to her gown, Adina once again felt the urge to pray. She knew deep in her heart that she needed prayer for sustenance more than she needed food or water. Still every time she would begin to close her eyes in prayer, the hurt and anger over her parents would return.

As Adina lay down on her pallet, she remembered fondly how she had learned to pray. It had been when she was in her late teens on the small flat roof of her parents' home. Adina had spent every warm night that she could lying on her back on the roof and staring at the stars. She had sensed for some time that there had to be someone or something greater that had placed the stars there. She had tried often to communicate with that someone. But she hadn't known whom or what she was talking to.

As she had lain there one night talking aloud to the sky, she had suddenly heard another voice.

"You have a heart for God, young lady." Adina sat upright. She had no idea where the voice had come from or to whom it belonged. Finally, she looked to her right. She could barely make out a dark image two rooftops away. She squinted her eyes until she was able to make out an elderly woman who was sitting in a wooden straight-backed chair on a rooftop two houses away.

Adina stood and moved closer to the old woman's roof. The woman did not get up. "What did you say?" Adina asked.

The old woman scooted toward the edge of her chair and leaned in Adina's direction.

"I said," the woman shouted in a voice that was high-pitched and childlike, "you have a heart for God."

Adina stood and walked toward the other woman's rooftop. As she arrived at the raised wall at the side of her own roof, Adina could see the woman better. Her hair was white as cotton and she wore it tied tightly at the back of her head. The elderly woman's face was wrinkled deeply but, even in the dark, Adina could see that her eyes were kind. The most striking thing about the woman was her diminutive size. It almost looked as if a small child was sitting in the chair. The woman's feet couldn't quite touch the ground, even though she had scooted forward. Adina stood quietly, intrigued.

"What's the matter, young lady?" the woman inquired. "You had no trouble talking a moment ago. I have been sitting here listening to you talk for some time now." The woman noticed Adina's look of embarrassment. "Oh, don't worry. I couldn't make out what you were saying. If I had I would have moved farther away. What you had to say was between you and Him."

"Me and who?" Adina asked.

"Why you and God, of course. That is who you were talking to, wasn't it?" the woman asked, smiling broadly.

"Well," Adina responded, looking at her feet. "I am not sure. One night many weeks ago, when I looked up at all the stars, I just felt that someone or something—"

"You felt His presence," the woman interrupted. "That's what I said in the beginning. You have a heart for God. You sensed God was near when you marveled at His creation. Many here in this city don't sense that."

"What do they feel when they look at the stars?" Adina asked.

The woman turned to face forward again. There was not much of a view in that direction. The nearby wall of an apartment house rose up to block the sight of the surrounding neighborhood. The woman's smile faded, a frown creased her eyebrows, and her bottom lip stuck out in a pout. Suddenly instead of looking elderly, the woman looked like a disappointed toddler.

"They feel nothing," she said. Then she hopped down from her chair and walked through the door leading into her house. Adina heard the door close and lock behind her. She wondered what had been wrong.

The next night, however, the woman was back again at about the same time of the evening. Before stepping out onto the roof, Adina peeked out from the threshold to see if the woman was there. She smiled slightly when she realized that she was. The little woman was barely visible over the retaining wall around her own roof as she sat in a smaller chair that night. Adina stepped somewhat tentatively onto her own roof and called out.

"Hello," Adina said in as pleasant a voice as she could.

"Hello, young lady," the elderly woman's childish voice answered. Adina smiled again at both the squeaky voice and the friendly feeling she got from the lady.

"I am called Adina."

"Yes," came the reply. "Yes, I know."

"How do you know?" Adina asked.

"I have been your neighbor for many years. From the time you were a baby, I have heard your parents call you by that name. I am Nayna, by the way."

"I am pleased to meet you, Nayna, but why have we not met before? We have been in this house nearly all of my life, and I don't recall ever having seen you before."

"Tell me, Adina," Nayna said. "Who lives in that house over there?" The woman pointed back over her shoulder at the house across the street. The house was opposite Adina's.

"I don't know," Adina answered.

"Neither do I. In this city it is not easy to know very many of your neighbors. Many don't want to be known and many a young girl such as you does not need to know. I was not sure I wanted to be known. That is until I heard you in prayer. Then I knew that I wanted to be known and I wanted to know you." Nayna pointed at Adina as if bestowing a title upon her.

Adina momentarily frowned and then smiled at the woman's interesting manner of expressing herself. After a moment, it occurred to her just what Nayna had said in addition to how she had said it.

"Nayna, what is prayer? And who is God?"

"God is the Someone and the Something that you sensed was there. Your sense was correct, for there He is," Nayna's hand swept across the sky. As she looked up, her nose crinkled and her broad smile returned. The old woman was looking at the sky as if looking into the face of a dear friend that only she could see.

"But my father says that there are no gods."

"Your father is half-right," Nayna said, still looking toward the heavens. "There are no gods. But there is God, and He is there." Again, the wrinkled hand swept at the stars as if Nayna could gather a handful and lay them on her apron. "And He is here, in this city and on these rooftops as well."

"I don't understand," Adina said, perplexed.

"Yes, you do, child. Yes, you do. Now, I must go in. The night dampness is setting in. It is not good for an old woman."

For the next several weeks, Adina and Nayna met almost every evening on the roof. Because of Adina's concern over what her parents might think, neither woman ever ventured to the home of the other. In fact, on the nights when Adina's parents decided to enjoy the evening air on the roof along with her, Nayna always stepped inside right away, never even speaking.

Adina once asked her why she always left so abruptly at the sight of her parents. Nayna replied that Adina's parents had made it quite clear when Adina was merely a toddler that they did not want to hear about God or even talk to Nayna. Nayna supposed she had offended them by mentioning God in almost every conversation she had had with them when they first moved in.

Whenever Adina had time to spend alone with Nayna, however, it didn't take long for Adina's questions to begin and for the talk to turn to God. Nayna would answer with her little-girl voice and intriguing phrases. Throughout their talks, Nayna was able to teach Adina much about God. She taught, for example, that what Adina had been doing all those nights, talking to the sky and watching the stars, was actually an attempt to reach out to Him in prayer. She taught Adina who God was and that He had created all things. Nayna taught just the opposite of what Adina's father had said. She taught that, instead of relying on one's own strength, one should look to God.

Then one night came the conversation that would change not only Adina's life but even the course of history.

"Nayna," Adina asked. "Have you noticed how tall I am?"

Nayna laughed out loud. It was a tittering laugh and full of mischief.

"Have I noticed? Child, how could one as small as me not notice one as lofty as you?"

"Does it bother you?" "Do you think I'm strange?"

Nayna looked quizzically at her young friend.

"Why would how tall you are bother me? Now perhaps if we were walking in the forest and there were only one piece of fruit left high in the limbs of a nearby tree —"

"Maybe my height doesn't bother you because you don't know where I got that trait from."

"You mean from the giant that sired you?" Nayna replied.

Adina gasped. "How could you know that? No one is supposed to know but my parents."

Nayna waved a dismissive hand toward Adina.

"An old woman with few visitors and no one to talk to, at least until God placed you in my path, cannot help what she hears through her windows." At that Nayna turned her head to the side and stuck her pug nose into the air, a clear indication that she felt she had nothing to be ashamed of.

"Child, if I were concerned about what you were like on the outside, I would be much more likely to be offended by your striking beauty than your height. After all, I am not as young and beautiful as I once was." As she said this, Nayna pinched her own cheeks and pulled back her skin at her forehead as if she could stretch the wrinkles away.

"What is important to me, and important to Him," Nayna thrust a finger skyward, "is what you are on the inside. And, Adina, your inside is filled with goodness and kindness and love."

Adina felt tears of joy well up in her eyes. She looked at her feet for a moment before looking into Nayna's eyes.

"I have heard of the awful actions of the one whose blood I share. I am so afraid of the pull that that might have on me."

"Giant or no giant, the pull of God is much stronger. And God has a firm grip on you. I know, He told me so."

Adina paused a moment and considered asking Nayna *how* God told her. But there were other questions she wanted answered.

"Nayna," Adina asked. "How did you find out about Him? How did you get to know God?"

"My friend Sapphira introduced me to Him. She is the wife of Noah. Do you know them, child?"

"No, do they live on this street?"

"No, they live a half-day's walk from here outside the city, but you can meet them someday. Sometimes they come to the city to see Noah's brother. Often, they stop and visit me. The next time they are here, you will finally come over to my home."

Adina first met only Noah, Sapphira, and Japheth as they had traveled into the city together. Soon, Japheth was coming to see Adina on his own. It was when he took her out to see his home that she met Shem, Prisca, and Ham.

The year Ham and Adina were to be married, Nayna was gone. She slipped quietly away one night in her sleep to be with her Lord. Adina had seen her just the evening before. She had been as bright, sprightly, and charming as ever. Not even Sapphira had any idea how old Nayna had been. But she and Noah came and retrieved her body and made sure that Adina was able to be at the burial.

Adina smiled at the memories of her dear mentor as she lay on her back on the pallet, just as she had once lain on the roof of her old house. She wondered how Nayna would advise her to deal with her hurt and pain. She didn't have to wonder long. There was no doubt about what Nayna would tell her. Adina sat up. She looked around the dark room, her eyes settling on the stand that held the wash basin. It would be the perfect height for an altar Adina thought. Unable and unwilling to resist any longer, Adina moved over to the wash basin and knelt there.

CHAPTER 18

The Day the Work Stopped

The day started out as any other had in the last weeks. The family went about their chores with little fanfare or discussion. When they were all fully engaged in their work, they were generally spread out around the ark. There was not much opportunity for interaction. Little did the family know, but everyone would work closely together on this morning.

Boredom was the catalyst. Of all the creatures on the ark, Japheth felt that the most hideous and disgusting to look at was the cockroach. The large cockroaches hissed each time he approached the basket they were housed in. He decided that this would make the roach the perfect accomplice.

Japheth overcame his repulsion of the four-inch insect long enough to hold it down and work the tiny lasso he had fashioned from cord around its midsection. The roach hissed incessantly at the unwelcome apparel. Japheth released the roach back into its basket and then shook his hands wildly and shrugged his shoulders to overcome a severe case of the heebie-jeebies.

He looked around to make sure the coast was clear. Then he walked out the upper deck to the point in the center where he could see from the top to the bottom of the ark. Japheth knew there was a water barrel there that provided perfect cover. He hid behind it with his partner in crime and awaited a hapless victim. It didn't take long before he spotted the perfect person.

Tamara was too familiar with animal life to be adequately frightened. Adina was too sweet. Shem would just lecture him for an hour on how risky it was to tie a string to the hideous roach. Sapphira, well, Japheth just knew better. Prisca, however, would be absolutely perfect. The timing would be perfect because she was coming down the front of the cages at mid deck right now.

Japheth determined that he would lower the insect rapidly as she went by. With a little of his fishing skills he should be able to land the roach right on top of her head. Much screaming and jumping about was sure to follow. It would be the first belly laugh Japheth had enjoyed since boarding the ark.

As Prisca approached, Japheth dangled his little friend over the rail. Just before Prisca passed beneath him, he played out his string rapidly. It was not until Prisca had already passed by that Japheth abruptly realized two things. One, he had mistimed the release of the roach and was going to miss Prisca completely. Two, the string Japheth was using was too short. As he tried to close his grip and stop the roach's descent, the end of the string slipped through his fingers.

Japheth looked over the rail to observe the roach's increasingly rapid descent just in time to see Ham step out where Prisca had just been and look up.

Ham called out, "Adina, are you up—" The hissing cock roach hit him squarely in his upturned mouth. Ham hollered loudly, slapped himself wildly in the face to brush away the intruder, and stumbled backwards, crashing through the gate of the monkey's cage.

Little One already didn't like Ham, and she certainly didn't want to stay around him when he was screaming and hollering the way he was now. Little One leapt from the top of one cage to another. Rowdy was at mid deck following Prisca around. When he realized animals had escaped, he felt it was his job to herd them. He began to bark loudly, which excited both monkeys and led to their own howls of counter-protest.

Suddenly, animals all over the ark were getting excited. Little One's male counterpart climbed easily down the vertical column to escape from Rowdy and was quickly intrigued at some fruit scraps in the goats' trough. He made quick work of the clasp holding their enclosure door closed. Once he went inside, the goats ran outside. Now there was a monkey loose on the mid deck and a second monkey and fourteen goats running around on the lower deck. Rowdy was doing everything in his power to keep the lot of them stirred up with his barking.

For his part, Ham had shaken off the effects of the roach, made a mental note that the roach had come down on a string, and placed the insect underneath an empty bucket for safekeeping. He then took up the pursuit of Little One. Noah, Shem, Sapphira, and the others came to see what all the commotion was about. Tamara began running to the rescue, calling to everyone that, if they would give her some time, she could get all sixteen animals back where they belonged.

"Would someone please get that dog to stop barking?" she yelled in exasperation.

Japheth rushed down from upstairs in an attempt to remedy his mistake, but before he could jump in to help, he bumped into the ample chest of his older brother Ham.

"Japheth," Ham said, jaw clenched. "Do you have any idea how some creepy black bug got a string tied around it and how it got dropped onto my face?"

Japheth swallowed hard before shaking his head vigorously that he did not. Ham apparently did not believe him because with a shove he sent his little brother flying into the chicken coop. Japheth's head made an ideal battering ram to break open the wicker door to the coop. Chickens came flapping into the air in a cloud of feathers.

The combination of chickens squawking, goats bleating, and monkeys just making a general mess of everything had every animal on the ark pacing and calling to one another.

Shem assumed his leadership role and began to chase the goats, occasionally diverting his attention to one of the monkeys. The two primates were now having great fun climbing freely from one deck to another, throwing whatever they could get their hands into. The result of Shem trying to catch multiple animals at once was that none were caught.

"Someone wait on the far end of the aisle and catch one of them," Shem bellowed as he crashed into a stall wall while rounding the corner at the far end of the lower deck.

Japheth, still shaking out the cobwebs from his head-first crash into the chickens, looked over the rail to see his mother crouched down, waiting to scoop up an oncoming kid. Sapphira must have sensed she was being watched for she looked up at Japheth with pursed lips and said, "Boy, when this is over—"

Japheth was surprised by his mother's agility as she literally dove for the baby goat, who bleated with delight as he cut left and flew past her. Japheth then looked to see his father on the walkway for the window, stalking an unsuspecting chicken as it perched on the rail. Tamara had Little One in a motherly embrace and was scolding her as she opened the door to a spare cage. Adina was at mid deck attempting to lure the male monkey her way with a piece of fruit. Ham was now at the lower deck and had the foresight to walk down the aisle toward the goats with a wide board that served as a moving gate.

Just when it seemed things were starting to get back under control, Rowdy would show up in one of the scenes with enough barking and fanfare to send the nearly captured animals in all directions. It seemed at least *he* saw the fun in all this mayhem. It was readily apparent to Japheth that no one else did.

"Japheth," Noah called from the walkway, "catch that dog and tie him up somewhere, or we will never get things under control."

Finally, after considerable effort on every family member's part, all the animals, including the cockroach, were back safely in their newly repaired enclosures. All the chasing and cage repairs had taken the better part of the day, and there was still a great deal of spilled food to be cleaned up.

At late afternoon, the entire family, winded and dirty from their efforts, assembled at the center of the ark on the lower deck. The animals were finally calm.

Japheth walked up to the group last, his head hanging. Shem and Ham stared at Japheth disapprovingly, their hands on their hips. Adina and Prisca, their arms folded across their chests, were clearly unhappy with their brother-in-law as well. Surprisingly, Japheth glanced up to see a slight smile on the faces of his mother and father. They had decided that, with no serious harm done, they would let the siblings handle the coming lecture.

"Do you need more work to do, Japheth? Is that the problem?" Shem asked. "Aren't we all loaded down with enough chores without you creating messes like this? We are not children, Japheth. We don't have the time or energy for your silly games."

As Shem admonished his little brother, Japheth was pleasantly surprised that Tamara came and stood beside him, taking his hand.

"Of all the dumb ideas you have had since this started, this was the dumbest," Ham spoke.

Japheth, who had been contrite until now, felt his face getting hot at Ham's description. "Well, maybe if you hadn't screamed and fallen backward like a little girl over a bug, things wouldn't have gotten so out of hand."

Sapphira suddenly snorted at this as she tried to stifle a laugh. But Japheth's comeback was not as well received by either of his brothers. Ham took a step toward Japheth, but Shem stepped between the two.

"And maybe if you had been doing your chores instead of fooling around we could all be resting by the fire after a productive day's work," Shem scolded again. "In fact, I think that is just what the rest of us will do now. As for you, you can clean up this mess and then finish feeding the animals that got skipped on this deck because of your shenanigans."

Japheth looked to Noah in protest, but his father only raised his eyebrows and nodded his approval, indicating his agreement that the penalty was just. One by one, the family departed. Only Tamara stayed behind.

"Tamara," Noah called out. "Come and join the rest of us. Japheth must be reminded that actions have consequences."

Tamara looked into Japheth's eyes reluctantly. As she took a step backward she slid her hand down the length of Japheth's arm and gave his hand a squeeze. Japheth leaned in to kiss her but only caught her cheek as she quickened her pace and left the room.

CHAPTER 19

Japheth Stumbles

By the time I completed the last of my sentence, the others were getting ready for bed. Except for a short supper break, it had taken me the remainder of the evening to finish the cleanup. I had had plenty of time to mumble under my breath about the unfairness of my punishment. As I completed the last bit of my labor, my thoughts went to other things.

I couldn't believe it had been over three months. That is not to say that it didn't feel like we had been on this ark that long. Indeed, it felt like it had been much longer than that. The never-ending chores, the stuffy air, and spending several hours each day with no view of the sun or sky were not helping our time on board pass rapidly. What I was having trouble believing on this night was that my wife and I had enjoyed little to no physical contact since before we walked up the ramp and closed the door.

How long is she going to let whatever happened to her come between us? I was unsure if it was just the attack she had suffered or the lack of privacy on this floating barn that was affecting her. Whatever it was, I was sick of waiting. I didn't deserve this type of treatment. I had taken Shem's advice. I had prayed about whatever role God would have me to play on this voyage and I had prayed for my marriage. By now, God should have been noticing how obedient I had been. He should have done something to change Tamara's bad behavior by now.

God also didn't seem to be hearing my prayers about a position of leadership. Nothing had changed in the pecking order of this family. Many times when we were all trying to solve some problem that had arisen in the day-to-day life on the ark, I had offered good solutions. I was as smart as either Shem or Ham, and my ideas would have worked. But no one listened to me. Sometimes they laughed and said my schemes were too elaborate and couldn't be done with what we had to work with. How could they know if they would work if they never tried any of them?

I tossed a pitchfork full of hay into the camels' stall and laughed despite myself when it landed on one of the camel's backs instead of in his trough. Then I walked over and hung the pitchfork on its peg and leaned against a water barrel. As I stood there with my arms folded, I shook my head at the thought of my sorry state. How could I ever assert myself with this family? When we got to wherever we were going would I always be the bothersome little brother whose wife ignored him? It angered me to think about it. I was as intelligent and as righteous in the sight of God as anyone on this vessel, and that included Father. I deserved more respect.

And why should Tamara continue to neglect me? I had been very patient. I had allowed her emotions time to heal. Still she ignored me. There had been lots of women back home, some even prettier than her, who had shown more than a passing interest in me. Tamara should have been thrilled to have me. I was good to her. I never treated her with disrespect the way Ham treated Adina. Why, I bet sometimes even Adina wished she had married me.

Puffing out my cheeks in disgust I turned abruptly and headed up the passage toward the kitchen. The passage was dark, but I didn't take the time to light a candle. As I walked, I noticed a shaft of light. It was coming from the storage room where Ham and Adina slept. As I passed by, I turned to see the light's source. Through the crack in the door I could see Adina on the far side of the room. She was bathing in a basin. Her back was to me.

The second I saw her, a voice inside my head told me to keep going toward my quarters. I knew I needed to go and find Tamara, so I took a step or two down the hall. My steps toward the kitchen were slow.

Sometimes I wanted to punch Ham. He didn't appreciate Adina. She was too good a woman for him. Then my thoughts went to Tamara. Why should I hurry to find her? She didn't want me around her. She had made that clear. I stopped walking. Shutting out that voice, I turned and looked back over my shoulder at the now tantalizing shaft of light. I determined that I wouldn't look. I would just go back to push the door closed so that Adina could have more privacy.

I sneaked back toward the opening, cautiously looking up and down the passage as I went. I stopped with the line of light from the crack falling across my chest. *There's nothing wrong with one quick glance*, I thought, trying to convince myself. I looked up and down the passage again. The voice had risen to a scream.

I continued to ignore it until suddenly the voice seemed to disappear. *Just a quick look*, I thought. *Don't make such a big thing out of it. Hurry up before someone comes.* I stepped still closer till the light fell across my eye and I saw her again.

I did much more than take a single peek. I stood mesmerized, leaning one way and another to see more than Adina's back. I had always known that Adina was more womanly than Tamara, but I had never seen a woman other than Tamara like this. My mind began to flood with thoughts. Rather than flee from them, I indulged them. I found my breath coming more

165

quickly. I lost all thoughts of anything or anyone else—that is, until Ham placed his hand on the back of my neck.

CHAPTER 20

A Family Lost

Noah had noticed when he went to bed that Japheth was missing. Sapphira, Prisca, Tamara, and Shem were all in their beds. Noah assumed Ham and Adina were as well. Where was Japheth?

He knew that his youngest son was frustrated and feeling that his brothers didn't respect him. Noah had sensed that even before the craziness of the day. Despite the trouble his youngest son had caused, Noah still had to laugh. Though the timing of his jokes was sometimes shaky, Japheth really was a joy. Noah liked to think that Japheth got his sense of humor from him. As a younger man he would have done something just like what Japheth did to Ham.

On the other hand, Japheth was always ready with some grandiose idea for an invention that would make life on board easier. He got that from Noah's younger brother, Jason. Jason had always been a man of ideas. The problem was Jason's intelligence and his independent nature had made it very difficult for him to listen to Noah. And his ideas, particularly the one's relating to his business interests, were almost always contrary to God's ways.

Noah had suffered rejection almost everywhere he went to talk about God's righteousness and the coming judgment.

No pain of rejection could compare, however, to that which he experienced from his own family. The rebuff Noah had suffered from his brother and his three sisters haunted him the most. It was a moment that he had replayed almost every day since they had entered the ark. As he lay back on his bed, Noah remembered it yet again.

Noah and Sapphira had gone into the city to Jason's home. It had been several months since Noah's brothers and sisters had all been together, and they were gathering for a meal. By that time, the main beam for the ark and much of its framework were assembled such that one could easily envision the shape it would have. Sapphira had begged Noah to spend the visit enjoying fellowship with his extended family. She implored him to avoid launching into a message or warning of the impending flood.

"You need time to rest your body and mind. And your family needs time to be with you without having to think about what is to come. You will have many more occasions to talk to them about such things. Just let today be a time to be together," she implored. And Noah had agreed. He determined that he would go to his brother's home with no agenda. He had no plans to speak out. *Perhaps if we can recall good times we have enjoyed in the past*, he thought, *they will be more likely to listen in the future.*

Except for warm greetings for his siblings, he had remained silent through the beginning of the meal. He had even sat quietly when his brother broke bread without as much as a mention to the Lord who had provided it. But once they all had food on their plates and started to eat, it became apparent that Noah's hopes for a quiet family meal were in vain. He had come with no agenda. His brother had not.

"Noah," his brother blurted, abruptly placing his fork down on the table. "We wanted to all be together for this first time in many months to ask you once again to please stop this insane talk about a great flood."

"Yes, and to insist that you tear down this monstrosity you have been building," his oldest sister added. "You can see it from any rooftop in town. It is already dominating the view on the main road into the city. People all around are talking every day about you. They tell me how sorry they are for me that my brother has gone mad. Have you any idea how tired I am of being a laughingstock?"

"I know how it hurts to be laughed at and made fun of—" Noah began to say.

"Noah, you silly fool!" his brother interrupted. "It is completely within your own power to put a stop to their mocking." As his brother spoke, Noah noticed how rapidly Jason became angry. He sensed that this had been eating at his siblings for a long time.

"No, brother, it is not within my control. God is in control, and He has given me the responsibility to warn everyone and to make ready for the flood."

"Do not speak that! Do not speak that, that drivel in my house!" His brother jumped to his feet and was red-faced; veins bulged in his bald head and in his neck. Noah and his wife were momentarily frozen by the intensity and sudden-ness of this outburst. Just as suddenly as he lost his temper, Noah's brother seemed to gather himself somewhat.

"If there is such a great flood to come, my brother, why does your God speak only to you? Why doesn't He come down here and stand in the street in all His glory and tell us of it Himself? Would a great God speak of such a thing through such a small man?"

At this, tears began to well up in Sapphira's eyes. She was heartbroken for Noah and the terribly difficult position he was in.

"Stop your crying, you silly woman," Noah's youngest sister hissed into Sapphira's ear. "You should have done more to stop this long ago. I hold you just as responsible as he for this lunacy!" Sapphira didn't respond; instead she kept her focus on Noah and tried to set her jaw and stop her tears to show him support and give him strength.

Noah's brother was not finished.

"Perhaps while your God is telling only you of the future, you could ask Him what businesses I should invest in and how I should assign my men."

"Please don't say that," Noah pleaded. "Please don't mock God. And He is not my God alone. He is your God as well. He doesn't want to see you killed in this flood. He has made provision for you on the ark. You must come with us." Noah looked over at Sapphira, and she gave a slight nod as if to agree that there was no need to hold back now.

The red returned to his brother's face and his hands balled into fists. His jaw muscles flexed and he began to shake.

"There is no reasoning with him," he growled to his sisters through clenched teeth. Then he grabbed Noah by his cloak and shook him. "There is no God speaking to you, you idiot! There will be no great flood, and there will be no ark. If you won't stop this, I will come with my men and shred your handiwork into kindling!" As he finished his pronouncement, Jason grabbed Noah's hair and pulled his head back with one hand. With the other he shoved hard at Noah's chest, knocking him to the floor.

This was too much for any of the onlookers. Noah's oldest sister pulled at Jason's arm, only to be shoved back into her chair. Then Sapphira came around the table to assist Noah. But as she approached, Jason knocked her to the floor as well. At this Noah, though nearly sixty years his brother's senior, came rapidly to his feet. The frustration of what he had endured at the hands of jeering crowds suddenly came back to him in a rush of emotion. Noah backhanded his brother hard enough to knock him onto the table. Food on wooden plates fell to the floor with a clatter.

Noah's piercing blue eyes suddenly contained a fire that he normally reserved for his most passionate preaching. His brother started to get up, but his anger had been replaced by fear. Noah held him in place by the shoulders and spoke with heretofore unreleased anger. He looked from his brother to the faces of the others as he spoke.

"You have all been warned repeatedly. I cannot force you to believe me. If you come to the ark for refuge, it will be given to you. But if any of you come to the ark to damage the work God has led me to or to harm my family, I will destroy you myself."

With that, he held one hand out to help Sapphira to her feet. He pushed her gently behind him and backed away before turning and walking out the door.

In Jason's mind, it was not just a matter of his family walking into the ark. He had much to lose should Noah's teachings about godliness take root with the people. He was a man of great reputation in the town for being a ruthless businessman. When Jason traveled through the city, everyone knew him. Some feared him. Most of the people loved him because he was instrumental in providing forms of hedonistic entertainment that previously had been unavailable. Noah fought against the opposing forces and loyalties in the lives of all the people as he tried to teach about obedience to his mythical God. If his teachings ever took hold, it would be a death knell to Jason's fortune.

Months passed, and Noah had not seen his family. Finally, the day after Methuselah died, Noah headed back to the cluster of houses where his brother and sisters lived. This time he went there alone. He felt he must tell his brother of their grandfather's passing and at the same time make one more plea for them to come with his family aboard the ark.

Nowhere was the challenge greater or the current against him any stronger than within his own family. Jason was in his garden watching the water cascade from a fountain as Noah approached. Though Jason's back was to the road, the sound of footsteps made him turn. The second he recognized Noah, he rose quickly to his feet and walked out the front gate. He came up the road to meet his brother. As Noah watched him approach, everything about Jason's demeanor and the way he moved revealed that he was still very angry.

"You're not welcome here," he called out, still closing the distance between them. "Stop where you are. Don't set foot on my property."

Noah stopped walking and raised his hands in front of him to indicate his resignation. "Jason, the time is at hand. The rain will begin very soon—"

"Shut up!" his brother shouted. His body shook as he grabbed great fistfuls of his own beard. "I will not hear your babbling ever again! Nothing can save this family from the damage you have done to it. I can never regain the status I once had. I will always be regarded as the one with the crazy brother!"

With his nose a fraction of an inch from Noah's, Jason lowered his voice and declared, "You have refused to stop your fool preaching. You insisted on continuing with this so-called ark despite my pleas. I beg you to do one thing that I ask." Noah waited a long moment for his brother to continue. "You and your family please crawl aboard your precious ark and rot!"

Spittle hit Noah's face. He recoiled more from aversion to the heartfelt nature of the statement than any physical repulsion. He felt as if he had suffered a great blow to his core. He stumbled back, but Jason, eyes red with anger and teeth clenched, continued to advance and shake his head as if answering yes to some unasked question. Out of the corner of his eye, he noticed his sisters and their families stepping out of their houses.

"That's right," Jason went on. "Go and die locked up in your crate. And the same for all who are with you! One of your new animals can tear your dead body apart for all I care."

Noah had been walking backward but turned to walk away for he realized from their demeanor that his sisters agreed with Jason.

"You're a pathetic disgrace!" Jason screamed after him.

As Noah walked purposefully toward his home, he could no longer see the road for his eyes were filling with tears. He chewed his bottom lip hard enough to draw blood, but he did not feel the pain. Every few steps a sob burst from his chest, only to be choked back. Though his feet felt as heavy as stones, he continued at a steady pace back up the road until he was just out of reach of the stones Jason was hurling. Noah lowered his head and saw his tears make tiny dots in the dust of the road. For a brief moment, he had a mental picture of Jason, his face beaming, sitting on Methuselah's lap when he was a small boy.

"Grandpa is gone, Jason," Noah said in a voice just above a whisper. Then he raised his head, focused his gaze as far down the road as he could see, and headed for the ark. He did not look back.

With a huge hand, Ham squeezed my neck hard enough to make me wince. Involuntarily, my knees bent as I tried to pull away from the pain. I swept my forearm around hard into Ham's elbow, but I couldn't break his grip. Ham squeezed harder and then, once he had shown me that he only let go when he was ready, pushed me away and into the wall. My shoulder was driven into the boards with a thud.

I began immediately to think up something to tell him. How would I explain what I was doing standing here looking into his wife's room?

"If you were about to throw a bug into my room, I'm not in there, stupid," Ham said, grinning. For a second, I thought

I smelled alcohol on his breath. But that was impossible. No strong drink had been brought on board. Then I noticed the lantern in Ham's other hand. The light from it had flooded the passage as he approached, masking the light from the crack in the door. My mind raced through this line of thought.

"Shem sent me to ask you again to move back in with the rest of us," I lied.

"Why don't you and Shem leave me alone and mind your own business. Besides you don't want me down there around your wives at night." As he said this, Ham winked and brushed past me as he entered the storeroom where Adina was bathing. She shrieked and covered herself with a towel as Ham opened the door abruptly.

"Ham, I was bathing! Couldn't you warn me you were coming in?" Ham ignored her completely and plopped down on their straw mattress. The pallet he had crudely fashioned looked much worse than it had when our voyage began. Straw was coming out and lying all around the floor. I felt sorry for Adina.

As I looked up at her, I noticed that my sister-in-law's face was flushed. She tried to cover herself. In spite of my own embarrassment both at being caught and finding myself in this position, I stood and stared dumbly.

"Japheth," she scolded. "Please leave and close the door!" She said this in a way that clearly indicated that she considered it obvious that this was the proper course of action. I felt like a cad for not having done it without being told. As I shut the door, the last thing I saw was Ham looking at me with a disapproving grin as he shook his head slowly. Oddly, in addition to feeling relieved that Ham had not caught me, I also felt a twinge of resentment toward my middle brother.

I walked as far as the entry to the kitchen area. I was filled with conflicting emotions and thoughts. Why did Ham make that lewd comment about being around our wives? Had he seen me after all? Surely not. He would have beaten me if he had. Or did he have so little respect for me as an adversary that he didn't care what I had seen?

And then thoughts of Adina filled my head. I replayed the image in my mind and forgot my other concerns. And then I replayed it again. Finally, I shook my head to clear my mind and stepped inside the kitchen.

The room was empty and the lanterns were off. I could see embers glowing in the fireplace. There was a partial loaf of bread and some cooked beans left from our meal sitting on a wooden plate on the hearth. Mother had undoubtedly left it out for me. I chewed as I sat alone at the darkened table. As I sat there, a voice in my head was so clear it was as if someone was sitting beside me.

What kind of man are you? I thought. *Did you not witness what the wrath of the Lord can do?* I was suddenly ashamed and a little frightened. I would not let that happen again. Adina was my brother's wife. He didn't deserve her, but she was still his. I would not let something like that happen again. It wasn't right.

The sleeping area was filled with the sounds of heavy breathing as I entered. Father was the only one still awake. He looked up at me as I entered. It was obvious that he had been crying, but I didn't want to talk about what was bothering him. I looked briefly at Shem and Prisca. Her head rested on his shoulder and his arm was around her as they slept. I crawled into my bed and snuggled next to Tamara. A moment later, without waking, she rolled to the far side of the bed and turned her back to me.

175

CHAPTER 21

Women of Strength

The women were all gathered in the kitchen preparing dough. It was the third day of the week and each week on that day they would bake.

The time the women spent preparing meals had become, for most of them, a welcome break from the more lonely work of animal care. It was a time for them to talk to one another. They talked of everything from their fears regarding the voyage to the difficulties of cohabitating so closely. While the men worked on the other decks, the women worked equally hard in the kitchen. Yet they enjoyed the time.

"Mother," Prisca asked as she kneaded dough, "do you remember when I first came to live with you?"

"Yes, I think of it often," Mother replied. "You looked so small and pitiful with your dirty face. And you were so skinny."

"If I know you, Mother," Adina added, "I'll bet the first thing you did was feed her."

They all laughed, knowing Sapphira's propensity to feed anyone and everyone who came to her home.

"Yes, I did," Sapphira replied a little defiantly but with a heartfelt smile. "And she certainly needed it. The poor thing had not eaten a good meal in days."

Reminiscing in this way was not painful for Prisca. She remembered how grateful she had felt to have the family bring her to their table as if she were their own. She remembered how proud she had been of her own little room they had made in the loft. And most fondly, she recalled how she had almost instantly been attracted to Shem.

"Remember how Shem smiled at me all the time?"

"Yes," Sapphira squinted up her nose and nearly squealed at the precious memory. "But he wouldn't talk to you for the longest. I think it was over a week before he finally asked you if you wanted one of the apples he had brought in."

"As if he just happened to have an extra, I suppose," Adina added as she put double handfuls of chopped vegetables into the kettle of boiling water.

"I am no longer a wife to Japheth!"

The words spilled from Tamara's mouth and brought every woman in the room to a standstill. The kitchen was awkwardly silent except for the sounds from the crackling fire and the bubbling kettle. Tamara had been so quiet on the voyage that the others had grown used to it. They had all but quit trying to engage her in conversation, feeling that perhaps she needed time with her thoughts. Adina had kept to herself the episode of Tamara's crying on her shoulder, feeling she might embarrass her sister-in-law if she shared it with the others.

Sapphira was the first to go to Tamara, placing an arm around her daughter-in-law's shoulders. Prisca followed quickly, feeling a little guilty that she rambled on so about her and Shem's happy memories. Adina at first looked longingly at Tamara from her post in front of the chopping block. Then she wiped her hands and came around to take both of Tamara's hands in hers.

"What do you mean, child?" Sapphira spoke first. "Of course, you are still his wife."

"Not in the way that I should be, in the way that I want to be. What once brought me joy and made my heart race now almost repulses me. And it is not Japheth. It is not him at all. I love him so."

"It is difficult for us all being cramped up together as we are," Prisca said, still not realizing the full extent of Tamara's statement.

Tamara began to cry. Adina rolled her eyes at Prisca's naiveté and added, "Tamara is still struggling mightily with the attack she suffered. I don't think any one of the three of us fully comprehend what she went through."

"Oh, my dear, I am your own mother-in-law, yet I have been so busy and so caught up in all that we have undergone that I took no time to talk to you about how you must be feeling. Foolishly, I just assumed you were slowly healing. We have all been through so much. But you have been through more than all the rest of us."

Tamara composed herself enough to speak in a choking voice. "I try not to think about it. I try to get past it. I know time has passed, but it seems like just days ago. Then I feel terrible to dwell on my problem in the midst of all the suffering and loss realized by others."

"The magnitude of others' losses does not mean that your problem is trivial," Prisca reassured her.

"When I see your mother I will slap her to her knees for sending you out into that dreadful city and to that type of place at night!" Sapphira said furiously.

Sapphira's anger had caused her to momentarily forget that neither she nor Tamara would ever see Tamara's mother again. She caught her mistake and blushed. Tamara began to sob deeply once again.

Adina spoke up. "This is more than any of us can help Tamara with in our own power. Perhaps we should talk to Father about it. But first we should pray to God on our own."

"Of course, you're right," Sapphira agreed. "Surely the God who made provision for us on this ark will hear our prayers. He chose us by His own hand to be here. I know that He loves us and cares when we are in pain."

Tamara spoke up again, "I have wondered if He did love me at times. I don't know why He let this thing happen to me if He did. But then I remember that He did make a place for me here with you all and Japheth."

Adina squeezed Tamara's hands warmly. "I was so devastated by the loss of my parents, Tamara. You heard what I said to Father that night. I was actually angry with God. Now, after much prayer, I am sure that He loves us all very much or we wouldn't be here. That is what is helping me to cope. To know that Almighty God cared enough for me to make a safe place for me here gives me such strength. Not only are we safe here on the ark from the waters, we are safe from the evil that tried to take you from us, Tamara."

With that, they all looked from one to another and smiled reassuringly. It was as if by speaking it that they all came to grasp the depth of Almighty God's love for them.

Sapphira did not know Adina with the same intimacy she did Prisca. And she did not feel the need to protect her as she did Tamara. Adina was too strong in spirit for that. But at this moment she felt very close to Adina and was happy she was here.

"Let's all bow on our knees right here in this kitchen," Sapphira said. "The men won't be up for awhile yet. Adina, would you lead us in a prayer for Tamara's healing?"

And so they knelt there, with the stew of vegetables that God had instructed them to store in the ark, with the pot boiling in the kitchen that God had inspired Shem to design. They knelt there in the center of the ark, drifting in the center of the vast body of water that covered the earth. They knelt with nothing to steer them but the One who had brought them safe thus far.

CHAPTER 22

Enchanted

"Japheth, would you like more stew?" Tamara asked. This was at least the third time she had waited on me during tonight's meal.

No! What I would like is a wife who doesn't jerk away when I try to put my arm around her or turn her face to the side when I want to kiss her, I wanted to say.

Tamara's little attempt at charity was not going to be enough to make up for the way she had been neglecting me. I knew she was tired from her chores on the ark. We were all tired. But that didn't excuse her behavior.

"Japheth, darling, did you hear me? Would you like more stew?"

Tonight's meal had been strange. The women looked at one another and smiled more than normal. I wondered briefly if they were planning to play some joke on one of us. Suddenly, Tamara's question got through to me.

"Uh no, I'm full."

I stood up without looking at Tamara and walked over to the hearth.

I had been doing much better. An entire month had passed since I looked in on Adina. I had managed to avoid doing it again. In spite of the cold reception I continued to receive from Tamara, I felt terribly guilty for what I had done.

Adina and I had once been interested in each other, but she was my sister-in-law now. I knew I mustn't have these types of thoughts. And I had fought and fought to not let my mind go in that direction. I had to be disciplined and fight my urges. I was standing by the hearth after another long, hard day of tending the animals and feeling somewhat proud of my efforts toward virtue when Adina walked by.

Though I had determined not to let my mind wander, it would have been obvious to any healthy man why I would be tempted. As she passed, I turned my face away from the others and smacked the heel of one hand into my forehead. I was doing it again! I turned to leave the room, but Adina spoke to me.

"Japheth, I have to help the others clean up after dinner. Can you please haul two buckets of water to my room and take a cake of soap? I'll need it later."

Was she teasing me? Did she know what I had done? Perhaps it was more than that; perhaps this was an invitation to join her in her room. But that wasn't likely. Adina was too sweet and too loyal to Ham to consider such a thing. I looked over at Ham now. He was sitting there stuffing his face. He had barely acknowledged his lovely wife all night. Why hadn't she asked him to draw her water? Probably because he would tell her to do it herself. So, because of his attitude, had she grown to appreciate me?

Adina had shown no hint that she was interested in me anymore. Yet many times I saw that the rude things Ham said hurt her. Perhaps she was attracted to me too but was simply afraid to show it.

Throughout dinner I fought to keep my mind on the little conversations going on amongst the others. Occasionally, I took opportunities to watch Adina as she smiled and talked, usually to the other women at the table. I was completely enchanted by her smile. When I would begin to watch her, I would look away abruptly, but I needed only to sit quietly for a few moments before forbidden images would begin to play across my mind's eye.

When dinner was over and the table had been cleared, we were all sitting around the living area. Mother was sewing in the rocker Shem made for her. Dad was in another rocker with his head back and his eyes closed. Shem and Prisca sat at the table playing a game with one hand while holding hands with the other. Ham sat on a stool that looked too little for him and carved something from a piece of wood. As the dusk turned to dark, one by one they began to head to bed. Shem and Dad headed up the ladder to watch the stars out the window and attempt to determine the course we were traveling. Tamara walked toward the animals. Finally, Adina got up and headed to her room.

I thought immediately of the water and soap I had taken to her room earlier. I looked around at the others to see if anyone left in the room had noticed my struggle. None appeared to. I debated with myself for several moments. Eventually, I made a definite decision that I would not be that kind of man. Tamara was going through some difficulty that I didn't understand, but I would wait for her to come back to me.

A few more moments went by. It occurred to me that I might have left the top rail down on the bears' cage. I determined abruptly that I had best go check, so I headed down the passageway to the animals' area. *It isn't as if I am just trying to walk by Adina's door. I have a legitimate reason to be in the passage,* I lied to myself.

As I passed Adina's door, I walked along the opposite side of the hall. My eyes were locked onto that familiar sliver of light from the door. I walked past, and my breath once again came rapidly. I felt silly that I was suddenly perspiring. I was going to make it without giving in. I was almost to the large door leading to the middle animal deck. Then I stopped. Tamara didn't appreciate me, and Ham didn't appreciate Adina. If this was the worst thing I ever did to Tamara, she could consider herself lucky.

In one step I crossed to Adina's door and put my face clumsily to the crack. I would just take a quick glimpse this time. It wasn't as if I was going to stay here and stare like before. I was disappointed to find that Adina was still clothed. She wiped a cloth gently around her neck and then folded it over the side of the wash basin. My breath came even more rapidly now. It was as if I had been running. I tried to steady myself and quiet my breathing.

Rather than disrobing, Adina pulled one end of the cord that held her hair up, untying the bun. Her hair fell across her shoulders and down her back. She leaned over to one side and shook her hair out as she combed through it with one hand. Next, she walked around to the other side of the wash stand and eased herself down to her knees. She closed her eyes, bowed her head, and folded her hands beneath her chin. Candlelight bathed her face, highlighting the curve of her full lips and accentuating her high cheekbones. The long lashes of her closed eyes made them seem even larger and more beautifully shaped than normal. But the image that I saw of Adina was no longer sensuous. Instead, she looked as innocent and pure as a little girl. I watched her a moment as her lips began to move in silent prayer.

I slumped back from the door and sat down heavily upon the floor. I reached up and grasped my head in my hands. What had I done? Adina had never shown me anything but kindness. She had been as nurturing to Tamara after her ordeal as my own mother had been. Yet I had snuck around in dark passageways and violated the privacy and trust of this beautiful, caring, godly woman.

In the past I had always thought Adina somewhat of a tragic figure. Suddenly, it occurred to me that she stood by

Ham and followed him onto this ark despite his harsh treatment of her because of a faith in God that I could only aspire to. Adina was far from pathetic, she was heroic.

And what of my own wife? Had Tamara done anything to deserve this type of betrayal? Her attitude toward me on this voyage was not one of neglect but rather reflected a grievous injury to her heart and mind. My response as her husband had been to abandon her. It had been only a month before when she had stood beside me when the rest of the family was angry with me.

I began to feel nauseous. I leaned back toward the door and again looked through the crack. This time it was not so that I could see Adina's nakedness but so that I could admire her in prayer. At the same instant that my focus returned to Adina, she stopped praying. She stared for a moment at the wall opposite the door with a frown. Then she stood, turned, and took a quiet step in her bare feet. I lost sight of her briefly until the door opened and she was standing before me.

CHAPTER 23

Shem's Concern

S hem and Noah sat on small stools that put them at just the right height to see out the window. Shem and Ham had worked together to build the stools, and they were being used by everyone at some time each day. The walkway by the window had become a kind of solace for anyone who needed a break or just needed some time to see the sky. In this instance, the stars were incredibly vivid and the moon, which had seemed closer ever since the flood, reflected off the still water.

"Ham is overfeeding the hippos and the elephants. We have been underway for one hundred twenty-one days. At the rate he is going we will run out of hay before we make it one hundred twenty more," Shem cautioned.

"They are eating all he gives them and they are not getting fat. The supplies will be fine," Noah replied.

"We don't need to wait for them to get fat to estimate their food usage. We only have four or five months left at the rate he is feeding them."

"And how many months should we have, Shem? Only God knows that. Neither of us is absolutely sure how much these animals need. Ham has been caring for them, and no food has been left in their troughs. They are not gaining or

187

losing weight. So we should trust that he is feeding them correctly. If that is the case, we will have enough food."

There was a long silence while Shem squirmed. He wasn't satisfied and had more on his mind. But he moved on.

"Many of the small animal cages are only being cleaned every third day. We should talk to the girls about that," Shem continued to press.

"I have been walking daily on that deck; I don't see a problem with the cleanliness."

"The weather is getting warmer, and we cannot afford to let odor build up. We have to keep our air from getting stale in the lower decks."

"As the weather gets warm they can increase the frequency of the cleanings," Noah replied patiently. "Why don't we let them make that determination? I certainly don't think any or our womenfolk need us to tell them when something smells bad." Noah chuckled.

"Father, every time I try to talk with you about matters concerning the day-to-day chores on this vessel you either don't answer or make light of it. Perhaps these particular issues aren't critical, but all the concerns added together may mean the difference in our having real problems later on or in our being prepared for the long term. You said it yourself: We don't know how long we may have to stay on this ark. You must start listening to me and taking me seriously."

"Do you really think I need you to present me with a list of concerns every time we are alone together? I already spend nearly every waking hour in prayer for our safe return to land."

"Praying is all well and good, Father, but we must be vigilant as well. Just as God chose to use us in constructing this ark, He expects us to work hard to insure that every creature and certainly every person on this voyage makes it safely to whatever awaits us."

"Obviously, I understand that we have to do more than merely float along and wait, Shem," Noah said, growing a little irritated. "But we needn't work ourselves into a frenzy over every detail either. God knew we didn't know everything about these animals when we started. I am sure He allowed for that when He guided us in preparing for this."

Shem sensed his father becoming exasperated with him and fell silent for a time.

"What's it like?" he finally asked.

"What is what like?"

"When God talks to you. What is His voice like?"

"You've asked me this before," Noah smiled slightly now. Seeing that Shem was still waiting for his answer, he went on. "Well, like I told you, it is a very clear and distinct voice that I hear, just as I am hearing your voice now. It is commanding, and I cannot help but place my face to the ground. I feel love from Him, yet at the same time I feel some fear."

"I never hear Him when He speaks to you."

"I don't understand why, but for some reason when He is talking to me or instructing me, people nearby don't hear. I found that out when I was preaching. Sometimes when I was most discouraged He would speak to me and then I could press on. But others standing all around me didn't seem to hear anything."

"Did you ever worry, Father, that these voices that only you hear are coming from your own mind?"

After all this time, after all they had been through during the years of construction and what God had already brought them through, this was the first time Shem had so boldly questioned his father. Noah turned sharply toward Shem, ready to defend himself angrily. But then he thought of how difficult this had to be for one who could not hear what he himself had heard. Noah's shoulders slumped slightly as he resigned himself that such questions would continue to come, even from his most supportive son.

"Am I so insightful and wise that my own thoughts could have brought us this far? Could my own mind have predicted a flood that didn't come until many years later?"

"No," Shem replied softly. "Only God could have guided us to this point. In fact, sometimes God speaks to me too. Not in an audible voice but in other ways. So why do I still feel so afraid?"

Noah placed a firm hand on his eldest son's shoulder and thought of how to answer such a question. Thinking of nothing, he simply sat quietly. The men couldn't see the bottom of the ark, but they could hear the water churning and lapping gently at its sides. The fountains that had once driven geysers high into the sky were still active but getting calmer each day.

At that moment, the world seemed so peaceful and quiet that it was impossible to think of the way these same waters had destroyed so much just months before. The moon and stars so vivid in the sky shimmered off the surface of the dark water, creating an almost surreal scene of two skies. Missing was the sound of night birds or the chirping of crickets. Even the slight breeze was silent since it had no tree limbs to blow through.

Shem broke the silence yet again.

"Where are we going, Father?"

"I don't know, Shem."

"Have you no word from the Lord about that? Any indication at all?"

"To be honest, Shem, I have not heard God's voice since those first critical hours when the ark floated away from its supports. That's when He told me to be strong and to just trust Him."

Shem found this news disconcerting, to say the least. He wanted to trust. As his father had said, all that was predicted so far had indeed occurred. But even with all that God had brought them through, it was so difficult to have no plan.

When they had constructed the ark they had to trust totally on God's guidance and on His timing to provide it. At least they had an end in mind.

Now they knew nothing. They had no idea when they would get to land, where the land would be, or what it would be like. They could only continue about their routine and wait on God. And the waiting seemed to get more and more difficult as they moved further in time from their miraculous survival in those first days.

"Not only have I not heard God's voice, Shem," Noah continued, "lately I find myself not wanting to hear it. It's as if this time on the ark is a time of a long-needed rest for me. And as long as I don't hear Him, nothing new is required of me."

"That's understandable, Father, with all you've been through. Still you are our only communication with God. I hope He speaks to you soon."

"You don't have to rely on me to hear from God, Shem. It sounds as if you have already discovered that He might choose to speak to you in other ways."

Shem pondered this for a few moments. But before he could respond, they heard a commotion downstairs. Someone was arguing. The shouting got closer as the parties involved came up the passageway toward the kitchen. Then at the bottom of the ladder, Ham's voice could be clearly heard. And he was threatening to kill Japheth.

CHAPTER 24

Brother against Brother

I kneeled there dumbfounded as Adina stood before me, clutching her robe at her throat. I had no words to explain my presence.

"Japheth, how long have you been out here?" she asked with a frown. "And why are you kneeling there in the first place?"

I stood up and continued to stare at the far wall of Adina's room like an idiot. My mouth was open, but no words came out. I heard a voice in my head telling me that I should have expected to get caught for doing something so seedy and stupid.

Adina looked around, and then with one hand still holding her robe closed just beneath her chin, she used the other to push the door to her room closed and looked at it from my vantage point. She saw the sliver of light immediately.

"Japheth! Were you watching me?"

Her face flushed. Her expression was more one of severe disappointment and hurt than the one of intrigue I had fantasized about. Adina took one step back from me, then two.

"I thought you were—I never dreamed you would *spy* on me. You of all people."

I was mortified. I felt I was falling into a deep well. I knew a dear friendship with my sister-in-law was slipping

away, but I couldn't come up with words that would save it.
I could not explain my actions because there was no worth-
while explanation. I knew I had to say something.

"Adina, I was spying on you, but I never will again." I
pleaded.

"I guess not, now that you have been caught," Adina
countered.

"No, it's not like that," I stammered.

"Then what is it, Japheth? What am I supposed to think
when I see my brother-in-law peering into my room?"

I didn't even know what I was saying now. Stupidly, I
attempted flattery.

"You must know how beautiful you are, and you know
how I once felt about you. And Tamara wants nothing to do
with me anymore. So, yes, I did spy. I am a young man. I
have desires, but I am ashamed of the way I let them control
me now."

Adina was unfazed by my attempt at rationalization.

"You and I are brother and sister now. No other thoughts
should be in your head. And obviously you don't understand
Tamara at all and what she is going through. Can't you see
how hard she is struggling with her feelings? She *does* want
to be with you. She wants desperately for things to be like
they were. She has been praying with us about this for some
time now."

I was so surprised at this news that I almost didn't notice
Tamara standing a few feet behind me in the dim light of the
passageway. Adina had only now spotted her as well. We
both looked at her.

"I thought I heard Japheth call my name," she said with
tears welling up in her eyes. "I came to see what he needed
and I heard—"

She turned and ran back up the passage toward the
kitchen.

"I didn't stop to think," I began awkwardly.

"That much is certain." Adina replied.

She raised one eyebrow and it was readily apparent that she was now more concerned with protecting Tamara than with her own embarrassment. She looked sternly at me for what seemed like a long time. Then her face softened slightly.

"Japheth, I know what kind of man you are. And I know this isn't like you at all. But you must think of others, not just yourself. Your selfishness has done serious damage. I am your brother's wife and your wife's dear friend. You have made a terrible mess of things."

"I know I have. And I cannot express how sorry I am already. But know that this didn't start only because I feel neglected by Tamara or was consumed with lust. I have never stopped caring for you. And I hate the way Ham treats you. He doesn't appreciate at all what he has in you."

"And I have noticed the way you glare at Ham sometimes when you feel he is treating me badly. There have been times when that look makes me feel better. But you don't know the Ham that I know. You don't see a side of him that I see. I love Ham, and I know deep down he loves me. Japheth, I am not your concern. And I am certainly not your responsibility. I can take care of myself. What I can't handle, God will. You owe all your allegiance to Tamara at this time when she needs your love the most."

Despite the fact that Adina was taking this better than could be expected, I could still feel heat as my face continued to flush. But embarrassment was about to be the least of my worries. From the other room, I heard Ham's voice bellow.

"He did whaaaattt?"

I didn't know it, but Tamara had run straight to the kitchen to my mother and Prisca as a flood of tears moistened her cheeks. She had blurted out what she had seen. She hadn't noticed Ham sitting at the table.

I had grown up fighting back against Ham's bullying. But when I heard the tone in his voice, I was gripped by fear. A knot formed in my stomach, and the nausea returned with greater intensity. I wanted to run to the far end of the ark. But I knew I had nowhere to hide. I had created this problem, and now I must face it. With my head down and my shoulders hunched as if walking into a stiff wind, I headed toward the kitchen to meet Ham. Adina grabbed my elbow to stop me.

"Japheth, don't confront this now. I've seen him this angry before. Better to give him time to calm down."

"I've seen him like this too, Adina," I replied. "He won't calm down any time soon. No, I have to face him."

I wasn't so much thinking things through as I was reacting emotionally to circumstances as they developed. Suddenly everything was spinning out of control. In just the last few seconds I had been caught in a terrible act by Adina, hurt my wife deeply, and angered my brother beyond control.

As I walked into the kitchen, Ham was already moving intently toward the passageway to find me. He looked up at me as I entered the kitchen and stopped. His jaw muscles flexed as he gritted his teeth. His eyes seemed as if they could shoot fire, and his huge fists were clenched tightly at his sides. "You've been looking at my wife while she changed in our room?"

We had no privacy on the ark. But what little of our own space there was had become perceived by each of us as our homes. I had violated Ham's wife and his home. I should have felt remorse. I should have been contrite. Instead, I inexplicably reacted in anger. That would prove to be a big mistake.

"Your wife," I scoffed as I continued to walk toward my brother. "Maybe if you would have treated her as your wife instead of some possession, I would have been a little more reluctant to look at her. Maybe if you treated her with some respect—"

I never finished that thought. Ham was across the room and on me before I had a chance to bring my hands up to deflect his first blow. He brought a massive fist in a round-house punch to the side of my head, knocking me off my feet. I landed on the edge of the table and felt a sharp pain in my side. Before I could hit the floor, Ham was pulling me up by the front of my tunic. This time I raised a hand to block him, but the force behind his punch was enough to drive my own fist back into my face. My nose spewed blood, and I felt as if Ham's forearm had broken mine.

So many times I had been angry enough with Ham that I had wanted to attack him and teach him a lesson. Now I had to face the fact that I was absolutely no match for him physically. My mind raced as I tried to think of a way to save myself. It was at that desperate moment that my mind cried out to God. Why had I not cried out to him when temptation was working on me? Why had I not asked for His help instead of relying on my own determination to resist my sinful urges?

Despite my mistakes, God heard me. For it was at that exact moment that Dad and Shem seemed to come from nowhere and pull Ham away from me.

Ham was incredibly strong, but Shem was nearly as strong. And Dad was honed by years of hard physical work. With Shem locking both his arms behind Ham's back and Father pushing back on Ham's chest, he was unable to break free. I rose slowly to my feet.

Despite the pain I had put her through, Tamara was quickly at my side with a cloth for my nose. A part of me wanted to push her away. My pride, already mortally wounded by my own actions, did not want to allow my wife to assist me. I wanted to be tough and stand up on my own in defiance of Ham's attack. But my ribs hurt with each breath. I was nearly in a state of shock from the combination of Ham's blows and my mind's reaction to all the damage I had done to my family.

Anger and defiance seemed to have literally been pummeled out of me. I now stood facing my whole family without the least idea of what to say or how to explain myself. I was through being angry, but Ham was not. He lunged at me, causing our father and our brother to tighten their grip on his arms and to pull him back hard. Pinned and unable to lay hands on me, Ham lashed out in the only way he could at that moment.

"*You* talk to *me* about the way I treat my wife? At least I am willing to fight to protect her from invasion. I didn't let my wife walk through city streets alone at night. My wife didn't get attacked at the winemaker's whilst I sat idly by."

"That's enough!" Shem said as he spun Ham around and pounded his chest hard into the wall of the kitchen. Father had to catch up to keep hold of Ham.

I forgot my bloody nose and walked toward Ham.

"Shut up!" I shouted. "Shut up and never bring that up again! I didn't know she was going. I thought she would be at her mother's. And why should I explain myself to you? You know nothing about what went on that night. As usual, you were off somewhere cavorting with your friends."

Ham's anger was far from appeased. That anger overwhelmed his sense of caution. With one side of his face being held against the rough boards of the wall, Ham's eyes burned with anger and he blurted recklessly.

"I would say I know more about what happened to Tamara than you do. I was there."

As soon as he had said this, Ham's face revealed that he wanted to take his words back. But it was too late. The sudden silence was overwhelming. Everyone in the room froze. Adina stood with her hand over her mouth, her eyes wide. Mother, who had been sitting as she comforted Tamara, now stood. A look of disbelief crossed her face. Shem and

Father were so stunned that they loosened their grip and drew back. Tamara broke the silence with a gasp. Ham turned to face us all. His eyes darted from one face to another. Then, with a look of resignation, he shook free from Shem and stepped away from the wall. He looked at the floor as he spoke quietly.

"While you were too busy that night working until all hours on this," he swept a hand abruptly around the room as he spoke, "I was there at the winemaker's. I was, uhh, about to come in through the back door. When I looked inside through the door I saw you, Tamara."

For perhaps the first time since before we boarded the ark, Ham looked Tamara in the eye. He then addressed her directly. She looked into his face and began to shake her head. I couldn't tell if her reaction was more of shock at Ham's revelation or an attempt to block out memories of that night. Ham went on.

"You were on the floor. Four men were holding you down, and two of them were tearing your clothes off. You had either fainted or been knocked unconscious. I feared you were dead.

"I had seen the men there before but I didn't know them. One of them had deep, fresh scratches on his face, and he yelled at me to get out. They probably expected me to walk away as others in the place were doing.

"Tamara, I know we have never been close. I suppose the two of us have never even had a private conversation. But when I saw you lying there like that and knew what those men were trying to do, I lost all control.

"I lunged at them and punched the man closest to me. He fell hard on his back and I dove onto him. I began to beat him about the head and face. His friends didn't care enough to stop their attack on you. So I turned on the next man. Then the other two seemed to realize I would eventually get around to them. It was three against one, and they tried to pull me off the second man. I have never been so angry. I literally couldn't see.

"The men were skinny and in poor health probably from years of inhalants and strong drink. I threw the other two off as if they were children. The man I had been beating got to his knees and began to crawl for the back door and entered the alley. I had the impression that he was the leader, so I went after him. The other two tried to stop me. Ultimately, we ended up in the alley behind the place. I beat them all badly. I know this, because some moments later I came to my senses and they were all lying there. The leader may have been dead.

"I was actually shocked. It was as if someone else had beaten them and I had just happened by. All I could think of at that moment was that I needed to get out of there. I didn't check to see if the man was dead, but I am not ashamed of what I did to him and his cronies. They would have killed you if given the chance. What I do feel ashamed of is that in my rush to escape, I didn't go back inside to check on you, Tamara."

Tamara suddenly spoke. Her voice was so soft as to be barely audible.

"I came to on the floor that night. My lip was swollen and bleeding, I had lumps on the back of my head that throbbed, and my dress was torn. My body was scratched and bruised in some places. And—and I knew that they—I just wanted to get away. I stumbled for a few steps, but once I got outside I was able to run. The next thing I remember, Japheth was picking me up and placing me in the ox cart to take me home."

Tamara's voice trailed off, and Ham dropped his head again to look at the floor. Finally, he said, "I left you there. I am so sorry. I was afraid I would be killed myself if I were caught."

"So that is why you never went back into town in those last days and weeks prior to our boarding the ark," Shem said. Ham nodded slightly.

"Thank you, Ham," I spoke with pain. "You surely saved Tamara's life. They would have killed her.

"Ham, I—I don't know what to say. I was already ashamed of my actions against Adina. But now they seem all the more grievous," I said.

Ham, his head still down, said nothing more but merely walked slowly out of the room and down the passage. Adina, after glancing at me briefly with a look that bordered on pity, followed. One by one, the others left the room and left me and Tamara alone.

"Tamara, I am so sorry," I began.

"I'm sorry too," Tamara interrupted.

"You have nothing to be sorry about."

"But I am sorry. I am sorry I let my mother shame me into ignoring your advice about the city. I am sorry I let what happened affect us so deeply. I am sorry—"

Before she could finish, I covered her mouth gently with mine and held her close. I felt her stiffen but then relax. I reveled in holding her and in sensing her forgiveness. We stood like that for a long while, in the center of the kitchen. She kissed me gently on my wounds.

As we stood there holding one another, we began to remember who we were as man and wife. I remembered there was good in me. Tamara's embrace confirmed that. And Tamara found some respite from feeling victimized. After a while we both began to cry softly, then we laughed for no reason. For a few precious moments, there was no ark nor any animals nor responsibilities that overwhelmed us, just a young man and young woman deeply in love.

CHAPTER 25

Ham's Fall

Though the confrontation between Ham, Adina, and me was cathartic for Tamara and me, it had a much more negative affect on the family as a whole. Feeling empowered by the spark that had been rekindled with Tamara, the next morning I went to Ham and Adina and asked again for their forgiveness. Adina, who seemed more embarrassed than she had the night before, nonetheless accepted my apology. As I expected, Ham was much more reluctant. After my apology, Ham only stared at me for a time and then, with a nonchalant wave of his hand, said, "Forget it."

Then he simply turned his head and refused to make eye contact with me. I had a small hope that he might apologize as well. After all, this was the second time he had come to blows with one of his brothers. And in both cases he had laid hands on us first. But when it became clear that no apology would come, I stepped back into the passageway and headed to my chores.

The next day passed and little changed. When we all came together for a meal, there was less conversation and what was there seemed forced. It wasn't that there was animosity between us, but there were hurt feelings and the embarrassment that comes from justifiable guilt. Despite my apology, I felt horrible for what I had done to Adina and the sleazy nature of my actions. Yet I still was angry at Ham. He had emasculated me in front of my wife, not by the beating but by accusing me of failing to protect her.

Ham likely felt bad for not telling Tamara what he knew sooner. Ham seemed self-conscious one moment and seething with anger the next. I suspected he felt badly about his violent response against me and his revelation of how he had handled Tamara's attackers. At the same time, he was clearly still angry with me. There was much tension between my brother and me.

As he had done so often before, Dad stepped in. He led us in prayer that night and for several more nights after that. He praised God for the mercy He had shown us and asked Him to heal relationships and to mend hearts. He prayed for Tamara's continued healing. Most importantly, he prayed that God would forgive our weaknesses. During the first couple of prayer sessions, Ham and I caught one another looking to see how the other was reacting. But over time we became more and more connected with what Dad was praying.

Over the next days and weeks, things gradually got better. Then we went through a period where we settled into a routine. The animal care, never easy, became more streamlined and efficient as we gained experience. There were moments when, after a hard day of labor, we were able to relax and sometimes even laugh together. Tamara and I continued to find healing for our relationship. Sometimes husbands and wives would drift away and seek privacy. No questions would be asked by the others. At most, the other spouses would look up at one another and smile with understanding.

It seemed we almost forgot what life had been like before the flood. Our life was here, aboard this vessel that God had provided. We were becoming conditioned to our very small world inside these gopher-wood walls. Hour after hour, day after day, the ark drifted on. Perhaps, if things could have remained that way, we could have learned to be content. Unfortunately events would soon transpire that would have everyone aboard, animals and humans alike, desperate to escape these confines, desperate to be anywhere but near one another.

As weeks became months, things began to change. What had been streamlined efficiency now became monotony. Since the flood, the weather had been very mild and had not been a factor in the daily survival of Noah and his family. Now the sun began to beat down on the ark and on the waters surrounding them. As the temperature and humidity inside the ark rose, all inside became edgy and irritable. Unpleasant odors increased. The animals, most of whom in recent weeks had seemed fairly content, now became increasingly lethargic. Their demands for water increased, which increased the workload to care for them.

As far as Shem could tell, everyone in the family except him seemed to be growing more and more lazy. He disgustedly slammed a lid down on one of the grain barrels. It was the third time he had closed it since yesterday. He was growing sick and tired of the others' lack of attention to detail. If the barrel tipped, there would be wasted grain and they needed to salvage every kernel. Why did he have to be the only one who realized the importance of these things? Even Prisca had grown sloppy lately with her chores. From the corner of his eye, Shem saw Japheth heading for the deck ladder to the middle deck.

"Japheth, there is a mess in the corner of the horses' stall," Shem scolded.

"I cleaned twenty stalls before lunch today, Shem. Perhaps I missed a spot!"

"We can't have that, Japheth. It is critical that we get all the waste into the pit. During hot weather we can't allow any of the waste to contaminate our air. Placing it in the pit minimizes the exposure to air and keeps down the odor," Shem shot back.

"I understand full well why we have the pits. And I am sure that all the air on this entire ark will be contaminated by one pile of horse manure," Japheth replied sarcastically.

"Take care of your area properly. That's all I'm saying." With that, Shem went to check on the other decks. Exchanges like this were becoming more frequent. The situation was little better in the kitchen where the women were sweating profusely while preparing dough. Father had urged Mother and the other women to prepare fewer cooked meals. Their diet recently had consisted of more cheeses and dried fruits. They baked wheat cakes on the fire once a week and ate them throughout the week to avoid building a fire any more often than necessary.

Prisca leaned back against the edge of the table and held a dampened cloth to her forehead, her eyes closed. She puffed out her cheeks and blew out a tired breath. Sapphira walked by and spoke, "Perhaps if you spent more time working now and less time leaning on the table we would have time for rest later."

"I just stopped for a second," Prisca shot back as Sapphira passed.

Once Sapphira was out of the room Prisca scowled in her direction and silently shook a fist. Between Shem and Sapphira she had about all the bossing she could tolerate. What had gotten into them? Shem had always been a bit bossy, but she had never seen her mother-in-law this bad. She was shaking her head and pondering the situation when Adina entered the kitchen, hauling a basket of dried fruit.

"I'm growing pretty tired of dates and raisins," she said to no one in particular. "I never thought I would miss Mother's vegetable stew."

Though Prisca shared the closest relationship with Sapphira, all the daughters-in-law had taken to referring to Sapphira as Mother now.

"I'd rather eat the fruit," Prisca replied, dabbing at her throat with a cloth. "I'll do anything to keep from working around this fire and heating our quarters any more than they already are."

"Yes," Adina agreed. "I wonder if Dad is certain that God didn't intend for us to have a back porch on this ark. At least then we could have more of a breeze." Both women huffed a halfhearted laugh and returned to their work.

Meanwhile, the men had all met at the boars' pen. Noah, Shem, and Japheth watched and offered suggestions as Ham attempted to repair some damage the hogs had done to the rack that held their hay and kept it from being trampled underfoot. In their zeal to feed, one of the large animals had pulled it partially off the wall. Ham was attempting to climb along the side of the stall along the outer wall. His intention was to reach the rack from above and pull it up to be reattached.

"Ham, don't do it that way," Shem cautioned. "It won't be a sturdy repair, and they'll have it pulled down again five minutes after we leave."

"Not the way I am going to tie it they won't," Ham persisted.

"You'll not get a chance to tie it when you're lying on your back after you fall from there," Noah added.

"I didn't fall with all the climbing we did to build this thing. I don't think I am likely to fall now."

Ham began to breathe heavier now with his effort to shimmy down the heavy poles of the stall wall. Inside, the boar stood up from where he had been resting and began to pace nervously. Of all the animals on the ark, this large boar had by far the worst disposition. None of the men wanted to enter the animal's stall and risk encountering his sharp tusks.

"Ham, this is going to take longer than if we simply let them out into the alleyway as I suggested," Shem said, becoming more irritated now.

Japheth weighed in as well. "We can hold them in place with the extra gates we have down below. Then we can take our time with the repair and do it right."

"We are not hauling those panels all the way up here," Ham grunted as he pulled the hayrack up and into place. He was lashing it there with a heavy leather strap. He straddled the corner of the stall with one foot resting uncomfortably on the top pole of the rear stall wall and the other foot on the adjacent one. Squatting, he held the rack with his left hand and pulled taut on the leather lash with the other.

It was as he pulled out a final bit of slack that his left foot slipped and he nearly fell into the stall. With quick reflexes, he caught the top pole with his hands and hooked his other leg just over the top pole. He hung there in an awkward position. Fortunately, with the exception of a pretty good scrape on the leg, his pride was the primary injury.

"See, I told you, Father. I am like a cat. I couldn't fall if I wanted to."

The other three men shook their heads and laughed as they moved forward to help.

"No, no. I don't need any help from the likes of you three." Ham was beginning to smirk at himself a little now. He placed the foot of his dangling leg onto one of the poles and began to pull up when he slipped again. This time, at the sound of the poles clanking loudly against the post, the big boar didn't hesitate. He rushed headlong into the area where the noise originated. His poor eyesight did not allow him to identify the nature of the threat he sensed. But he was an animal devoid of fear. As he got close to the corner, his eyes made out flesh and he attacked with fury.

Ham screamed as the tusk plunged into and through his calf muscle. The boar twisted his head furiously, attempting to do maximum damage to his would-be attacker. Flesh was separated from bone as Ham scrambled desperately to pull free. Instinctively, he kicked at the boar's head in defense.

But even Ham's powerful blows glanced harmlessly off the massive skull of the four-hundred-pound boar.

For a few critical seconds the other three men were stunned to inaction. Shem moved first, grabbing a nearby pitchfork and racing toward the stall. As though they had been awakened by Shem's movement, Japheth and Noah moved as one to grab Ham.

While Noah worked to pull Ham over the side of the stall by his arms, Japheth wrapped his arms around Ham's waist and lifted the larger man. Ham screamed louder as his leg was pulled between the boar's tusk and the lift from the men. At that moment, Shem arrived and rapped the boar hard across his muscled back. The boar squealed in protest and withdrew for an instant. It was just long enough for Noah and Japheth to pull Ham's leg free and over the top rail of the stall. All three tumbled down and into the floor, with Ham lying on top.

Sapphira and the other women came running, having heard the commotion all the way from the kitchen. Sapphira recoiled at the site of Ham's leg lying awkwardly across Japheth's chest. Then she whirled to catch Adina before she got too close. Prisca and Tamara continued forward and huddled over the men to block Adina's view. Soon Tamara returned to take Sapphira's place at Adina's side.

"Mother, perhaps you should help Prisca," Tamara said, trying to be as discreet as the situation would allow.

Sapphira had been sought after in their former lives for her understanding of healing. Among other things, she used many herbs and homemade pastes to help heal a multitude of wounds and ailments. With great gentleness and strength, Sapphira took charge. She did not hesitate to bark out orders to both the men and women. The purpose was not only to help her with Ham's care, but also to occupy the minds of the others to keep them as calm as possible.

In an amazingly short time, Ham was lying on his bed with his leg wrapped and in a crude splint. The bleeding continued but at a much slower rate than in the first few minutes after the accident. Sapphira had given him a special tea to help him sleep, and she herded the others quietly into the kitchen.

"He will sleep until morning," she informed them. "Praise God the bone is not broken and most of the damage is in his calf muscle. If we can keep fever from coming on him, he will heal from this. I don't know how well he will walk."

At those last words, Adina placed her face in her hands. Tamara put an arm around her and drew her close. Prisca placed a hand on Adina's back.

"How long before he can take back his share of the work?" Shem asked.

"Shem!" Adina was shocked at her brother-in-law's callousness.

"Obviously, I am sorry Ham got hurt, Adina. But someone has to think of the implications to the rest of us — to our survival. I am not sure how much you understand about the precarious balance between how much work is required daily and how many of us there are to complete it."

The others stood silently for awhile looking from one to another. It was clear that they hadn't thought of that aspect. But in the coming weeks, Ham's absence would become a paramount concern.

CHAPTER 26

Arduous Work

Ham sucked in a deep breath as he laid the crutches Shem had made for him against the table. He gingerly lowered himself onto the side of the bed and stared at the crutches for a moment. He couldn't help but puff out his cheeks in a sarcastic chuckle. The crutches were extremely well crafted. Shem had even gone to the trouble to smooth the wood till it practically shimmered. Must his older brother be good at everything? The crutches just made Ham feel all the more pathetic.

He had just made his way from one end of the kitchen to the other and was exhausted. He, the strongest of his brothers, now had to view a lap around the ark's kitchen as a major victory. At least he was no longer lying flat on his back. In the first three weeks after his injury he had been consumed with fever. He had thought he would die, as did Adina. Yet Mother had assured them he would get better.

Three days ago his fever broke and he had ignored Sapphira's warnings to rest and let his wounds heal more thoroughly. Instead, he had tried to assume some of his work duties. Leaning on the crutches as he worked, he had passed out before he could even finish putting food in one trough. Now, after going two more days without fever, he was beginning to wonder if even his exercise in the kitchen had been a mistake.

As he lay back on the bed, he began to feel as weak as a kitten. He was sick of this bed. He was sick of the view of the ceiling. Ham had been the most reluctant family member when it came to boarding the ark and later in regard to his chores. Now he longed for the opportunity to clean a stall. Why, he would even be glad to clean that ornery boar's stall. He smiled when he recalled the story of how Shem had needed to be restrained that day so that he did not strike the poor boar a killing blow on the spot. Despite all their disagreements, it was nice to know that his older brother would still jump to protect him in a pinch.

After he lay there awhile longer, he began to think. Why did he have to think so much? He had had plenty of time for that in recent weeks. He began to remember yet again where his mind had gone and the voices he had heard. Once again, he began to feel fever grip his body. He had grown familiar with the dreaded feeling. He feared the fever for the visions it might bring. Were the voices that he heard real? Or was he just hallucinating? Ham stared at the ceiling without really seeing it as he had over and over during this past month of recovery. He hoped for sound sleep, but within his slumber he began to drift in and out of consciousness.

As his eyes opened, Ham momentarily saw the low ceiling above his bed in the ark. But slowly the rough hewn wood transformed into the boards that made up the ceiling of a tiny storage room under the stage at the theater. Perhaps it was a bit of a stretch to call it a theater. It wasn't a theater in the classic sense, though one could certainly be entertained here. Ham laughed at his little joke for a second.

Then it occurred to him to wonder why he was lying here on this dirty floor. Oh yes, now he remembered. The men had put him in here. They had unceremoniously thrown him in here actually. Ham wished he hadn't remembered that because, along with that memory, came the recollection of how badly his back hurt and his head throbbed and how his stomach churned and—oh no, he was going to be sick again!

He couldn't move. He couldn't get out of his own mess. Suddenly, his joke didn't seem funny anymore. In fact, for the first time since he had been a small boy, he felt like he might cry. The roots he had purchased were to be ground into a powder and swallowed. He had swallowed quite a lot along with his usual strong drink. He had never combined the two before. The combination had done something to him. Something was terribly wrong. When the men had come to drag him from his table in the theater, he could barely lift his arms to defend himself.

He couldn't remember what he had done to make them angry. But they had wanted him out of the theater immediately. He could remember being loud and everyone turning from the stage to look at him. "My uncle Jason owns this place!" he barked. Then he could remember actually being on the stage himself.

What would his father and mother have thought of him if they had seen him here? They likely couldn't even imagine such a place existed. Even for Ham, with all his past wild ways, his recent trips to this place constituted a new low. Now he was going to die here in these pitiful and filthy circumstances.

He would never see Adina again. Adina, she would be so heartbroken. Why? Ham didn't know.

The voice he heard just then was not audible as a speaking voice would be. But still he heard it clearly.

"Ham, you are not of these people. You don't belong here. Deep in your heart you know better. Now get to your feet and get home!"

Had that been God? Was this the type of experience Dad had been describing when he said that God had spoken to him? He didn't ponder the question long for he was suddenly finding strength. Whatever the source of the voice, he had to get out. He had to make it back to Adina.

Ham rolled over on his side then made it to his hands and knees. He crawled around the tiny dark room until he felt a door just barely large enough for him to squeeze his shoulders through. Once through, he had to drop down a couple of feet to a floor behind the stage. He landed with an awkward thud. Then he rose stiffly to his feet and began to stumble directly to doors that led to an alley.

He didn't recognize the alley and, when he staggered to the main street, he realized he was in an unfamiliar part of the city. He needed to get moving. If he could make it to an area he was familiar with, perhaps he could hide somewhere and come to his senses. He could not afford to be seen by the group of violent men who beat him up. Even if Ham had been sober, he could not have stood against them. He remembered now. He owed them money, which they were determined to collect. Thankfully, they didn't know where he lived for they were the first men Ham had ever been afraid of. In his current physical state, it would be especially difficult to defend himself.

He stumbled and fell for awhile as he tried to make his escape. As the cold night air began to revive him, he could remember more of his ordeal. He recalled the men who put him in the back room talking about coming back for him later. He had seen enough to know that when they came back they intended to make a macabre game of killing him. They would likely make it the finale of the night's entertainment.

Ham was scared. Slowly he made his way into a part of the city that was more familiar. He made his way to a fountain and splashed water on his face and into his mouth. The water seemed to revive him a little. He then slipped down an alley and slumped into a corner and slept. When he woke up he felt his strength returning.

It had been a woman's scream that woke him. At first he confused it with what he had heard in the show earlier. Only something was different about this voice. It sounded strangely familiar. He stepped to the door and looked inside. As his eyes adjusted to the light, he was horrified to see his own brother's wife. She was fighting desperately as men hovered over her, grabbing at her. They were hurting her. Ham pulled himself up and tried to shake his head to clear the fog that seemed to shroud him. He took another step toward the door. But rather than kick it in, he pushed it open a crack and looked in. Tamara's screams were louder now, and Ham pulled his head into his shoulders at the sound.

He wanted to spring into the room to help Tamara, but he thought he saw one of the men who had beaten him up. If one was there the others likely were as well. Maybe they knew he came here a lot. Maybe they even knew Tamara was his sister-in-law and that is why they were attacking her. They would kill him if he went in there. He had seen what these men did to people. They would torture and kill him.

Ham took a step into the threshold. He could just see Tamara. She was kicking desperately and crying out for help. He just couldn't tell how many there were and who they were. What if they saw him? He couldn't make himself go in. He was shaking now all over. He had to get out. He had to be away from this place and those men.

A groan escaped Ham's chest as he pushed away from the doorway. He began to run as fast as he could with no idea where he was going. His breath came in shallow pants. He heard a cry that sounded almost like a small child. Over and over, he heard the short staccato cries before he realized the sound was coming from his own throat. He ducked down an alley and threw himself behind some crates.

He had to hide. He needed to get away. His hands grasped the sides of his head, and he squeezed as if he would cave in the sides of his own skull. She would be all right. Japheth would surely come looking for her soon and maybe Shem as well. They could get her out. Ham owed those men money, and he couldn't go in there. The men wouldn't know Shem and Japheth.

Ham began to cry. Tamara had looked so frightened. He had never wanted to see anyone look that scared. Surely Japheth would be there any minute. Ham's breaths were coming faster and faster now, but he didn't feel as if he was getting any air. He couldn't see anything but Tamara's face. They were hurting her. Right this second, as he was sitting here crying like a baby, they were hurting Tamara.

Ham's breathing began to calm. What good would it do? What good would it do for him to live if it was to be like this? What kind of man was he? Ham's eyes bulged as he drew in a large breath and held it. He sprang to his feet and ran headlong for the winemaker's shop.

He was at the shop in seconds. The front door, which had been locked by the winemaker moments earlier, seemed to explode in a shower of splinters as Ham burst through. Ham realized instantly that none of the attackers were the men he feared. They were merely common hooligans all much smaller than Ham. Ham became enraged. He was angry with the men and furious with himself. He fell upon the men. He didn't think; he only reacted.

He ended up back in the alley standing over three of the men. All were groaning, unable and unwilling to get on their feet. The fourth man lay behind the bar not moving. Ham looked down at his bloody knuckles as if they didn't belong to him. He had no recollection of the beating he had inflicted upon them.

He looked back over his shoulder and thought about Tamara. He had left her there alone for critical minutes because of his own cowardice. He couldn't face her. He didn't know what to do. He walked back around to the front door and looked down the street. Far in the distance he could see the crowd parting. It was Japheth fighting his way toward the shop and Tamara. Ham looked back inside and saw Tamara, bleeding but pulling herself to one knee.

Ham didn't want to be caught there. He didn't want to explain what he was doing in the winemaker's shop in the first place. Besides, he thought the others could be after him any minute.

He made his way over the hills outside the city to the grassy field behind his house. He crossed the field until the lantern light from his own house was within a few dozen yards. Adina would be there, and he had to fight the urge to burst inside and fall at her feet, look into her deep, loving eyes, and beg her forgiveness. He had never wanted to be near her this much. He resisted the urge. He couldn't have her see him this way. He was filthy and he stank.

Ham drew water from his well and poured it over himself. He found the cake of soap that always sat on the rafter of the little well house and washed as best he could. He wasn't concerned about his appearance. He wanted to wash the stench from him. He wanted to wash away where he had been and what he had been doing. How could he have gotten into the sick habit of going to that theater? And why did he ever start partaking of the things they sold there?

He dried himself with a cloth that hung on a peg by the well. With his face buried in the cloth, Ham thought of Adina again. He looked up over the cloth at the window of his home. He knew Adina would be there. She would be waiting for him, worried. She was always waiting.

He let the towel drop to the ground as he walked toward the window. He approached quietly. This was not what he wanted. He wanted to rush inside and throw himself at her feet and sob as he begged her forgiveness. He wanted to hold her close and feel her arms around him. But his pride wouldn't allow that.

Ham peeked through the window of his own home. There she was. She was pacing the floor and twisting her fingers together as though winding some unseen thread around a spool. She looked nervous. She sat down in a chair and picked up some clothing she had been trying to mend. But as quickly as she took the sewing up, she sat it down again. As she did so she turned her face toward the ceiling and she began to whisper. Ham couldn't make out the words, but he knew that his beautiful, kind wife was praying for him.

Once again, Ham fought the urge to run inside. Involuntarily, he reached his hand out toward her. He did love her. He knew he was fortunate to have her as his own. Yet he was always afraid. He was afraid some day she would look into his eyes, see him for who he really was, and never want to be near him again. And he resented her for it.

He moved back toward the field. He wondered how he could let her see what he really was. Adina was so good. Her heart was pure. Ham felt that he didn't deserve her forgiveness. He didn't deserve her.

With his head down, Ham walked back out into the field until he was near a large oak that had been left standing in one corner. He lay down in the soft grass and his mind began to replay the images of the evening. He had seen things in that theater that previously his imagination couldn't have conceived. He didn't realize it at the time, but many of the gratuitous images would never completely leave him. They would return to him over and over in moments of weakness. They would help illuminate a path that would lead to spiritual compromise and be a lynchpin in future battles waged in his heart between what his flesh wanted and what he knew was right.

At the same time, Ham wondered if the ground herbs had made him paranoid or if that too was part of who he really was. How could he have left Tamara there? Even for a second? What had happened to her during those critical minutes while he hid and groveled like a coward?

He lay there in the grass, now wet with dew and tossed about, hoping for sleep to overtake him. How could he, the son of an honorable, God-loving man, have arrived at this place in his life? He believed in God. In fact, he had made peace with the fact that God was real when he was still a boy. Yet, his brother, parents, and wife went too far. It seemed one or the other of them was constantly praying or bringing up God.

Ham did not want that kind of life. He believed in God and he knew that God cared about him, but he saw no need to immerse himself in religion. He wasn't the type. His family encouraged, even pushed, him to get to know God. They wanted him to pray all the time or at least pray a lot. They said that was the way to have fellowship with God. How could a man have fellowship with the God of the universe? And what was wrong with just acknowledging God without being absorbed by some presumed fellowship?

Except for his trips to the theater and his drinking, Ham felt like he was a pretty good person. The things he had taken at the theater were a recent addition. He would make sure he never did that again. To Ham, there seemed to be no reason he couldn't start over tomorrow. He would continue to believe in God and just stay as he was without going overboard. Then the same voice he had heard in the dirty theater storage room forced him to admit something to himself.

"Ham, you haven't stayed as you once were," the voice spoke again in his heart. "I called you to Me as a young teenager but look how much further you are from Me today."

Ham tried to block out what he was hearing. Yet after the night he had just had, he had to admit to himself that the longer he had attempted to maintain the status quo, the further away from God and what his parents had taught him he had found himself. It was as if there were only two direc-

tions in his life. He either had to grow in his relationship with God or continue his downward spiral. Ham looked down at his torn clothes, tasted the soured alcohol and vomit on his breath, and for a moment, saw himself with clarity.

He looked back once again toward the house and noticed that the light from the windows grew dim and then went out. Adina was going to try and get some sleep. She would not rest well if she were worried about him. He should go to her and let her know he was alright. "Why do you have to be so good?" Ham asked aloud.

Ham didn't really believe he was a pretty good person. When he was with Adina, he felt completely inferior. Despite the fact that she did nothing but love him, the way she conducted herself made Ham uncomfortable. It was if some light emanated from her and accentuated that his life did not reflect that same light. Ham resented her for that most of all. He realized that he resented all of them. And yet he knew that too was wrong. That is why he lashed out. That was the real source of his anger.

At some point, sleep overtook him for he awoke with the sun breaking over the horizon, his clothing wet with dew. Ham immediately recalled the events of the previous night and began to put them into a different perspective. He had been a fool to think that he had heard the voice of God pushing him to leave the theater. After all, what would God be doing in a place like that? Then he thought for a moment about the timing of what had transpired. If the voice had not motivated him to leave when he did, perhaps he would be dead right now. And was it a coincidence that he fell asleep in the alley behind the winemaker's? If he had not been there at the right time, what would have happened to Tamara?

Abruptly, Ham brushed this off as well. As much time as he had spent at the winemaker's in recent months he could probably go there blindfolded. And besides, why would a Holy God have anything to do with him when he was in the

*state he had been in that night? He would go in and change
clothes and forget this whole thing had happened. He made
a deal with himself then and there that he would never go
back to that theater. He would not allow himself to sink that
low again. Everything, he decided, would be fine.*

Ham sat bolt upright in bed, his mind shrouded in a
feverish fog. That night of lying in the field sobbing had
been months before. In the time since then, and before the
flood, he had indeed avoided going back to the theater. But
that was more out of fear of being recognized as a trouble-
maker than anything else. He was glad he was able to help
Tamara, but what kind of hero was he really? He had left her
there alone. Even when he did something right it seemed it
was all wrapped up in mistakes.

Rather than face his own failings and take his family's
advice on looking to God, he had figuratively thrown up his
hands and given up. Ham now realized that, had it not all
been destroyed and had he not been provided a place on the
ark, he might be there still. On his own, he would have never
broken away from it. If an escape had not been provided, he
might have stayed in that life until it killed him.

Thinking back to his confrontation with Japheth, Ham
now knew that he had been angry at more than just his
brother. He was angry with himself as well for the shame he
was living with. He was ashamed of how he had lived prior
to the flood and ashamed to be on the ark. Why had he been
given passage with his wife and family, all of whom seemed
so much more deserving? And why had all of the friends he
had run with been left behind to slip beneath the cold, surging
waters of the flood? Tears welled up in his eyes again as he
searched for answers. He had little time to ponder further, for
suddenly, he was thrown from his bed and onto the floor.

CHAPTER 27

Landfall

I stumbled as I struggled with the sack of grain I was attempting to carry. I was in my twelfth hour of my fourteen-hour day. We had been working like this for a month, and I didn't know how much longer I could continue. Ham's injury and accompanying illness had upset the balance of work more than any of us had anticipated.

The heat had been oppressive for the entire four weeks. Frustration and fatigue were at an all-time high. We barely spoke, and when we did it was generally to snap at one another. Yet, just when I didn't think I could endure another day, things suddenly got much better. It began with the simple blessing of a cool breeze.

"Well, Japheth, I see you've done it again."

I rolled my eyes at the sound of Shem's nagging voice bellowing from the passageway. I knew from his sarcastic tone that he had found some perceived shortcoming in the completion of one of my chores. No doubt he was looking all over the ark for me so that he could describe, in painstaking detail, the error of my ways. I simply kept working, hoping that he would walk all over the lower deck looking before he finally found me. But I found no such favor; in less than a minute, I saw him round the corner by the large cat's cage and head my way.

"What is it now, Shem?" I asked, making sure that my tone adequately reflected my disdain.

"You've left hay strewn down the aisle for me to clean up while you rush on to dump grain in the troughs. I've told you before, Japheth, rushing through your work and doing it halfway is just as bad as not helping at all. It just creates more work for the rest of us," he said as he stomped toward me. I had had enough of him treating the rest of us like errant servants, so I bristled at his comment.

"I wasn't going to leave anything for you to do, Shem. I've told *you* before that I get all my feeding done and then go back and clean everything at the same time."

"Well, that's a poor way to—"

"Shem! Japheth! Stop your quarreling and come stand at the window with us," Mother called to us from the top of the ladder to the kitchen. Her voice was faint as we were nearly at the opposite end of the ark and a deck below her.

Shem started to protest but, when we realized it was Mother's voice, we just shot each other a surprised look and began jogging for the ladder. We climbed rapidly up into the kitchen and then went up the ladder from there to the window. We arrived to find that everyone except Ham had made it up the ladder. They were all looking out and smiling. Tamara turned to me as I stepped over the top rung.

"There's a cool breeze coming in, Japheth!"

There was excitement in her voice and she looked like a teenager pushing herself up on her arms and standing tiptoed as she let the breeze blow through her hair. I slipped my arm around her waist as I came alongside her. I immediately felt the rush of cool air as well. The dampness and humidity that we had been enduring was suddenly being driven away by the winds, and we took the air into our lungs in deep breaths. Over the next several minutes we all found ourselves laughing at the least thing. We were like children again, teasing one another and feeling almost giddy.

Perhaps God brought the breeze first so that we would all be paying attention, for suddenly our revelry was interrupted. We were all thrown forward and nearly into a heap. At the same instant, a loud groaning sound was heard from the ark. Even the animals got stirred up, many of them calling and vocalizing all at once. Then, with a higher-pitched grinding sound from the hull, everything stopped. We all looked at one another for several seconds, stunned.

"Is anyone hurt?" Father spoke first. "Ham, are you all right?" he hollered down the ladder.

"Yes, I'm coming up," Ham answered. "I had some pain in my leg when I was thrown from my bed, but I think I'm okay. What happened?" He continued to talk as he struggled up the ladder with much help from my father and Shem.

One by one, we all checked ourselves. Upon realizing we were fine, it began to occur to us what had just happened. Once we did, our euphoria could not be contained. Though there was never a great deal of movement by the ark on most days, the contrast to now could not be denied. For the first time since the floodwaters rose, the ark was completely still. We had run aground!

After months of being cooped up in the ark, we progressed from happy to giddy to near hysterics.

"Japheth! We've landed!" Tamara said, her eyes wide.

As she said this, everyone first strained to lean out the window in an attempt to see the surface beneath the ark. We all knew better. The only view from the window was of the roof covering one half of the ark and of the far-distant horizon. Suddenly, as if someone had given a signal, we all stood and stared at one another. I think it was Shem who first said what the rest of us were already thinking.

"The door," were the only words Shem uttered.

With that, we all ran as a group for the ladder. I was so excited I couldn't think clearly. I clumsily climbed, slid, and fell down the ladder. I don't even recall running down the passage for the door, only that we were all pushing, shoving, and trying to be the first to see the door. Even Father, normally the voice of calm and reason, wore a look of joyful anticipation. But his excited expression quickly turned serious as he pushed past Shem and me to look at the door. It was still sealed.

"I'm sorry, everyone," he stated. "I reacted too quickly and let my emotions get the better of me. God would have given me instructions if he wanted us to make so bold a move as leaving the ark."

"Father," I began. "We've landed somewhere. If God had intended for us to stay on the ark, we would still be floating and drifting."

"Japheth, we don't really know that we are on land. All we know is that we hit something," Shem interjected.

"Well, of course, we've hit land, Shem," Ham interjected. "The floor feels solid beneath us. There is no sensation of movement at all. That wouldn't happen simply because we hit something."

"I'll get the axes," I said as I took a step toward the supply room. "We need to get this door opened and see what's going on. Then we can make a rational decision."

"You're not touching this door with an axe, little brother."

I didn't care for Shem's condescending tone one bit. At least I was man enough to make a decision and follow through. He was the one who wanted to keep sitting in this ark and wringing his hands. I was opening my mouth to let him know exactly what I was thinking when Father spoke.

"Shem's right. We don't know what's out there. We don't even know how high the water is around the ark. Cutting into that door might well be a disaster."

After all we had endured, after all the trials that Father's listening for God's voice had brought us through, I was so quick to let my wants overtake me. Until now, a word from Father was enough to make any of us stop, evaluate ourselves, and listen to his counsel. Now following my lead, even the women began to question Father.

"Noah, don't be so stubborn," Mother scolded. "We have all heeded your wishes throughout this ordeal. Now we may finally be near the end and you want us to continue to live as we have been?"

"Father, I want to feel grass under my feet again," Adina added.

Tamara joined the growing chorus of dissent. "Yes, Father, I want to see these animals running, flying, and being free. I don't just want that, I need that. I can't stand the thought of staying on this ark another night."

I watched Father's face and those piercing eyes as he listened. His jaw was becoming set in that all-too-familiar way. His countenance was the same as it had been the night he had talked to us about building the ark. At the time none of us, except Shem, really believed he had instructions from God. The next morning, looking just as he looked now, he had started before daybreak, by himself, clearing the area we would need to build the ark. While the work was far too demanding for one man, it was clear that he would not plead or beg for our help. He would simply do it alone—or die trying.

Now as I saw that look again, I was perturbed when I sensed he was going to simply ignore all our wishes.

"Father, I'm sorry," I started. "You are free to do what you feel is right for you and Mother, as is Shem. But I must think of my own wife. I am going to make an opening. I'll make it at the top of the door. That will be well above the water line. Then if I see dry land outside, Tamara and I are walking out of here."

Ham added insult to injury. Looking at Shem he commented, "For once, Japheth is the smartest one here. You're all stupid if you don't listen to him."

Having Ham on my side should have given me pause. Instead, I turned my back to my father and my chest began to swell. He had not interrupted or tried to stop me as I was speaking. I had been decisive and stood up to my father, and Tamara saw me do it. I took a few slow steps toward the supply room and the axes. When Dad still had not stopped me, I quickened my pace. Before I could reach the supply room door, however, Dad's calm yet authoritative voice stopped me cold.

"So was it you then, Japheth? Or perhaps it was Ham."

"What do you mean? Was it me or Ham that what?" I asked, perplexed.

"Was it one of you who sealed this door? Did you keep us all safe with your ingenuity and foresight?"

With that, he stepped over to the bundle of fodder and threw it across the passage, revealing our latch. I wondered how long Dad had known.

"How did your giant latches perform, sons?"

As he asked this, Dad stared at Ham then me. I felt my face begin to flush with embarrassment. The latch, still hanging there open as it had from the beginning, seemed to be a monument to my lack of faith. I thought I had learned something when I saw the door sealed that night with Tamara. But my behavior over the last few minutes, and during a large part of our journey for that matter, showed that I still had growing to do. Dad wasn't done.

"It was God and only God who closed this door. It was He who sealed the water out. And only He will decide when it shall be opened."

Father said no more. He took a moment to look into everyone's faces. He made little eye contact because, with the exception of Shem, each of us stared at the floor.

CHAPTER 28

The View Outside

Ultimately nothing changed in the family's daily routine.
Animals still needed the care they had required when
the ark was adrift. If anything, as the days and weeks wore
on, the animals seemed to have an increased appetite.
Animals that previously had been lethargic now spent more
and more time pacing restlessly in their enclosures. Many
of the animals that were babies when they boarded the ark
now began to engage in play with their stall mates. Their
behavior seemed to be a precursor to mating activity. Even
Rowdy was spending most of his time near the female dog
on board.

"We had better get off this ark soon," Ham had once
commented. "We certainly don't have enough food or labor
to care for a bunch of pups, kittens, and calves."

Despite his normally unshakeable faith, Shem began to
look nervously at their food supplies. The rate of usage was
definitely on the increase, and the supply bins were seventy-
five percent empty.

As the supply of food dwindled, Shem tried to take
comfort in the fact that the breeze that had blown steadily
since the day they struck land had to be helping to dry things
out. The horizon as viewed from the window remained

completely covered by water. Yet the occasional creaking or shifting of the ark gave some indication that the waters were continuing to recede.

Judging by the calendar Noah kept in the ark, it was the first day of the tenth month when Shem called to him from the window. "Dad, come quickly."

The call was to Noah but by the time he had made his way up to the window, Shem was already surrounded by his entire family.

"Look, Dad! What do you make of this?"

There was no mistaking what they were seeing. Mountain peaks were clearly visible in the distance. It was apparent from what was revealed that they were only seeing a small portion of the mountains that these peaks belonged to. Initially, Noah thought they were merely large rocks protruding from the surface. However, their mass and distance from one another indicated that there was much more land beneath the surface.

It was the clearest confirmation to date that the water was indeed receding at a fairly rapid rate. It had only been twenty-four hours since anyone had last checked the horizon and nothing was visible above the water line at that time. Initially, Noah and his family were almost as excited as the day they struck land. Then the questions began.

"Those are mountaintops. I'm sure of it," Ham said.

"Yes, they certainly appear to be," Noah agreed.

Shem added, "I've been studying them for some time, and I don't recognize any of their shapes. Either the water changed the shape of the mountains near home or we have drifted far."

"I would say we've drifted," Noah answered. "Those peaks look rocky. I don't think water would have had enough of an effect to change them significantly. Certainly it would not have changed them so much that they would look this different. None of these look even vaguely familiar."

Beginning that day, watching the peaks became a daily, sometimes hourly, event. As more and more of the mountains were exposed, the family was amazed at the rapid rate at which the previously rocky-looking surfaces sprouted lush vegetation. By the end of that same month, the mountainsides were almost completely covered in greenery.

Each family member spent time each day straining his or her eyes for a more detailed look at some of the strange-looking plant life in the distance. It was difficult to tell, but it seemed that there was shrubbery or perhaps ferns, grasses, and greenery that might be the size of trees back home.

One night after the chores were complete and the evening meal was finished, Shem asked Noah to walk down to the lower deck with him. Both men had to be mindful now of how close they got to certain enclosures. The dragons had grown during their time on the ark and, like many of the animals, had been much more energetic in recent weeks. At times, they now showed signs of aggressive behavior. Likewise, the large cats prowled anxiously inside their cages, often growling at passersby. This was in sharp contrast with months prior. At times during earlier parts of the journey, Shem had worried that the animals were sick since they spent so much time sleeping.

"Dad, I think we must consider very seriously nailing the shutters closed," Shem began.

"Why, Shem?" Noah inquired.

"Look around you, Dad. At a time when the animals are eating more and needing more care than ever, no one can seem to stay on task for looking outside."

Noah looked at the floor as if slightly embarrassed, then countered, "You have a point. But everyone seems so much happier now. With every foot that the water recedes, their hopes increase."

"Yes, and their willingness to work dwindles away."

"No, I won't allow it. It's too harsh, too extreme."

Shem pressed the issue. "Do you have direction from God to close the shutters?"

Again Noah looked embarrassed, this time avoiding Shem's eyes and instead staring blankly at the animals.

"Actually, I never had direction from God to open them in the first place and that has concerned me. I didn't think it through at the time. I didn't bother to consult Him. I know I should have."

"We have to be very careful now, Dad. We *must* be coming to a critical period in whatever God has planned for us. There has already been a near-uprising once when we struck land. Nearly everyone was ready and willing to take matters out of God's hands. We have come too far and fared too well under God's guidance to take off on our own now."

Before they could debate the matter further, Japheth came walking down the aisle. It was apparent by his pace and the bounce in his step that he was excited about something. He began to shout down the aisle.

"Ham and I have a great idea," he blurted.

"Oh, great," Shem said under his breath. Noah couldn't help but chuckle as he awaited the rest of Japheth's revelation.

"We can build a boat," Japheth continued breathlessly as he came alongside the two older men.

"Now hear me out. Don't roll your eyes and close your ears simply because it was our idea. There are plenty of places where we could take a board or two from an interior wall. In no time we would have enough wood to make a passable raft or, better yet, a small rowboat. Ham and I would make the journey. In a day, we could be up to the nearest peak. Who knows what God may have provided for us there? With all the plant life we can see from here, there may well be fruits, nuts, or other fresh foods. We could bring back more wood for the fire, maybe even fodder for the animals."

Noah and Shem looked at one another and said simultaneously, "Time to seal the window."

He used the long claw of one forefinger to skewer the dung beetle that was scurrying along the floor. This one was a stowaway; it wasn't protected. He held the still squirming beetle up for a moment and admired it before biting off the head with his pointed teeth. He sucked the rest off his claw and chewed while he pondered. He had just been listening to Shem and Noah's discussion and was now being told by the Prince that it was time to leave.

Though the trip had been a crushing bore, anything was better than going back there. He shook his hoary head as he thought of it. There was nothing there but torment. It didn't matter, though. He wasn't being allowed to do much of anything here. One little possession of one stupid boar, and that was all. And that had only lasted a few minutes.

He had to get out before they closed the window. He couldn't be here then. He would have never been here in the first place if Noah hadn't opened the window prematurely. The little man felt self-satisfied that he had at least made an effort to undermine the family. He couldn't end the voyage for them. That would have never been allowed by Him. But at least he had taken a step that would make the family more miserable.

In three long leaps the little man had vaulted himself from the lower deck all the way to the window. He squatted there, hesitating for a moment. He hated the water, but he would have to dive through lots of it as water was now between here and there. Oh well, he might as well get it over with. He leapt hard from the window and glided through the air for several hundred feet. Then, when he was over one of the deepest sections, he grimaced and plunged himself in. It would be a long, long dive down. He would descend to the bottom and then through to the other side. He dreaded it. It was time to return home.

CHAPTER 29

A New Word

Japheth had finally given up. It had been nearly a month since Noah had closed the window shutters, drove in pegs, and forbade anyone from opening them until he said otherwise. But for two entire weeks, Japheth kept badgering his father with his talk of building a boat. In fact, the little craft kept growing. Japheth and Ham's imaginary craft had grown from a raft to a dingy to a boat capable of making multiple trips even to the farthest mountains visible. Finally, the two brothers seemed to realize Noah meant that building a boat, or leaving the ark no matter how unselfish the motive seemed, was out of the question.

"No means no, boys," Noah concluded as he left his younger offspring in the passageway near the kitchen.

Noah was in the middle of his nightly walk to insure all the decks were secured. As he walked through the kitchen, he took a moment to offer kind words and encouraging hugs to both Prisca and Tamara. This had become routine for him, even during the most stressful times.

As the days dragged on, so grew Prisca and Tamara's concern for their father-in-law. They knew Noah had reached a breaking point when he first saw the world under water from which he had not fully recovered. To the women, he was not the man and the leader.that he had been prior to that time.

After Noah walked beyond earshot, Prisca asked her younger sister-in-law, "Tamara, does Father seem different to you?" The two were preparing cakes for an upcoming meal. Prisca was readying dough as Tamara soaked some dried apples. After a little soaking, the apples would be fried with honey and spices, providing a delicious filling for the cakes.

"Yes, very much so," Tamara responded. "I can't quite put my finger on it. It's almost as if at times he seems scattered. It's as though he sometimes can't get his thoughts together. I don't know how to describe it."

"He seems indecisive. And that is a complete departure from the father who Shem grew up with and the man who you and I have always known," Prisca said.

"Yes, indecisive is the word I was looking for. But at the same time Shem seems to be taking more and more of a leadership role."

"Are you kidding?" Prisca asked with an exaggerated roll of her eyes. "I know he must be a pain to you all sometimes, Tamara. But I really believe that if any of the brothers can take on Father's role, my Shem can."

Prisca stared off into space momentarily, an adoring look in her eye. Then her brow crinkled into a frown.

"I mean no offense to Japheth," she blurted.

"No, I understand. And I agree. Still, with all he has brought us through and with the relationship he shares with God, I would feel more comfortable if Father could get back to being his old self."

They looked at one another and nodded in agreement. Then there was a moment of awkward silence. Neither woman wanted to delve any further into the frightening possibilities if the family were to lose Noah's connection to God. They had both realized the frailty of their faith when they wanted to go charging out the door at the first sign of striking land. The grass under their feet indeed; a plunge into deep waters would have been more likely.

The next morning Tamara went below deck to see the horses. As she recalled her conversation with Prisca and the gleam in her eye as she spoke of Shem, she was somewhat envious. "Perhaps if Japheth and I could get out of here and have some privacy, I too could be with child," she said to the mare as she approached.

"Prisca has been sick for every morning now for two weeks. Mother says she is carrying a baby, which will be the first one born in the new world God is creating for us. I am happy for her. I really am. And it's not as if she has gloated about it. But I get tired of seeing the way she positively beams when she recovers from her morning illness and makes eye contact with Mother."

Like all the animals, the horses had become more and more fractious in recent days. Tamara entered the stallion's stall carefully. He startled her as his lips fluttered a soft whinny. She put her hands on her hips and gave him her best angry look.

"You know I hate it when you do that," Tamara pretended to scold him.

As she reached out to pet his soft nose the stallion surprised her by lowering his head down over her shoulder. She didn't know that a horse was capable of an embrace, but that was most certainly what this was. She wrapped her arms around his large neck and gave him a hug. The mare, as if suddenly jealous of all the attention the stallion was receiving, sauntered over to nuzzle Tamara's back. The woman returned her affection by reaching out to scratch her ears.

"I bet you both miss running free along the hills," Tamara said. "Don't worry. You'll be doing that again soon."

Her assurances were somewhat halfhearted. She secretly wondered if they would ever get to leave this ark. She dropped her arms from the stallion's neck and walked over to scratch the mare on her jaw.

"Adina hasn't said anything yet. But if I don't hurry and get pregnant, even she and Ham will have a child before us."

"Tamara, come quickly!" I cried down the ladder from the kitchen.

"Tell her to hurry up, Japheth. I can hardly wait," Adina pleaded.

"Where is she anyway?" Ham asked impatiently.

"Don't ask foolish questions, brother," I answered. "I am sure she is brushing that horse or talking to those housecats as if they can understand her."

"I wouldn't be so dismissive, son," Dad said. "She definitely has a way with the animals that goes beyond any of us."

At that moment, Tamara entered the room and slid her arm around my waist.

"I have a feeling someone was just talking about me," she said as she gave me a peck on the cheek.

"Well, isn't that sweet." It was Ham again. "Now do sit down. Dad has something to tell us that he promises will be exciting."

Everyone found his or her customary seat at the table and stared up at Dad expectantly as he stood at the head of the table. He began by reminding us that it had been forty days since he had sealed the window, and now he finally had a word from God.

"God has instructed me to open the window today. From there, I will release one of the ravens. If he finds nowhere to perch, he will have to come and perch on the ark to rest from flight. But a raven is not particular. Even if he finds a perch still slimy from the floodwaters, he will land on it. Since there are no predators left alive outside this ark, we will know that when he doesn't return, he has found a perch to roost on and something to eat."

Once the raven failed to return, Dad told us he would release a dove.

"The dove feeds from the ground and will be much more particular about where she puts her feet than the raven," he said.

Each time the dove returned he would put it back into its cage for another seven days. On the day that the dove did not return, Dad would know that there was dry ground available.

"Once that happens," Father explained. "God has directed me that it will be time to remove the covering from the ark."

A cheer went up from us all. We leapt to our feet, hugging, kissing, and shouting thanks to God. Even Ham turned his face skyward and shouted to the top of his lungs, "Thank you, God!"

Father joined in our celebration for awhile. Then he shushed us.

"Once the covering is removed, we will again wait upon God to give us guidance."

Though Father still smiled as he said this, it was if his comment quenched the joyful spirit in the rest of us. We thought we were setting a day to leave the ark. Instead, we were being told how long we would have to wait until we could remove the covering and then wait some more.

Father didn't seem to realize the negative impact this realization had on the rest of us. Instead, he left the room hurriedly to collect the raven.

CHAPTER 30

Father and Sons

The other men and I were all sitting around the window, waiting. Shem and Ham had claimed the stools as usual. I had made a passable seat on a wooden storage box. Father sat on his bench, which we had moved up from his seat at the head of the kitchen table. This had become a tradition for us in recent weeks. We would meet here to wait on a bird.

For days and days and days, we had waited upon a raven. Now we waited on a dove. She had been sent out twice. This was now the third time she had been released. And it was the longest she had ever stayed gone without coming back.

"Perhaps she drowned," Ham said sarcastically.

"That's not funny, Ham. Keep in mind that God directed us in this. He would not let anything happen to her," Dad said, as Shem and I agreed.

Ham rolled his eyes then looked at the floor. We were all quiet for awhile longer.

"What do you all suppose it will be like?" I asked.

Everyone looked at me and I knew immediately from their expressions they had been pondering the same thing. What would the world look like when we first stepped out of this ark?

"I have no idea what to expect. I really don't," Father answered first, anticipating that we would all look to him. "I have prayed about it. I have meditated on it. But I don't have any insight on that at all."

I knew that if Father did not have a vision of what to expect, none of us would.

"We've had so much work to do we have barely had time to put much thought into it, I suppose," Ham commented. Oddly, his comment seemed to be the most pleasant one any of us could remember from him in a long time. We all smiled and nodded in agreement.

Shem added, "I had thought it would be just like back home. But the more I think about it, that doesn't seem likely. If God wanted to start over with mankind, it seems to me that He would start over with His creation as well."

There were raised eyebrows and, again, nods of agreement all around. No one added anything further, and then Ham spoke.

"Why am I here?" he asked.

His question took Shem and me by surprise. My eyes darted nervously around the room. Father, on the other hand, seemed to have anticipated it.

"Ham," Father began. "You are here, as we are, because God ordained it to be so."

"God wanted a new world, right, Father? I mean that's what you told us. He wanted a world without all the wickedness and godlessness that was present before. So he should have chosen people like the three of you. But I am not like you. I can tell by the way you look at me. I am not as good as you."

"Ham, we have never said that," Shem protested.

"You don't have to say it, Shem. I can sense it from you."

"Ham, that's not so. Perhaps what you are sensing comes from within you," Shem continued.

"No, he's right," I blurted. Everyone looked up at me. I sat there embarrassed by my own bluntness for a moment before I continued.

"Ham is right. I have thought in the past that I was better than him. In fact, I have thought that I was quite a good man. I had just been celebrating my goodness when I walked down the hall and ended up spying on Adina."

I dropped my head to the floor and felt the heat travel up from my neck to my face. I found myself wishing I had kept my mouth shut or that I had thought longer before speaking. But the words were out there now. I knew I had to elaborate.

"Shem and I had been talking. I began to think of myself as a leader in this family. I even went so far as to think what a leadership role might mean in a new world. I felt I deserved such a position. Looking back, I think I got so caught up in being impressed with what a good person I was that it ultimately helped me to fail."

I looked up again. Shem looked serious but expressionless. Ham was listening to me as if I was speaking in some language he could not comprehend. Father was the only one who smiled knowingly.

"Japheth, if you have come that far in your thinking, then your behavior with Adina will prove a useful learning experience."

"Thank you, Father, for your sympathy!" Ham stood up now, clearly irritated.

"I don't mean it like that, Ham. I don't mean to be unsympathetic at all. What Japheth did was wrong. But the fact that he realizes his mistake and what led to it will help him to avoid such behavior in the future."

"Well, I am so glad my wife was here to provide such a valuable lesson," Ham protested. "I wonder if you would be so understanding if I had been the one caught spying, but let's get back to the point. Japheth admitted that you all are better than me. So my question remains: What in the name of God am *I* doing here?"

Ham was getting angrier by the second.

"I never said we were better than you. I said I *thought* I was better than you. And I am sorry for that, Ham."

"Yes, I understand that you're sorry. You said as much before when you came to my room. How nice for you that you were able to clear your conscience. You're lucky I didn't rip into you again."

I wasn't angry, yet I too came to my feet. I wanted to elaborate, but Father stood and put his hand up to stop me from speaking. Then he placed a hand on Ham's shoulder.

"Ham, my son, why are you always so angry? This is not just anger at Japheth. You are angry with yourself."

Ham jerked away and stepped to the window. He rested his forearms on the sill with his back to Father. Undeterred, Father continued.

"Ham, the reason you are on this ark is because God has hope for you. He wants great things for you."

Ham kept his arms on the sill but turned his head to face Father.

"Well, how wonderful to know that I am not beyond hope," Ham retorted.

"Oh, stop trying to show us all how tough you are!" Father spoke more sharply. "You asked why you were here, and deep down you must really want to know. Let me tell you something. God's hope for you *is* a wonderful thing.

"Do you think I am blind, son? Do you think I don't know the kind of life you were living before we came into the ark? Your mother and I have both lain awake at night praying that you would stop living as you were. God wanted you to stop too. He provided passage for you and got you away from the city so that you could change.

"He wants you to return to Him, Ham. He wants a fellow-ship with you. Isn't that wonderful? Almighty God wants fellowship with you just as much as He wants it with all of us. He wants that relationship just as much as He wanted one with your ancestor Adam. It's what you were born for, my son. God had too much confidence in you to give up on you and let you drown in the flood."

I was so moved by Father's words to Ham that I couldn't keep quiet any longer.

"Ham, you like to tease me and call me the dutiful son. But we all learned that I am far from perfect. When I tried to be good on my own, I failed miserably. But when I looked to God for my guidance and strength, things got so much better. Now I have a renewed relationship with Tamara, and I feel closer to God than I ever have."

I was talking to Ham's back. He had turned back to look out the window as Father spoke and had not turned around again. We waited a few moments, but Ham did not speak. I noticed that his knuckles were white from his tight grip on the windowsill. Suddenly he pushed himself away. Keeping his back to us, he started for the ladder.

"None of us is perfect, Ham." Shem said suddenly. He had been quiet up until now, merely listening to us all. I got the impression that he had wanted to speak up several times but he hadn't known how Ham would receive his words.

"I need to think," Ham said over his shoulder. Then he was down the ladder and gone.

The three of us stood and stared at the hatch and the top of the ladder.

"He sounded choked up," I said.

"Do you think he heard you, Father?" Shem asked. "Do you think he understood?"

"Of course he did, Shem. He'll come around. You'll see."

Ham grunted with effort. He pulled the bag up from its hiding place in the manure pit with one hand as he swung himself up onto the floor of the lower deck with the other.

He sat the bag beside him and dangled his feet into the pit as he rummaged inside for a flask. The first two were empty, and Ham threw them angrily down into the manure below. On his third try he heard the liquid that had grown more and more precious to him gurgling inside. The cork was wedged tightly in the flask and it made a loud pop when he pulled it free. He brought the bottle to his lips then hesitated and lowered it to rest on his thigh.

"So there is hope for me after all, is there?" he said to no one.

Ham raised the bottle to his lips and took a long swallow. Then he gritted his teeth as the liquid burned its way down to his stomach.

"At least that little pervert Japheth was honest. They all think it. They are all so high and mighty that it makes me sick!"

He said the word sick loudly enough that some of the animals startled and shuffled in their stalls. He raised the flask to his mouth again and poured it down his throat with such vigor that some spilled over his cheeks and down his chin. He wiped his face with the back of his hand and waited for the heat in his throat to subside. Then he looked around at the animals with a sarcastic smile.

"Guess what, everybody! Shem and Japheth are not perfect! What a surprise!" He laughed at his humorless statement. "What have any of them ever done that I couldn't equal? I worked on this box plenty. Except when I was hurt, I have worked as hard around here as anyone. I'm bigger, stronger, and tougher than any of them. When we step out of this floating coffin there are going to be a lot of unknowns out there. Then we'll see. I might just show them all a thing or two."

Ham raised the bottle in the direction of the passageway in a mock toast to his brothers. After taking another long swallow, he held the bottle out as if seeing it for the first time.

"Ahhh, that's good," he said. Then, as he brought it to his lips again, he heard the sound of footsteps. He fumbled with the cork and the bag, but before he could put it back into its hiding place, he looked up to see Adina.

His wife looked at him and then at the bag. Ham clearly saw a look of disappointment cross her face. He was familiar with it. He had seen it before. She asked no questions. Instead, she seemed to gather herself with a deep breath. Then she smiled, and her disappointment was replaced with a look of excitement.

"The dove is back! And this time she's brought something with her."

CHAPTER 31

The Way Out

After the dove returned with an olive leaf in her mouth, Father knew that the land surrounding the ark must be productive enough to sustain us. On that day, he had brought the dove back into the ark, where he kept her for seven more days. Now that he had released her once again, she stayed away even longer than before. By the following afternoon, she still had not returned. I climbed up to the window to check on her, only to find Father already there and looking out.

We could see that, off in the distance, mountainsides were more covered in green than ever. Yet with the position of the ark, which apparently was on a high mountain peak, and our restricted view from the window, we still could not see the ground closest to us.

"Still no sign of her?" I asked.

Father didn't answer. He just stood, looking off into the distant sky.

"Do you see her out on the horizon somewhere, Father?

I was squinting, but I still didn't see her. "Which direction is she?"

"Japheth," Father said. Then he grew quiet again.

"Yes, Father, what is it?" There was even more silence.

"Japheth, I think it's time you go and get those axes."

I stood there blinking stupidly for one minute, then two. I wasn't sure I had heard him correctly. Well, I knew I had heard him correctly. I just didn't know if I could believe what I heard.

"Go get the axes, Japheth. It's time we made an opening in the side of this ark!"

I backed away from my father as if he had struck me a blow. Then I backed away one more step. Suddenly, I felt something rise from my throat. I whooped as loudly as I could and leapt into the air. I went tearing down the ladder, screaming to the top of my lungs.

As I tore through the kitchen, the women stared at me as if I had gone mad. But as I headed down the passage to the tool storage room, I cried out, "Father says for me to fetch the axes. We are going to open a door in the side of this ark!"

Like me, it took the women a moment to absorb what they had just been told. Once it registered, they too began to whoop and holler. By the time I gathered the tools and ran dragging them down the ladder to the door at the lower deck, everyone but Father was already gathered there.

Shem and Ham held out their hands for axes. As we each got a firm grip on the handles, I noticed Father walking up from my rear. I could sense that he was smiling. Each of us three brothers looked at one another, waiting to see who would take the first swing.

"Well, go ahead, Japheth. You made the big announcement," Shem said.

But I was reluctant.

"Father, would you care to do the honors?" I asked.

"Not at all, son. Please, go ahead."

I drew the axe back and then hesitated again. I eased the axe down slowly then finally held it down at my side.

"I have been waiting for this day for what seems like an eternity. But now that it's here, I almost hate to scar her."

I smiled a crooked smile and looked at the others. I expected them to laugh at me or scold me. But each of them seemed to understand. I noticed that Ham and Shem had lowered their axes too.

"We worked hard on these walls. Getting the lumber to fit together tight and taking care that they didn't leak," Ham said.

"And they've protected us through some violent storms," Shem added.

"We've been safe within these walls," I continued.

I looked at everyone's faces. We had been through so much together. Storms had raged against us from the outside. And at times we had raged against one another. We had shared so many meals as a family here and clung to each other for life in the early days of this journey. I pulled the axe back up to my waist and held it there in both hands.

Then before I could doubt myself again, I swung with all my strength into the wall. The axe sank in deeply, and I struggled briefly to pull it free. Shem and Ham stood watching. I swung again and then again. The wood was strong and tough. But suddenly sunlight broke through the cut I had made.

The light coming in seemed to awaken my brothers because suddenly they went to work with their own axes. Soon chips of wood were flying everywhere. Ham seemed to rattle the entire vessel with each of his mighty blows to the wall. It didn't take long until we had a window-sized opening at just the right height to look out.

The sunlight streaming in seemed to awaken something within the animals. Almost simultaneously, they all began making their natural calls and vocalizations. The male gorilla beat his chest and jumped from one side of his enclosure to the other. The lions roared, and the elephants trumpeted. Suddenly it was so loud within the ark that we could barely communicate with one another. We began to laugh nervously, but the cacophony was almost frightening for us. With our attention diverted by the noise, our axes had stopped. We took this opportunity to have our first close-up look at our new world.

There was just enough room for Shem, Ham, and me to put our faces to the opening. What we saw stunned us. Nothing looked the same. Though much of the ground outside was still rocky and barren, there were also plants that were the likes of which we had never seen. There were ferns taller than a man. Huge flowering bushes and shrubs were everywhere. Plants with leaves so huge that they could shelter a man from rain were placed in strategic spots. It almost looked as if we would not be able to walk down the mountain to the valley below for all the greenery.

We were standing there trying to take it all in when Father walked up and, with a smile on his face, pushed his way up to the opening.

"It's completely different," Shem said.

As Father stood there, the smile gradually left his face. Then he began to shake his head as if answering some unasked question.

"No, no. Not yet," he said as he backed away from the opening.

"Noah, what's the matter," Mother asked.

"It's, it's not right, that's all. It's too soon. Things aren't ready. We mustn't—"

"We mustn't what, Noah? What is it?"

Father reached up and pulled at Shem and my tunics. He pulled us back away from the opening. I felt the woodchips beneath my feet as I stepped back. I had to step quickly to avoid falling as Father tugged harder.

"Step away, Japheth. Get back, Shem. Ham, no more chopping. It's, it's still too wet. In fact, perhaps we should patch this—I suppose we must—It's not time right now."

Father waved his hands around his head as he walked away as if bees were buzzing around him. He headed back up the passage and then called to us.

"Get back to your feeding! Back to your chores! Let's feed the animals an extra ration and perhaps they'll quiet down."

Oddly, none of us had argued with Father that day. Instead, each family member lingered at the opening in groups of two or three. Then we did precisely what Father had told us to do. We went back to work.

They had been on the ark just forty days short of one year. They all imagined they would run off this vessel as soon as the opportunity presented itself. Now it had been seventeen days since they had cut part of the covering off the ark, and still no one had made a move to leave.

It took the better part of that first day to get the animals calm. The family actually couldn't do much at all to calm them. They eventually quieted on their own.

Since then the animals' appetites had increased tenfold. Food supplies that as recently as two months ago had seemed overly abundant were rapidly dwindling. The dried meat had run out months ago, but all the animals that normally ate that were now trained to eat grain, hay, or fruit anyway. Although they had several different varieties of each, at the rate they were feeding, it would all run out in six to eight weeks. Still, the family did not push Noah to let them leave the ark. Even Shem, who had been so concerned with supplies and logistics, seemed to go mindlessly about his work.

They never covered the opening they had made in the side of the ark. It became a routine occurrence to walk by or look from across the deck and see one or two of them gazing out. They were fascinated by what was beyond their line of vision. They all wanted out of the ark. But they were afraid.

This family that had stepped out on faith to enter the ark and had held onto that faith through rolling waters and catastrophic destruction could not bring itself to complete the opening. They were afraid of what would happen when they stepped beyond the walls of the ark. And though no one spoke of it, they were even afraid of what might come in.

Like the ark, they entered a period where they were without a rudder. Noah, though he had grown progressively weary during the latter months of the voyage, had always provided needed leadership. Now he sometimes sat for hours on his bed with his head down. As he had in the first nights of the flood, he let his hair become unkempt. As he sat with his head hanging, it covered his face from view.

Noah's family immersed themselves in their work even more deeply than normal. Some tasks were done multiple times or either to meticulous detail. Perhaps most significantly of all, no one prayed. For the first time in years, they didn't want to hear what God might tell them. He might tell them to step out into the strange world beyond the walls.

Finally one day, Shem looked at Prisca and her growing belly. He had a child on the way and, despite his own fears, he knew what he must do.

It took him some time to find Noah. His father was sitting on the floor in the dark corner of the tool room. His knees were drawn up nearly to his chin, and his fingers were laced into his gray hair. He seemed on the verge of a breakdown. Shem placed a hand on each of his father's shoulders and spoke softly to him.

"Father, the supplies are dwindling. We have to consider—"

As if awakened from a bad dream, Noah reached up quickly and grabbed Shem by both forearms. The look of fear in the old man's eyes was apparent.

"Shem, where are we? Where has God placed us? I don't know what's out there. I don't know what is safe to eat or even if there *is* food to eat. We have no shelter. I see no trees from which we can build shelter."

"Father, you are exhausted. You have carried us all for so very long. You went through so much in trying to save your brother. You lost Grandfather after hoping so desperately to bring him with us. You are frightened. I am as well. We must look to God. He has brought us safely here. We cannot doubt him now. We have given ourselves to Him up to this point. We cannot wrest control away. Come."

Shem placed an arm behind Noah's back as if to pull him to his feet. Instead, he only pulled him to his knees and together they began to pray. Shem prayed on behalf of Noah and the family that day. But over the succeeding days, like an athlete recovering from injury, Noah became more and more involved.

As had been Shem and Noah's routine in the past, they set aside time each day for prayer. Within a week, Noah had resumed the leadership role in the prayers. As the days wore on, they were joined by Japheth. They moved to the kitchen table where the entire family could participate. Though Ham was frequently absent, the rest of the family joined hands each day in prayer. Still, there was no word from God. That is, until forty-six days after Japheth had first buried his axe head in the covering of the ark.

On that day, the family had been in silent prayer together during the noon hour. The only sound was of quiet whispering as each member petitioned God for direction or assurance. Ham had come into the room as Noah said "amen" and everyone looked up. Noah looked into each face. His countenance seemed stronger now and more like the Noah who had entered the ark that day more than a year ago. Finally, Noah's gaze locked on Tamara.

"Tamara," Noah said. "I know you have grown very fond of many of the animals on board."

Tamara only smiled and nodded.

"I noticed you seem to have a particular favorite with the horses."

Again Tamara nodded, only more vigorously this time.

"Everyone has been so critically important to the workings of this ark and to this voyage. You have each worked incredibly hard. But we have all benefited in a special way from Tamara's gift with the animals. She was integral in getting the animals to eat what we could provide even before the first one set foot on the ark. And she has been crucial in keeping many of them in good spirits and good health since then."

Noah stood from his seat and leaned forward as he rested his hands on the table. He leaned close as he lowered his voice almost to a whisper.

"God has spoken. I have allowed us to huddle in fear long enough. Tamara, I give to you the honor of choosing the first animal to set free. And they will be free today!"

CHAPTER 32

Destination

W e were all up and in motion immediately. Shem, Ham, and I headed for the opening and the axes. Tamara headed for the lower deck and, my guess was, for the stallion. We began to work frantically. Using ladders and hoists, we soon had an opening large enough for even the elephants to walk through.

As they had before, the animals began their songs with the sight of the sunlight that now flooded the lower deck. I had not realized how dank it had become on this deck until the fresh air began to rush in. This too energized the animals. All began to pace nervously in their enclosures. Many literally climbed the walls.

When we had finished, we three brothers stood there, chests heaving. During the work, we had all removed our tunics and now our bare chests were covered in sweat. It felt good to work with such vigor.

Shem tossed his axe to one side and Ham followed. I rested a hand on the handle of mine like a cane. We didn't speak but only looked at one another. Then, as if on cue, we took a large step and were standing outside. The ground was spongy but was as dry as when we had left. We walked slowly away from the ark, pushing chest-high ferns aside as we went. When we were a hundred yards or so away, we turned to look back at the huge box that had been our world for the past three hundred and seventy-one days.

None of us had words for such a time as this. We looked from one to another and then back at the ark. Shem grabbed me in an embrace and then reached for Ham, who took a step back from him and held out his hand to let Shem shake it. As we looked the ark over, we saw Mother and Father looking down on us from the center of the window. They each stretched an arm out toward us and, with a beaming smile, Father held up a fist in victory.

On the first day that the flood waters rose, I thought nothing could ever be as awful as what was happening outside the ark. Now I didn't think things could be any better.

And then I heard the sound of horses' hooves thundering on the wooden deck of the ark.

The stallion had bounded from the enclosure that had held him so long. He thundered down the passageway toward the opening, with the mare following close behind. The horses, never breaking stride, leapt from the deck and to the ground below.

Though my wife made it to the opening only seconds after her chosen animals, I saw a look of disappointment as she looked out and saw that both horses had disappeared into the heavy vegetation. "I'll never forget you, my friend," Tamara called to the stallion.

My brothers and I stared at a trail of freshly broken ferns that revealed the horses' route of escape. Rowdy and his mate stood beside us, their ears perked up in the direction the horses had gone.

"I guess I'll never see them—," Tamara began. She stopped as we both noticed something. Almost a half-mile away on a distant ridge of this same mountain was a green meadow. There, none of the large ferns or leafy plants grew. Instead, only brilliant green grass swayed slightly in a light breeze. In what seemed like far too short a time to have covered such a distance, the stallion burst from the foliage in the distance and into the meadow. He whinnied loudly and reared magnificently on his hind legs.

Seconds later, the mare was running through the grass as well. She reached down without breaking stride and grabbed a mouthful of the succulent grass as she ran. The stallion, as if basking in our admiration, found the high point of the meadow and reared once again, pawing at the air with his front hooves.

Tears streamed down Tamara's face. She clapped her hands together and pressed them to her mouth. She laughed, then cried, then laughed some more as she watched the horses run free.

I looked back at my beautiful wife, and I was overcome with emotion. I trotted over and held out my hand to help her down from the deck. Instead of taking my hand, she placed her hands on my shoulders and jumped into my arms. I swung her around and held onto her tightly. Her long hair billowed in the soft breeze and covered my face.

Adina and Prisca made their way down to stand beside Ham and Shem. Shem threw his arms around Prisca as he embraced her and the child she was carrying. Adina quickly walked to Ham and placed a hand on her husband's shoulder. Then I looked back yet again at the ark. My parents' glowing faces were still framed in the window above. I cherished the moment. I will never forget it for the rest of my life. We had made it! With God's guidance, we had made it home!

Ham was back in the ark standing in the doorway on the morning following the big parade. After Tamara had let the horses go, a continuous procession of animals departing the ark lasted all afternoon and well into the night. Now, with the family outside working on the altar Dad had insisted upon, the ark was mostly empty.

As the others laughed and joked in their labor, Ham had snuck back inside the ark. He only intended to be gone for a few minutes so that he could enjoy a little toast to the new world. He had been disappointed and a little surprised to find the last flask down to just a few drops. He hadn't bothered trying to dispose of the leftovers from his stash. No one would ever look in there again, he suspected.

He would do what he had to for awhile. He would obey his father today and help build an altar. And he would be equally obedient in the days after that. He took solace in the knowledge that his days of answering to Noah and Shem and of feeling inferior to Japheth were drawing rapidly to a close. One of the four of them would rule this new world, and Ham had been thinking for weeks of ways to insure that that someone was him.

Ham smiled to himself as he thought of the possibility of having his father and brothers serving him. Wouldn't that be a pleasant change of pace? As he mulled over that thought in his mind, he felt a shiver go up his spine as if danger was approaching. He shook off the sensation and hopped to the ground. For now, he must do his duty.

The deceiver stood invisibly just inches behind Ham as he walked off the ark. As Ham smirked with satisfaction over his plans, the deceiver leaned in close. But he wouldn't show himself to Ham or the others. No need to just yet.

Ham certainly was big and strong—for a man at least. For a moment, he seriously considered crushing all of Ham's bones and leaving him lying there for the others to find. After all, this little voyage never would have happened if Ham hadn't interfered and had just let the others finish Tamara that night. Then Japheth and Shem would have torn into the city bent on revenge, both been killed, and this entire little exercise would have come crashing down.

The deceiver decided that he must not hurt Ham. He knew that God wouldn't allow it now. Besides, Ham still had a great deal of potential. He would work on him some more in the future. Even though Ham had ruined the plan he had for the girl, he still could have stopped this little voyage at least a dozen times. But he'd barely been allowed to *do* anything once the door of the ark was sealed.

Surely God did not underestimate him to such an extent that He thought a little water and a wooden crate would stop him. He had found it all quite amusing really, watching all those fools clutching at their throats, gasping for breath, and clawing at the water. He laughed again at the thought of it.

Still, as he looked at all the wilderness around him, he couldn't help but feel some regret. He would have to start all over now. It was a shame when he had come so near to achieving it. He had very nearly created hell on earth.

He'd been too bold, that was all. Yes, he had tried to do too much too soon. He wouldn't make that mistake again. From now on, he vowed, he would be the picture of discretion.

It was time to move along. Noah was nearly finished with his altar, and the deceiver was not about to be caught here when all *that* started. He would come back later. As he slipped down the hill through the greenery, he smiled again at that thought. Oh, how he would come back to visit.

By the time the deceiver reached the valley at the foot of the mountain on which the ark rested, Noah had completed his prayer to God. Now the deceiver crouched low as he moved along, shrinking in fear at the sound of *His* voice. God was declaring a covenant with man, and this time He could be heard by Noah and his entire family.

The authority in God's voice was still paralyzing for the deceiver. No matter how many years passed, the sound of it struck the same fear in him. It was the voice that had called out his name—Lucifer—on that day with Holy indignation. Moments later, God's mighty hand had swept him and the others from heaven and cast them all down. It was the same voice that pronounced the curse on him in the garden.

Lucifer could not overcome the fear of His voice! And he hated God for it. He continued to move away, more rapidly now. He began to run as he tried to escape it. Finally, when he felt he was a safe distance away, he uncovered his ears and slowed his pace. It was at that precise moment that he cried out and cringed as he felt an intense burning sensation on his back and shoulders.

Lucifer didn't know it then, but it was a mere sampling of what would come thousands of years in the future. In confusion, he spun around to see who or what had afflicted him. There was no one there. What he saw instead confused and startled him.

Apparently he had just passed through something. But why had it caused him such pain? Lucifer stared at the ground behind him in wonder at the heretofore unseen display of the soil bathed in the brilliant red, orange, yellow, green, and blue beams of a rainbow.

THE END

In the early 1980s, I attended a class taught by Dr. R. Charles Blair on "Ancient World History in Bible Light." As we studied about conditions prior to the flood, there were several questions raised in my mind as to what was it like for a man like Noah to hear the word of God and be obedient. Did he have doubts? Did he question his sanity and what he was hearing? Did his family ever question his sanity? What was it like to be standing inches away, behind a wooden wall, and hear the screams of people begging to be let inside the ark when the waters began to rise? What was it like to hear friends, neighbors, and even relatives standing on the other side and begging for mercy? How could Noah have resisted the urge to open the door? Then I remembered. It was God who closed the door, and Noah could not open it.

The class and questions in the above paragraph are the basis for a story that took more than twenty years to develop and for God to bring all the pieces together. It started with Dr. Blair's class and continued with the study of God's Word, but there were still several pieces missing. Then Pastor Kenneth Puckett gave me a tape of Ken Ham speaking at a church in Memphis. After listening to the tape and visiting the Answers In Genesis Web site (www.answersingenesis. org), more pieces of the puzzle were put together.

Finally, God brought Chris Skates and me together, and we began to collaborate on the story of Noah and his family. Chris has a real passion for truth and is an extremely talented storyteller. His creativity and ingenuity were inspirational and amazing as the book developed. It has been a joy to work with Chris and develop both an entertaining and educational story based on Biblical truth.

Our goal from the beginning was to provide as much insight as our imagination would let us regarding the story of Noah and the flood without contradicting Scripture. The flood was the single most tragic event in human history to occur after the sin committed by Adam and Eve. There were millions and possibly billions of lives lost during the flood, and only eight people survived. While this story seems like a fairy tale to many people today, God has warned us this will happen again. Not the flood, but the destruction of all people outside the safety of the ark of Jesus Christ.

We hope that you have found the story of Noah and his family entertaining and enlightening as to the possibilities of life before the flood and what it was like to live in a wooden box for over a year with thousands of animals to feed. We believe that Noah and his family were normal people just like you and me who had dreams, made mistakes, struggled with sin, and worked hard to live an obedient life. They had failures as well as successes. They were ordinary people with an extraordinary God who provided for their deliverance from a very wicked world. As you read about the past, we pray that you have thought about the future and how the story of Noah relates to today. Our prayer is that you find grace in the eyes of God, just like Noah.

—Dan Tankersley

I had prayed for nearly two years, "Lord, give me a story to tell." While I was immediately intrigued and excited by Dan's concept for this novel, it was only after the prologue that I began to believe that this was the story for which I had asked. I am blessed to have had this opportunity. My own concept of Noah and the ark has been forever changed by the experience.

For so long, those of us in and out of Christendom have considered the recounting of Noah's ark a lovely children's story. Other secular books, very loosely based on the Biblical account, have attempted to tell the story as a satire. Still others have depicted Noah as a highly self-righteous, judgmental man who felt those that drowned deserved their fate.

We feel that none of these depictions is likely close to what occurred. Far from a happy or satirical story, the Bible illustrates that Noah and his family suffered through the largest natural disaster in all of history. The loss of life that occurred outside the ark remains unprecedented. Likewise, nowhere in Scripture is it even implied that Noah was judgmental or that he never attempted to warn others about the coming flood.

Noah was told that only he, his wife, his sons, and their wives would enter the ark. However, this statement by God can be interpreted to be more prophecy than commandment.

Nowhere does God tell Noah that he cannot tell others or warn them or even try to get them to come along. Noah received word of the flood more than one hundred years prior to entering the ark. Are we to believe that during all that time Noah never mentioned the flood or tried to warn people? If you had received this word from God but, like Noah, had no instruction from him to keep it quiet, would you have warned friends, neighbors, and co-workers?

Another assumption that is often made is that Noah was a perfect believer. Once again nowhere is this implied in Scripture. The Genesis account states that Noah was "righteous" and "blameless," but it doesn't say that he never experienced doubt, frustration, or even terror.

In the final analysis, we feel that Noah and his family were just people. Believers who were capable of standing steadfast in a world consumed with sin? Certainly. Men and women of tremendous faith? Absolutely. But they were human nonetheless, and we have depicted them with individual personality strengths, weaknesses, and frailties. Many of these traits would manifest themselves in ways that would change the course of humanity after their voyage was over.

One of the greatest challenges in writing "The Rain" was speaking about a world that was consumed by sin without creating a work that was overly graphic or offensive. I tried to conjure up images of what the city Cain built would have been like. Unfortunately, I did not have to use my imagination. Most of the evil perpetrated in this story was based on real-life events that were broadcast on the news as this story was being developed. Just a few examples:

- In Chapter 4, the women were pelted with feces when the crowd in the city turned on them. That scene was based on eyewitness accounts of the treatment of modern-day missionaries.
- Dan and I heard a statistic that 50 percent of Christian men are in a struggle with addiction to pornography.

So it seemed plausible that at least one character (Japheth) might give into lust.

- The most difficult chapter to write was the story of Jerah and Shelah. That passage was written through tears after I had seen multiple news accounts of child abuse in the course of a single week. If child abuse is that prevalent in our world today, might it have been so pervasive in Noah's world that God decided to destroy His creation and begin again?

What we have attempted to do is incorporate all these possibilities. Most importantly, we have tried very hard to never contradict Scripture. This is, of course, a novel and some poetic license was taken. For example, Scripture states that Noah was to put one window in the ark. It does not indicate what the length of the window was. In our ark, the single window ran the length of the vessel. In addition, we made no attempt to have the characters speak in any type of period dialect or with any type of Biblical-sounding phraseology. For ease of reading, modern vernacular has been used throughout.

In the end, this is just a story. It is our version of how things might have occurred. We believe the Bible to be the infallible, inherent word of Almighty God. Therefore, we believe the Biblical account of the great flood to be literal. We do not contradict this account, but we do embellish it. It is our fervent hope and prayer that we have done so in a way that will allow the reader to identify with the characters and their plights.

Ultimately, we hope that you see the ark as it was intended, as a metaphor of Jesus Christ. He is your ark. In a world where storms may rage and dangers abound all around you, He is your refuge. He is your provision.

—Chris Skates

Acknowledgements

M any people contributed to the development of the book. Our spouses, Judy Tankersley and Tracy Skates, were instrumental in helping establish the foundation for how the book would develop. Pastor Kenneth Puckett, Dr. R. Charles Blair, Jack and Patsy Marshall, LeGail Tudor, and Dorine Sisco provided valuable insight and suggestions. We are indebted to them for the time they spent reading and responding to our survey on the early drafts of the book. We especially want to thank Dr. Blair for the hours he spent editing and his encouragement to us as he read the story. We also want to thank Kimberly Henderson, president of LiveLines Editing, (www.livelinesediting.com), in preparing the final manuscript for submission to the publisher.

Printed in the United States
200116BV00002B/112-1026/A